THE ~~I~~

ETHEL ARCHER (1885-1962) ~~...~~ man, was born in Sussex, and ex~~p...~~ of fourteen for asking questions in Scripture class. In 1908 she married the aspiring artist Eugene Wieland, and lived with him in West London. The couple made the acquaintance of Aleister Crowley, joined his A∴A∴ magical organization, and set up a publishing company called Wieland and Co., to publish Crowley's periodical *The Equinox*, as well as other texts, including Archer's first poetry collection *The Whirlpool* (1911). She published two other books, *Phantasy and Other Poems* (1930) and the occult novel *The Hieroglyph* (1932).

DANIEL CORRICK is an editor and literary historian with a specialist interest in nineteenth-century literature, especially the evolution of Gothicism and the Decadent movement. He has worked on a number of volumes including the collected fiction of Montague Summers, and unpublished works of Edgar Saltus and Edward Heron-Allen. In addition, he has edited several anthologies, including *Sorcery and Sanctity: A Homage to Arthur Machen* (Hieroglyphic Press, 2013), and *Drowning in Beauty: The Neo-Decadent Anthology* (Snuggly Books, 2018). He can be reached at: https://dccorick.com

SNUGGLY BOOKS

ETHEL ARCHER

THE HIEROGLYPH

WITH AN INTRODUCTION BY
DANIEL CORRICK

THIS IS A SNUGGLY BOOK

CONTENTS

INTRODUCTION

MOST readers will have heard of this novel and of its author through mentions in one of the many biographies of the famous poet and magician Aleister Crowley. Archer herself freely admitted that the three central characters are based on her recollections of herself, her husband and Crowley during the period of their close friendship in the years prior to the Great War, the "Hieroglyph" of the title being a thinly veiled pseudonym for the mystical journal *The Equinox*, on which the three collaborated. Nearly a century later there is no shortage of novels about Crowley and characters based on him; following his transformation into a pulp villain by Dennis Wheatly and his imitators in the pulp horror boom, and gradual rediscovery as a counter-cultural icon, the man who half-jokingly styled himself "Mega Therion" has become the single most recognised figure of modern western occultism. This novel, however, offers a rather different perspective from what came later. It was written and published at a time when Crowley himself was still very much active in the foreground of the British occult scene. More so, Archer's interest in his teachings can be seen to reflect the concerns of a generation. In this respect the novel is also about Archer herself, as a poet, as a wife and as a thinker—a High Modernist *Roman à clef* with all the tropes and preoccupations of that movement, from complex psychoanalytical family dynastics, conflicts in dynamic between the sexes and ultimately a quest for spiritual attainment.

A lengthily account of her life and background would be unnecessary, for the reader will find much of it presented under the thinnest of veils throughout the course of the novel. It will suffice to give a few salient details for the purpose of framing.

Ethel Archer was born in 1885 in Sussex, the daughter of a local clergyman, Osmond Andrew Archer. Her maternal grandfather, John Elanan Sinyanki, was a Jewish convert to Christianity who served as a minister in the East End and wrote treatises on Byzantine history; her uncle, the Uncle John of the novel, was a friend of Oscar and Constance Wilde, whom he allegedly tried to interest in Spiritualism. She began writing poetry at an early age, a practice that was encouraged by her family but not by her teachers. A biographical aside given years later in *The Poetry Review* recounts how she was expelled from school at the age of fourteen for asking questions in Scripture class (something her father had encouraged) and sharing a cigarette with another girl. In 1908 she married the aspiring artist and illustrator Eugene Wieland, and set up home with him in West London. The impoverished yet happy early years of their marriage spent in the stereotypical artists' garret formed the basis of a novel, *The Lovers*, by the American writer Elizabeth Robins Pennell. Soon after their marriage, the pair made the acquaintance of Crowley, then known primarily as a poet, and his lover Victor Neuburg, probably through the newly founded *Equinox*.

Archer and Wieland quickly became close to Crowley, with the latter serving as his secretary and setting up a publishing company, Wieland and Co, to release further issues of the journal, as well as other texts of magical import from its contributors. In 1911 they published Archer's first collection of poetry, *The Whirlpool*, the cover of which featured an iconic design by Wieland (Crowley contributed both an introduction and an anonymous review in the journal). The couple's relationship with the occultist had cooled by the time of the war, though Archer still maintained friendly correspondence with him. Following Wieland's death from wounds received during the Battle of Loos, Archer's poetic output slowed, although she continued contributing book reviews and prose pieces to the *Occult Review* throughout the following decade. The beginning of the thirties saw a revival of her literary energies, with the translation of a long essay on reincarnation, and a long awaited second collection of verse, *Phantasy and Other Poems*, which was published in limited edition by Neuburg's Vine Press. Later in the decade she became involved in political causes, opposing the invasion of Ethiopia by Fascist Italy, a stance which prompted Crowley to postulate a spiritual connection between her and the exiled Emperor Haile Selassie. She continued writing verse into the fifties, though a proposed third collection of poems failed to appear. Archer died in 1962 following a stroke.

The period in which the novel is set was one of the most fertile of Crowley's life; it came after years of travel and spiritual experimentation following his ill-fated attempt to seize leadership of the Hermetic Order of Golden Dawn, and saw him establish his own magical society, the A∴A∴, informally known as the Silver Star, which attempted to synthesise the ritual praxis of the older Order with the ideals of his new religion of Thelma. Under the imprint of Wieland and Co. were published some of his most important works including the four volume set *Liber ABA*, which incorporates *Magic in Theory and Practice* and *The Book of the Law*. It is telling that Archer chooses to present the Crowley of *The Equinox* period far more in the guise of an empirical psychonaut interested in testing the mind-expanding potential of meditation and hallucinogenic substances rather than that of a ceremonial magician transmitting initiatory secrets. Her own presentation is that of an artist seeking to comprehend the nature of inspiration and genius through mysticism. Consequently, Archer's interest in magical practice lay in the possibility of achieving a transcendent state of consciousness as discussed in the first volume of the *Liber*. A diary she kept at the time records a series of lucid dreams she believed to be astral journeys achieved through yoga and meditation. Some of the passages therein however—"Three strange looking black dogs came slowly out of the garden. . . and thinking that they were elementals I banished them with the pentagram of earth"—"I tried in vain to tear the thing away and finally got rid of it by assuming the God Horus. Invoking Thoum-ash-neith and doing 'the Enterer' I got away"—show that she was amply familiar with Golden Dawn rituals and Crowley's development of them.

Archer's recollections of the A∴A∴ and the *Equinox* set is a valuable record of the breakdown of that group resulting from the scandal following the Rites of Eleusis. These were a series of seven mystery plays written and performed by Crowley and several acolytes to a paying audience, favoured members of whom were given an opportunity beforehand to partake of a liquor punch laced with mescaline to enhance the experience. The initial motive was to raise funds for further publications; though Archer here suggests that it was also a means for the occultist to observe the effects of psychedelics on a willing public audience. Initial responses to the first performances were positive but then a society newspaper called *The Looking Glass*, hereto devoted to horse racing and theatrical gossip, published a three-part series of articles on Crowley accusing him of all sorts of depravity. These articles are included as an appendix, as they are one of the first instances of Crowley achieving public infamy. It is amusing to read the author's portrayal of the performance evenings as holocausts of innocence against Archer's witty depictions of the idle, pleasure seeking audience members faintly disappointed in their quest for wickedness.

In reality it was not the scandal of the articles alone which spelt the collapse of the A∴A∴ but the subsequent trial which followed. Amongst other claims the author of the *Looking Glass* article alleged that Crowley had engaged in various "unmentionable immoralities." Concerned that this perceived slander would lead to others associated with Crowley being labelled homosexuals, several members of the A∴A∴, including the order's co-founder George Cecil Jones, urged him to launch a libel suit against the paper; Crowley, perhaps wisely recalling the case of Oscar Wilde, refused to do so, though Jones did, losing his suite on the grounds that, although the paper had in effect libelled others by association, Crowley himself had not rejected its charges.

Archer is selective in how she presents this aspect of Crowley and avoids making any overt reference to homosexual activities. She would have certainly been aware of it, for the master-slave aspect of his relationship with Neuburg is introduced within the opening paragraphs and becomes a running joke throughout the novel. This reticence is partly dictated by the mores of the time; even though Archer is happy to dissect her former mentor's sins, both real and imagined, she probably felt open reference to homosexual relationships, even in passing, would be a step too far, not to mention also potentially damaging to others such as Neuburg.

There may be a further, veiled factor. In descriptions of her feelings towards Crowley following the death of her husband one is struck by this passage, amongst the most ambiguous and enigmatic of the novel: "If there were anything queer about the man (and she had often felt that there was), might he not start experimenting with Blitzen, now that conditions were favourable?" That she at that time feared he might exert some form of malign necromantic influence on her departed husband is unsettling enough, but what led her to consider this and what motivations might she have suspected? That he practiced magic was hardly something she would have been uncertain about. Given Wieland's physical beauty and the psychologically complex portrayal of her husband's relationship with Crowley, one wonders if Archer sensed a shadow of erotic tension, or at least awareness on the part of the latter, and felt uneasy about it.

The chapters dealing with the war and her husband's service are partly composed of Wieland's own letters home. Some of this material appeared before in bowdlerised form in Pennel's *The Lovers*, with many of the darker and more sexual explicit lines removed. Modernist accounts of the trenches and warfare have almost become a cliché in themselves (one thinks of Robert Graves' *Goodbye to All That!*), but Wieland's messages and Archer's responses upon reading them possess a certain apocalyptic quality, not only a sense of impending personal disaster but also of the possibility of a better future for humanity ruined. The values the couple shared and thought of as modern, those of free love and a new Aeon of higher consciousness, were necessarily revaluated in the face of equally modern mechanised warfare. For Archer the loss of her husband was more than the loss of a beloved partner; it was also the loss of a creative centre in which her artistic powers were able to ground themselves and develop in a stable manner required for working within the world. The next decade saw her struggle to overcome not only the grief of his loss, but also that of the Bohemian environment of the *Equinox* set. She did not reject her "modern" ideals, but what was modern in the 1910s was not modern in the 1920s, and she found herself painfully out of step with the post-war intellectual and literary climate. Yet attempts to recapture what was meaningful or important in the spirt of *The Equinox* beyond comradely fun are seen to fail or to be risible, as in the case of the new artist colony and Neuburg's quasi-pagan rituals on the Sussex Downs.

It is in the final third of the novel that the plot leaves the realm of thinly veiled autobiography for that of the ideal, and thereto ideal resolutions not often found in life. The greatest controversy and interest lies in the fate she envisages for her Crowley counter-part. It is this feature of Archer's novel that gets mentioned in many of the secondary texts on the subject, so this introduction will treat it a little more openly than would otherwise be required. *The Hieroglyph* is not a rejection of the A∴A∴ or its practices. Her ending for Crowley is redemptive but not penitent: he is neither seen to recant nor regret his magical activities, only his worldly failings and his inability to achieve the grand awakening of human genius. He is not Durtal retreating to the monastery to heal from his encounter with Satanism. His situation is a culmination of the aspect of his nature which Archer admired most starting from the days of *The Equinox*, and which would endear to him to the Counter-Culture generation—that of the rootless, mystical explorer who tramples conventions and crosses continents in the search for enlightenment. Even in the period at which he was presenting himself as a prophet through *The Book of the Law* Archer depicts him first and foremost as a spiritual seeker. One feels it is precisely because he has gone through such activities, rather than in spite of them, that he can reach this place.

In our world, at least, Crowley continued on his Promethean path, further experimenting with magic, drugs, sex and everything else from painting to gastronomy well throughout the thirties and into the post-war years. Yet that he remained in friendly correspondence with Archer until the end of his life nearly two decades after the novel's publication suggests he did not take the fate of his fictional self in bad part. For her at least his image plays the role of the ideal cosmic pilgrim, the Fool of the Greater Arcana, achieving a level of spiritual attainment which others—including herself—have not, thus ultimately justifying his claims to be a holy guide to humanity. She may have seen his religion of Thelma as a means to an end rather than an end in itself, but his notion of "genius" or True Will obviously had a significant influence on her later work and self-understanding.

Although the true significance of its cast and plot were known to very few when it was first published, *The Hieroglyph* is a record of a unique moment in English history, when cultural change and the dying of old institutions brought a generation to such a peak of spiritual restlessness that they saught illumination through the practice of magic. It is a memoir of a talented woman's unconventional beliefs and character, and her conflicts with a society which neither tried nor cared to understand. It is an account of the last glow of *fin de siècle* Bohemianism and youthful potential cut short by the horrors of the Great War. And of course it is a record of the influence of one Aleister Crowley, the man who styled himself the Crowned and Conquering Child, on the minds of his acolytes, in this case, it must be said, a supremely inspirational one.

—Daniel Corrick

THE HIEROGLYPH

CHAPTER I

"ARE you a Sadist or a Masochist?"

Iris Hamilton appeared to reflect for a moment; then lifted the cigarette with which she had been absent-mindedly about to burn the wrist of the man beside her.

"I don't know," she said lazily, "possibly both, it depends on the circumstances." Then turning to look at her companion more carefully, "What is a Sadist?" she asked.

"A Sadist," he said slowly, and she noticed the slight drawl and the still slighter nasal twang—"a Sadist is a person who likes to *hurt*, a Masochist is a person who likes to *be* hurt. Most women," he added maliciously, with a tinge of evident satisfaction in his voice, "are Masochists."

"Which accounts for the fact that most men are Sadists, I suppose?"

"Of course. But it doesn't always follow that this is the case. Newton, for example, my subeditor and Chela, is a hopeless Masochist. I give him as much as he can stand," he added grimly, "sometimes a little more, but it's all for the good of his soul. If he didn't work it off in this incarnation he'd have to in the next."

Vladimir Svaroff, poet, philosopher and occultist, exhaled the smoke of a peculiarly fragrant cigarette and smiled to himself. The expression of his mouth was suggestive of one who has just sampled a rare and delicious wine. His eyes contracted tightly and a scarcely perceptible squint appeared. He looked at Iris with a curiously blank expression and she felt a slight shudder pass across her. For a moment she saw him as a prosperous monk whose grandfather had been a Chinese god; the god predominated. Then the picture faded as quickly as it had come, and she saw in its place a rather good-looking man of about thirty-six years of age, sunbaked with travel in foreign lands. A man with a good-shaped head, small, well-set ears, a singularly sensitive and beautiful mouth, and curious hazel eyes. The hands, she noted, were small and delicate as a woman's. She had heard much about him; she wondered if all she had heard had been true.

She decided that he was interesting; which was the highest compliment at this stage that she could pay to any man. All her life she had longed for male companionship; most of the men she had met had bored her by making love. At such times a segment of herself had seemed to stand apart, coldly analytical, critical. She was utterly indifferent to it all; it left her unmoved.

Svaroff promised to be different. At the present moment he looked extraordinarily young; his mouth was slightly pouting. Iris thought it the most beautiful mouth she had ever seen; his eyes invited her. Bending down she kissed him on the lips, softly, daintily, deliberately. In just such a way she would have kissed a beautiful statue or passed her hand over some soft material whose texture pleased her. The action was curiously impersonal and, though sensuous, devoid of conscious sex.

It was the first time in her life that she had ever kissed any man but her husband. Had Svaroff responded she would have been surprised and disappointed. She was glad that he did not. Here, at last, was a person who could understand her. She felt stimulated and pleasantly intrigued. One does not ask permission of a rose before one inhales its perfume; in just such a way she had kissed him. The next moment she forgot.

As for Svaroff, the curves deepened at the corners of his mouth and his eyes grew a shade darker, but beyond this he gave not the slightest indication that anything unusual had happened. He realised with the unerring intuition that made him at once both dangerous and charming, that it was the artist in her, not the woman, which had just betrayed itself. The woman, he guessed and rightly, had never been awakened; indeed, he doubted if the sex were there to awaken. She suggested, he thought, a nymph or a dryad, something non-human at all events, he reflected, and his poet's mind played pleasantly with the idea. He noticed the small features, classical but suggesting a spirituality seldom to be found in the Greek statuary; the morbid little mouth, the long hazel eyes strangely flecked with red (for the first time he realised that they were the same colour as his own), the cloud of dark brown hair, curling, electric, soft as gossamer, that framed the shadowy little face—and then he thought of the volume of her poems that he meant to publish: erotic phantasies and strange love lyrics that might well have graced the pen of a modern Sappho—both mystical and realistic, subconscious and unconsciously equilibrated.

She was certainly an unusual type and one that scarcely fitted in with his Weineger theories. Except that one does not think of age in connection with a nymph or dryad he would have placed her at about seventeen. Once again the curious blank expression came down like a shutter upon his face.

They were in Svaroff's flat overlooking Victoria Street and it was a hot June morning in the year 1912. They were lying on a low padded seat in the glass-covered balcony that jutted out from the larger room behind them. About them were scarlet cushions. The sun streamed through scarlet blinds, making reflections like pools of blood upon the white woodwork. From below rose the roar of the street traffic. The air danced with scarlet vibrations.

"I think," said Iris, referring to his last remark, "that if one likes anyone very much one usually wants to bite them, but I didn't know it was called Sadism. I often bite the Boy's ear, he likes me to," she added naively, "but I don't care to be bitten myself. I like to be hugged so hard that it really hurts. But the Boy will never do it hard enough, he says he's afraid of breaking my ribs. I think I should rather like to be killed by a grizzly bear or a boa constrictor. It's a lovely sensation, feeling yourself growing smaller and smaller until finally one becomes nothing or everything. I'm not quite sure which it is," she added vaguely.

Again Vladimir noticed the curious impersonal note—it was as though she spoke of someone else, and her body had nothing to do with her. Though speaking of such intimate things she was strangely remote; it was as though she had placed an invisible barrier around herself. He felt himself being attracted in quite a new way.

"And who is the 'Boy'?" he asked.

"My husband," was the answer. "Didn't you know? Hamilton is my maiden name. I use it for writing, but really I'm Mrs. John Strickland, though that also is a *nom-de-plume*. Somehow I never think about it, and I take it for granted that people know. I wear the badge of slavery round my neck."

Laughing lightly she showed him her wedding ring which hung on a little silver chain. He looked at her incredulously.

"I'm nearly twenty-one," she said, in answer to the unspoken question, "and we've been married for nearly two years. The Boy's the most wonderful person in the world and I've never known a moment's boredom, and we've never had a single quarrel."

"How very dull that must be," said Svaroff.

For a moment Iris felt that she hated him. Then she remembered.

"It isn't at all," she said. "When you meet the Boy you will understand."

The extraordinary enthusiasm in her eyes and voice made Svaroff feel suddenly old.

"Perhaps," he said.

They had started by discussing poetry and publishers, they had ended by talking of herself and Sadism.

Iris picked up a gilt-edged volume bound in white vellum containing some of Svaroff's earlier work, and for a few minutes completely forgot his existence. She felt hurt and annoyed. *The Shadow of Isis* claimed her attention.

When she looked up again Svaroff was watching curiously.

"I like this," she said, picking out the poem that he, too, had secretly thought the best in the book, though he had not told her so.

"I'm glad you like it," he said simply.

Taking a fountain pen from his waistcoat pocket he wrote her name in the volume and handed it to her with a boyish smile.

"I say, you *are* a brick."

Her delight and astonishment were unmistakable. It made Svaroff feel young again.

"Am I? Well, read your Shelley and Keats and you'll do some first class work yet, but you must read," he told her. "Don't be afraid of plagiarising, you are not in the least likely to, but read you must. Poetry is as necessary to a poet as exercise is to an athlete, never forget that. And, by the way," he added, referring to a sheaf of manuscripts, "I see you end that sonnet on an adjective. Always avoid doing that; it is weak. Endeavour to end on a verb or substantive. Another thing it is as well to remember, avoid inversions, and always write in such a way that if your verse were to be punctuated as prose it would need no correction in regard to grammar, and the sense would remain intact. Definiteness need not be rigidity."

So, quite easily and naturally, he restored the balance.

He glanced down at his dancing pumps. "I really think we might have some lunch. I'm starving. If you'll excuse me I shall only be a few minutes, and in the meantime if you want to look at any books there are plenty here." He took her into the adjoining room and indicated the well-filled book-cases: "These are mostly scientific; these are poetry and fiction."

Smiling enigmatically he walked across the room and let himself out by another door, closing it carefully behind him. She heard him walk across the inner room and a second door closed. Freed momentarily from the spell of his strange personality, she had time to look about her.

A room, she reflected, betrays the character of its owner and occupant, and this was far from being a common one. She noted with pleasure the perfect mean between luxury and restraint, the absence of unnecessary detail, with undeniable comfort, the semi-ecclesiastical austerity side by side with evidences of strange perversity and barbarity.

The floor was painted black, and, save for one enormous leopard skin before the fireplace, entirely devoid of rugs. The walls were covered with a dull sugar-paper blue. The doors and the woodwork were white, the blinds were scarlet. On the wall beside the fireplace were drawings by Beardsley and Osman Spare. Above the mantelpiece hung a large ivory and ebony crucifix, the figure carved from a single tusk, a magnificent specimen of early Byzantine work. On the mantelpiece itself were several images of Buddha, and Egyptian and Chinese gods, the latter of jade, the former of some dark greenish metal. Swinging from the centre of the ceiling was a wonderful silver lamp or censer. In the middle of the room were a couple of Oxford chairs upholstered in blue to match the walls, and a long, low, leather chair as well. Against the wall by the windows a large office table with revolving stool. At the north side of the room and facing the fireplace were the books-cases referred to, containing many first editions bound in white vellum. Verlaine, Baudelaire, Swinburne, Oscar Wilde, were a few of the names she noted. On the top of the cases them-selves were some busts of Rodin.

On the wall facing the balcony was a long roll of scarlet silk, embroidered with gold Chinese letters, the scroll of a Thibetan temple. A large crocodile grinned from a far corner of the room—at the back of the book-case was a python skin.

This much she had time to notice when the door heading on to the landing and at right angles to the book-cases opened suddenly, and in burst a hatless, curly-headed youth. His eyes, which were wide open and very grey, seemed full of the lost memories of woodland places.

"I say, Holy One," he began, "I've just met . . ." then catch-ing sight of Iris he stopped abruptly.

At the same moment Svaroff entered by the other door. He had changed his shoes and was wearing a fur-lined overcoat—in spite of the warmness of the day he shivered slightly.

"This, Mrs. Strickland," he said, indicating the new arrival, "is Newton, my mad sub-editor."

The new arrival collapsed into a chair and broke into a peal of irresponsible laughter that was somehow strangely infectious. There was something very faun-like about him; he looked absurdly young. Iris found herself smiling in sympathy.

"He is not really, is he?" she said. "He doesn't look more than sixteen."

"I am ashamed to say he's twenty-six," said Svaroff.

At this the boy went into another peal of laughter, he dou-bled himself up, he appeared to think it a was a huge joke. Svaroff looked at him with an expression half of pity, half of amazement; in just such a way he might have regarded some strange insect whose contortions pleased and puzzled him.

"Will you *never* grow up, Newton?"

"I hope not," answered the other.

"What about Clay?" said Svaroff.

"Oh, Clay's not so dusty," was the reply.

Svaroff turned to Iris. "Forgive my talking shop for a moment, but I must just settle a few things."

Then, turning to Newton, "Have you come to any arrangement with Clay? Did you explain the new type and the extra copies we wanted?"

"Oh yes, I mentioned it, but he said he could not possibly let us have them before the middle of October. He began to explain to me why but I told him I was a poet, not a tradesman; then he said something, I forget what, so I walked out."

"What did you do with the extra sheets?"

"Oh, I left them on the table."

An ominous silence followed.

Svaroff looked steadily at the figure in the chair a full half-minute. His face was a mask, his eyes had contracted slightly. The other began to writhe uncomfortably, but he returned the look without flinching.

"Well," he said at last, with a strange mixture desperation and defiance, "what would you have had me say?"

"It's not so much what I would have had you say to-day," said Svaroff, "but what you'll have to say to-morrow, that matters. Of all the hopeless, doddering, drivelling idiots it's ever been my luck to encounter, you're the biggest, Newton."

He had quite forgotten that Iris was present.

They continued to regard each other antagonistically for the space of several seconds.

"Well," said Svaroff, "since you've made such a hopeless mess of things you had better get on with the other proofs, and you can add Mrs. Strickland's 'Felon Flower' and 'The Dreamer.' They're both to go into the next number."

"But I say, Holy One, I've just met the Brixton Flapper, and I've promised to take her to tea."

The look of withering contempt that Svaroff cast at his sub-editor would have shrivelled up anyone but the imperturbable Newton. For a moment he did not reply. Then he said in a dangerously quiet voice:

"I think you had better start on those proofs now. I shall expect to see them finished by the time I come back."

What exactly happened then, Iris does not remember, but she thinks that Newton made a grimace. Almost before she could realise it Svaroff had made a dive at the recumbent figure, and, quick as a cat, had grasped it by the collar. A slight scuffle ensued, and the struggling Newton was borne ignominiously along the floor and thrust into the inner room, Svaroff locking the door as he did so. He threw the key on to an adjacent chair.

"Remember," he said, making a pause between each word, "I shall expect to see those proofs finished when I get back; V.H.O., Newton." He uttered the three letters with peculiar emphasis.

A kick on the door was the only answer. Iris wondered if he were *really* angry; it was difficult to tell.

"Come, Mrs. Strickland," he said. "We shall never get off to-day."

As he walked to the door, Iris noticed he was limping. Half-way down the stairs she turned to him.

"Isn't it rather mean to lock the boy up on such a beautiful day as this?" she said.

"Oh, he can easily get out by the other door." Svaroff explained. "Only he'll never think of that! You don't know Newton." He turned and looked at Iris with what she called his blank expression, then he chuckled. They had just reached the street door.

"If it's not a rude question, what does V.H.O. mean?" she said

He smiled mysteriously but with evident enjoyment

"V.H.O. means Vow of Holy Obedience,"

He hailed a passing taxi, and they got in.

"Drive to Oddenino's," he said shortly.

CHAPTER II

WHIRLING rapidly down Victoria Street, Iris remembered with cinematograph-like suddenness all that had happened that morning. How in answer to her letter Svaroff had written asking her to bring her verses, and how arriving a little too soon, she had found him "reclining" on scarlet cushions in the glass-covered balcony or annexe that he called the sun chamber, a vellum-bound volume of Keats beside him.

How he had apologised most charmingly for his apparent laziness, saying there had been a symposium the night before and really he was awfully tired, and how she had thought that he looked it. She remembered, too, the strange elusive perfume, faintly medicinal but wholly delightful, that had met her on the threshold of his rooms; incense evidently, she had thought, but quite unlike anything she had known in church, the merest shadowy ghost of a perfume, yet potent as an unseen presence. It had made her feel strangely excited and not a little frightened. How he had made room for her on the couch beside him, and how she had sat down noticing he was dressed in black in deference to some recent loss, and how nice the black had looked against the red. How he had discussed her work, sympathetically, as one who understands, and how he had accepted her three favourite poems, saying that he must see more.

How in the pause that she had said:

"Do you remember Laura?"

And he had said: "Petrach's Laura?"

"No," she had said, "I mean Lara Sinienski," and how he had looked at her blankly till she had said:

"I'm Laura's niece—she doesn't know I had written. I know that it's ages ago, but I thought you might remember," and how after that he had dropped all pretence and asked:

"Where is Laura now?" and she had told him.

How she had also told him of her youthful infatuation for Laura.

"She was always so gay. I used to send her all my earliest poems; I really think I was in love with her!" And how Laura had first introduced her to his, Svaroff's poems.

"She used to read me your letters too—some of them," she had informed him. "I thought they were wonderful!" And then she remembered his expression of amusement and horror.

"But you must have been a child!"

"I was twelve," she told him.

Then she had asked him: "What happed to John the bull-dog and Ayesha the Great Dayne? Laura told me you used to wrestle with Ayesha—was she really six feet four?"

"I believe so," he had answered—"she was pretty big. They are both dead now. What a memory you must have!" He had looked at her admiringly.

"Well, I was interested," she had answered. "I believed you were a sort of magician, and I've often thought of that weird house in Scotland and of all the things I heard about it."

Then he had made a Latin quotation; and she had nearly burned his wrist.

She thought of it all, and then she thought of Newton. She turned to Svaroff.

"I see what you mean by V.H.O., but I don't quite understand it."

"Of course you don't," he answered. "I'll explain. It's a matter of discipline. Newton has promised to obey me implicitly for the next five months. It's an excellent plan and a very good way of seeing that things get done. Newton's the laziest, good-for-nothingest son of Israel that ever rejoiced in the name of Benjamin. He's the dirtiest too," he added as an afterthought.

Iris said nothing; she thought it was rather mean of him. Svaroff turned to her.

"Did you notice his hands?" he said. "They are just like a monkey's."

"But he can't help his hands; he didn't make them."

"No. But he can keep them clean! V.H.O. ensures his washing them at least twice a day; it also ensures his paying an occasional visit to the barber's. He'd never go if I didn't make him—he's as vain as a girl about his hair."

Svaroff, Iris noticed, had not much hair himself.

She felt amused.

"I don't know," she said, "but somehow I feel rather sorry for him, he looks so lost; he belongs by rights to woods and forests, not to towns."

"He *is* lost," said Svaroff, "and I'm trying to save his miserable soul, but if that were not sufficient, he forgets everything I taught him, and the first time I let him go out, he talks of taking the Brixton Flapper to tea."

The unutterable contempt and disgust that Svaroff managed to throw into his voice was worthy of a better cause. Iris laughed. Svaroff looked at her obliquely.

"Wait till you know Newton," was all he said.

They had arrived at Oddenino's. Just outside Svaroff paused.

"If you prefer it we'll go downstairs," he said.

Iris said that she should. They found a table at the extreme end of the room not far from a counter where the waiter hovered with his dishes. It was in a direct line with the stairs. They sat down. If there were other persons there, Iris failed to see them. The place seemed to her to be perfectly empty. This was what she liked, for she had never yet accustomed herself to feeding in a restaurant. Being of an extremely sensitive temperament she found that the presence of many strangers around her invariably took away her appetite and made her feel nervous: had she been an occultist she might have said that "crowds impinged on her aura"; as it was, she merely felt it subconsciously. In the same way she had noticed that there were certain individuals who made her feel ill. She didn't know why, but crowds invariably devitalised her.

"Please don't ask me to choose anything," she said to Svaroff. "I simply can't understand menus, and when the Boy is with me he always chooses."

He saw that she really meant it, and chose for her the most delightful lunch imaginable. Starting with iced melon they ended up with Peche Melba and some wonderful soup of Svaroff's own invention. The waiter positively purred. The admiration and respect he felt for Svaroff seemed little short of worship. He kept discreetly out of earshot, but when wanted appeared as if by magic even before there was time to summon him. He reminded Iris of the genie in the *Arabian Nights*, and had Svaroff clapped his hands and the table disappeared into the floor, dishes and all, it would scarcely have surprised her. Once, it was towards the end of the meal she found him looking at her with his strange blank expression. It made her feel a little uncomfortable and she asked him of what he was thinking.

"Absolutely nothing," he answered. "As a matter of fact I was watching that man balancing the plates; it's marvellous—how he does it. Had he gone on the stage he might have been a second Cinquevalli! Are you ready? If so . . ." Svaroff rose. He paid the waiter, and the man helped him on with his coat.

They walked very slowly across the room. At the foot of the stairs Svaroff turned to Iris.

"May I lean on your shoulder?"

She remembered his foot suddenly.

"Does it hurt much?" she asked.

"It does rather." He spoke a little absently.

She lent him her shoulder willingly.

"I'm so sorry, "she said.

He looked at her with quiet amusement.

"I really believe you are," he answered. Then he said: "Have you been to the Academy yet?"

Iris said that she had not.

"Well, if you think you can survive the awful strain we might go there. My late brother-in-law," he explained, "is exhibiting several portraits and I rather want to see what he has made of R. . ." Svaroff smiled to himself. "Do you know K's work?"

Iris said she was not quite sure.

"Well, K. is a success. He ought to have been a journalist. He always discovers the thing that is 'going,' and goes just one peg higher. At present you can scarcely tell him from Seargent. He will always get his work taken," he added, "but I don't altogether know that I should call him an artist. He's too facile—too like a chameleon."

Iris enjoyed the exhibition immensely.

They looked at K.'s portraits and she began to understand what Svaroff meant. The man *was* a chameleon.

Referring to C. and problem pictures, "He's not even photographer," he said.

Iris agreed with him—but she liked some work of Sims, and she told Svaroff so.

"Yes! Sims is all right."

Speaking of art generally, Iris said she liked Velasquez, and thought she should like to live with "The Buffon."

"So, I imagine, would a good many persons," he told her, "but there is only one Velasquez—genius is solitary. Yes, I was in Spain three years ago," he said in answer to her question, "and I used to go every morning to the Prado and gloat over Velasquez."

At about four-thirty he suggested that they should have some tea, "And I think, too, we might let out Newton," he added.

They drove back to his flat. As they were going upstarts he chuckled audibly.

"I wonder if he's still there," he said.

Iris felt that they were a couple of conspirators. Svaroff was for all the world like a naughty schoolboy.

He walked silently as a cat; he opened the door slowly, and looked in. For a moment he said nothing. Sitting hunched up in a chair, his head on his knees, a far-away expression in his grey eyes, was Newton. His hair stuck out like a couple of horns, he looked more faun-like than ever. For a moment or two he remained gazing at Svaroff with unseeing eyes. Then suddenly, as though he had made a great discovery, he said gleefully:

"You forgot to lock the other door."

"Of course I did, you young idiot, but how long did it take you to find it out?"

Newton ignored the question.

"I've finished your beastly proofs," he said.

"Oh! There's still hope for you, Newton.

"It's more than there is for you," said the other impudently.

But Svaroff refused the proffered batt.

He sank into a chair, and Iris followed his example.

"I believe," he said, speaking with exaggerated politeness, "that you said something about taking a lady to tea; if so, don't let me keep you."

It was an obvious dismissal, but Newton refused to see it. An obstinate expression spread over his face.

"Thanks, but I've changed my mind. I don't care about going now."

Despite his air of indifference Iris divined that he was very unhappy. Had such a being been capable of weeping she would have said that he was on the verge of tears—but as it was, in his case it would of course, have been laughter. She thought of him, boxed up the whole of that summer afternoon wading through oceans of proofs—she had seen the enormous pile of them—and then she thought of the delightful time she had had with Svaroff. She felt sorry for Newton. Perhaps, too, Svaroff felt a little touched. Anyway, there was not a trace of V.H.O. in his manner when he next spoke.

He looked plaintively at Iris. "Mrs. Strickland is dying for some tea; aren't we to have any, Newton?"

Newton was up in a minute, his face cleared as if by magic.

"Good old Guru," he said. There was absolute affection in his tone. He went into the other room, and through the closed door Iris heard him singing: "I love Holy Guru his coat is so warm and if I don't hurt him he'll do me no harm."

"What can you do with such a being?" said Svaroff, but Iris noticed that there was a sound of protection and something very like love in his voice. She guessed that subconsciously he was very fond of Newton—certainly there was some strange sympathy between the two in spite of their obvious differences. Svaroff went into the annexe and brought out a small black table, upon which was a brightly polished silver tea-tray with a Queen Anne sugar bowl and teapot. It looked, she thought, as though it had been a wedding present. The cups, which evidently did not belong, were very beautiful. They were white, and the design was a golden peacock with spread-out tail. It was a dull Sevreslike gold, and the pattern spread right round the cup, the head of the bird being at the handle. The pattern was slightly raised. Iris admired it very much.

"I designed it," said Svaroff; "they were made for me at the Army and Navy Stores." He spoke to Newton, who was just coming in with the electric kettle.

"Are there any Bath Olivers, Newton? I can't have anything else."

"I'll see," said the other.

As he fixed the plug into the wall he spilt some water.

"Never mind," said Svaroff, "At least it's not in the circle this time."

Iris wondered what he meant and then for the first time she noticed a large red circle painted upon the floor, at the four angles of which were Hebrew letters.

Newton laughed. "You ought to have seen Arthur this morning," he said. "Ever since I told him the circle was to keep in the devil he has been afraid to come into the place. He walked round this morning as gingerly as a cat by a grating of hot bricks." Newton's metaphors had telescoped a little. "He has a very real dread of you, Guru," he added.

"Well, I wish he would keep the place a little cleaner, that's all," said Svaroff. "However, if you managed to get him to clean the silver, and that is more than I can do."

"By the way," said Newton, "Harrington Hobbs looked in this afternoon; he's so inflated with self-esteem that one of these days he'll burst like the frog in the fable. I asked him how Buddha, was but Buddha has taken quite a back seat, he's Krishna now; when he reaches the Ain Soph he'll die of spontaneous combustion. Did I tell you of the lovely joke that Ivanoff played on him?" Newton went on. "I wish you had been there."

Svaroff gave a fat chuckle.

"No, what happened?—I noticed he had not been coming here much lately," he added, with a glance at Iris.

"Well," said Newton, "you know how he's been Buddha and the Universe and all sorts of things. A few weeks ago, when he was boasting that he had complete control of the elements, and nothing, absolutely nothing, could harm him, Ivan asked him if he would put it to the test. 'Of course,' said Hobbs, 'anything to convince you.'

"'Well,' said Ivan, 'I don't want you to risk it if you have any important engagement—a wedding or funeral, or anything like that.' 'No,' said Hobbs, 'I'm only going to a tennis tournament to-morrow.'

"Ivan sighed as though a great weight were off his mind.

"'All right,' he said, 'I'll give you something to take to-morrow morning at eleven minutes past eleven. It won't absolutely kill you, but of course you need not take it if you are afraid.' That made Hobbs swell himself out enormously, which was what Ivan wanted. 'I'll take absolutely anything,' he answered.

"'Very well,' said Ivan. He gave Hobbs powder in a little paper packet." Newton smiled impishly at the recollection.

"Well, you haven't told us what happened," said Svaroff.

Newton looked hesitatingly at Iris.

"Oh, I forgot," he said. "Next time I saw Hobbs he was looking very pensive.

"'How did the tennis tournament go off?' I asked him.

"'I didn't go after all,' he answered. 'I wasn't feeling up to the mark.' But he doesn't connect it with Ivanoff even now," said Newton. "He's hopeless—you'll never teach him."

"What was it that Ivan gave him?" Svaroff asked.

"Hg CL, six grains," was the answer. "Hobbs is certainly unique."

By this time the kettle was boiling, Svaroff made the tea. They drank it in the Russian fashion, and Svaroff made it delightfully. Iris thought it was the nicest tea she had ever tasted.

"Yes. It's a special kind; I always get it at Fortnum and Mason's," he told her, turning to his faun-like companion, who was already miles away, gambolling in some lost Arcadian forest. "Newton, you son of Choronzon, pass Mrs. Strickland the biscuits."

She noticed that he did not get up to do so himself. Lounging in the depths of his long low chair he looked the very picture of comfort. She, too, felt very comfortable and most agreeably lazy.

Newton, returning for a moment from his Pan-Arcadian pastures, withdrew his calf-like innocent gaze and hastily passed the tin. He had been looking at Iris for the last five minutes. The expression of his eyes suggested that of a young child or untamed animal, there was a total absence of self-consciousness. Already he was busy reconstructing their pasts and a wonderful poem would be the result. But in the meantime there was tea.

"I'm so sorry, Mrs. Strickland, but I've got a very wonderful poem," he stated naively.

"Well, I hope it is better than the last," said Svaroff, but the expression of his eyes was very charming, and belied his words.

He refrained from disturbing the boy again—but without in any way making it obvious that he did so. Iris felt again the very strong bond of sympathy between the two. In spite of their schoolboy raggings they most undoubtedly understood each other.

He talked instead to Iris. They discussed Time and Space.

"There is no such thing as Time," he told her; "it is all a matter of point of view, and that rests always with yourself." He glanced at Newton.

"That's why some persons have such a very bad time; they have no sense of perspective. Have a right perspective and you are in tune with the Universe, but *Do what thou Wilt* shall be the whole of the Law." He smiled mysteriously. "You ought to read *Alice in Wonderland*."

Iris thought of her father, the Rev. Cedric Hamilton, and of some of their early discussions.

"I've always thought that Time and Space were the same," she said; "because if you speak of Time you always think of distance and if you think of distance you always imagine Time; but it all depends where *you* are—but the Reverend says that though the two are inseparable in thought, they are not the same. I never *could* make him understand," she added.

Then, seeing that Svaroff did not answer, she continued "Of course there can't really be any Past or Future, it's all Present, because if you look far enough into the Future it's really the Past, and if you look far enough into the Past it's really the Future so that it all comes back to yourself. It must be——" the phrase came to her in a flash, "an ever-extended and eternal present."

She was rather pleased with herself.

"Yes, that's it," said Svaroff.

Then she told him about the Reverend.

"He was born," she said, "just exactly two thousand years too late—he ought to have lived in the time of Socrates—he'll never adjust himself. He turns day into night and night into day and you ought to hear him argue. But he is a most unsatisfying person to talk to, because whenever he finds himself being cornered in an argument, he always says: 'Define what you exactly mean by so-and-so,' and he goes off on a sidetrack; then he proves that you didn't say what you meant. By the time he is finished, what you meant to say has completely gone out of your head, and it leaves him in possession of all the field, which of course is what he wanted. Is that what is called a Sophist?" she asked innocently.

"It does sound rather like one." Svaroff smiled.

"Well, I think it is decidedly mean," she answered. "The Reverend says he is a metaphysician but metaphysicians make me feel tired."

She told him a lot of amusing things about the Reverend. How when he had a special service he would set all the alarm clocks the day before, and how they usually went off at the most unexpected moments; and how once, when the Persian cat had got into the drawing-room in the middle of the night and had walked over the keys of the piano, everyone in the house had thought the same thing, that the Reverend had gone mad.

"They were such weird chords," she told him, "and we heard the same ones three times, and then an awful silence."

"I can quite imagine it," he said.

And then a neighbouring clock struck six. With a start of dismay Iris rose to her feet. For the first time in their married life she had completely forgotten the "Boy" for more than an hour. She felt positively guilty. But she would make it up, she thought hastily—she would tell him all about her wonderful day. How pleased and interested he would be!

She began pulling on her gloves.

"Why this sudden energy?" said Svaroff smoothly.

"I had no idea it was so late," she answered, "I'm nearly as bad as the Reverend; Blitzen will think I am lost."

"But I thought we agreed there was no such thing as Time," he reminded her.

"Yes, I know," she said, smiling, "but in the mean-time . . ."

"Ah! The mean is the very Devil, any extreme is better; but the middle path when it is merely the *safe* path is fatal—it is neither hot nor cold."

He was looking at her steadily; she began to feel vague.

"But mightn't it transcend them both?" she said lightly, yet scarcely knowing why she said it.

Svaroff squinted. "Verily out of the mouths of babes and sucklings," he said sententiously. "Yes, in the *final* test it might," he admitted. Then, questioningly, "I wonder how much you really know?"

But Iris was getting out of her depth, so she held out her hand.

"I've enjoyed to-day tremendously," she said.

"So have I," he answered, with equal frankness.

He walked with her to the door. Outside on the landing they paused simultaneously as each remembered something.

"To-morrow I have to go out of town," said Svaroff, "but the day after we shall be having a symposium, an experiment to invoke Isis. Will you come? Do! Who knows, perhaps you will see Newton *as he really is?*"

"I should love to," she answered, "but may I bring the Boy?"

"Of course—bring as many as you like," he replied.

Iris hesitated painfully as the recollection difficulties assailed her with sudden force.

"Can you give me any idea as to when the verses will come out," she said, colouring uncomfortably. "You see we're in a frightful hole. We had a beastly blue paper this morning and I don't quite know what is going to happen!"

She tried to speak lightly, but the effort was more real than apparent. How she hated having to speak of these things. Why was money ever invented? It was the first time in her life she had ever had to discuss money with a stranger—for a brief moment she felt that she was unclothed. But Svaroff's expression was one of genuine concern.

"My dear Mrs. Strickland, why ever didn't you tell me before," he said. "I'm afraid it's too late to do anything to-night, but the cheque shall be sent the first thing to-morrow morning. The verses won't come out till September, but there's no reason why you shouldn't have the dollars in advance." He ignored her thanks.

"The book should go well," he said, "it is *poetry*—but you ought to write more, you know. Let yourself go, don't be afraid! You have found your moorings; try to write a long poem."

"Do you really think I could?" she said.

"Of course," he answered.

"I'll promise to *try* then, but I don't promise to succeed."

"Good! I shall keep you to it," he threatened.

"What, V.H.O.?" she said, laughing.

He looked at her gravely. "I'm not at all sure that it wouldn't be the very best thing possible for you. I'm not at all sure that you're not even lazier than Newton." The Chinese mask had descended upon his face. "By the way," he said musingly, "do you know that that clock struck *seven* just now, not six?"

"Good heavens, did it really?"

"Yes. But don't worry." He re-entered the big room and spoke to Newton. "Tell Arthur to call a taxi."

Ten minutes later Iris reached home.

CHAPTER III

FROM the point of view of most sane persons the parents of Iris ought never to have married. It therefore follows logically that from the point of view of most sane persons that Iris herself should never have been born. That they did marry and that she was born came to pass in this wise. To the union of her maternal grandmother with John Sinienski Iris owed her mixed blood. The Polish rabbi had fallen in love at first sight with Agnes O'Connor, the beautiful Irish girl from County Cork. Agnes was an orphan, and there had been no obstacle to the marriage, and they had been united within a month.

A converted Jew and now a priest of the Anglican Church, he had wished at first to take his bride to the land of his adoption, where together they would help to convert his brethren. Already he had travelled as a missionary to Syria, Palestine and to Egypt. They would go, he hoped, to Russia, but first to Poland, for Poland had been the land of his birth. But Agnes his wife had no such wishes. The thought of travel terrified her. She was fragile and beautiful, she was weak and determined; her will prevailed.

John Sinienski settled in London, and three children were born from the marriage—John, Emily and Laura. John, the eldest, was at Oxford and Emily and Laura were down for the Commemoration when Cedric Hamilton, then in his second year, had fallen in love with Emily. He had met her walking with her brother and sister in the gardens of Worcester College. Cedric's father had made a love match; Cedric followed the family tradition.

Emily was seventeen. She was shy and wild and slender as a wood nymph—she scarcely looked fifteen. Her waving bronze-gold hair had entangled him in its meshes and made him a prisoner from the first: her playing of Chopin, Rubenstein and Schumann had fastened the knots. It was inevitable.

The year after Cedric left Oxford he took Holy Orders—two years later they were married. For a year or so all went happily. They had similar tastes, the companionship was perfect. But when persons of similar tastes have entered into the bonds of matrimony, when those tastes are poetic and aesthetic, and neither party is blessed with private means, it does not require a Daniel to prophesy the ending.

Cedric should never have married—his ineradicable bachelor habits were incompatible with the responsibilities of family life. His few remaining relatives, for his parents had died when he was a child, washed their hands of what they considered an improvident marriage. Phlegmatic in temperament themselves and utterly devoid of imagination, they neither understood nor wished to understand the meaning of love and passion. Where they could have done much towards helping his advancement, they stupidly refrained from doing so. Not that Cedric ever solicited their help, for it was not in his nature to ask help of anyone, but they could see how matters stood, and—they looked resolutely the other way. Cedric had a strong streak of obstinacy—he had also a habit of caustic repartee coupled with an incapacity for any sort of compromise that clashed with his innermost convictions—a rather dangerous combination. He was a poet, a metaphysician and a musician—the very last thing then that he should have been was a priest of the Anglican Church. His intellect, which was very far above the average, his quick brain and subtle wit made it impossible for him to understand and sympathise with the lesser brains of his congregation and with their often narrow prejudices, their stupidity and their provincialisms. Unfortunately, without ever so intending, he made them feel conscious of the difference between them. This was a fatal mistake.

Cedric was lacking in the time sense, he was often late for services, an excuse was ready to hand. Cedric changed his curacy six times within the first two years. And when he took a chaplaincy in the East End of London, Emily returned to Oxford.

Of the seven children born to Cedric two had died in infancy. Iris was the last but one. Her brothers and sisters went in pairs—she was the odd one. From the very first she was always solitary and she showed her independence; but at this time she was not unhappy. Her mother was a charming hostess, she played magnificently, and the most delightful and interesting persons came to the house. They were mostly friends of her Uncle John, and Iris, who was five years old and very pretty, came in for a good share of attention. Dressed in white muslin, with a broad blue sash and the shiniest of black patent leather shoes, Miss Iris would be taken by nurse down to the drawing-room. That a certain brilliant Professor of Psychology came on purpose to see her, Iris never doubted for a moment. They were the greatest friends, and when he subsequently wrote from Munich that he was sorry he was unable to pay his customary visit to Iris, Iris was highly delighted.

He hadn't forgotten her. Iris remembered him so well that when fourteen years later she met and married her husband, it was partly because of the resemblance.

Of her father Iris remembered little at this time, but she loved her mother passionately and she was conscious early of an atmosphere of worry and the wish to protect her mother.

When one day she came unexpectedly upon the latter and knew that she had been crying. Iris felt that the world must surely come to an end.

A few days later Iris called her father a "Pharisee." There had been a discussion at the dinner-table and Iris, who had been listening quietly as is the way with children, suddenly delivered her verdict. It is probable that the verdict was justified, for to her amazement she, received a stinging blow upon the ear.

"Really Cedric, you should learn to control yourself," said her mother, "you might seriously injure the child." Then turning to Iris, "you had better leave the room."

Iris got up slowly. She was recovering from influenza. The blow, as unexpected as it had been heavy, would, had she not been seated, have undoubtedly knocked her down. But it was not the pain she minded, it was the indignity. Iris was nearly nine. She walked slowly to the door. At the door she delivered a Parthian shot. She looked at the Reverend Cedric with unutterable scorn.

"Don't forget that I am a lady although I have the misfortune to be your daughter," she said icily, and she was gone.

The next day the Reverend Cedric apologised. It was well for him that he did so, for Iris would never have spoken to him in this world again. She was certainly an *enfant terrible*.

"Are you fond of poetry?" said a grown-up visitor once, on seeing Iris was reading.

"Yes," said the latter, "Uncle Osric writes poetry."

"Does he?" said the visitor; "and what does he write about?"

"Oh, love and moonlight and that sort of thing," was the answer, but the irony was quite unconscious. And once, when many years later she had been discussing poetry with her father and he had said:

"I am glad, dear, that you are beginning to understand me a little."

"Yes, I *like* you well enough," she had replied, "but of course I'm not in love with you.

Nor did she realise that she had said anything extraordinary. Her innocence was amazing, for she was nearly fifteen at the time.

She was certainly an unusual child. She lived in a world of her own. From the early days when she spent hours lying in the long grasses of Port Meadow trying to see the wind to the day when some years later she seriously wished to enter the lion's cage at the Zoo, it is doubtful if her sisters ever understood her. She preferred trees and animals, especially wild animals, to human beings, and above all else she loved the wind. She felt that she was akin to it, as she was also akin to the flowers, but to some flowers more than to others. The water-lily in particular attracted her. She couldn't say why, but she felt the fascination so strongly that she was for ever trying to reach the white cup-like blossoms, and she often dreamed about them; perhaps it was because they were out of reach. In later years she thought it must have been their aloofness and their coldness that so attracted her: for when she kissed their damp smooth petals, so unresponsive in their chill purity to her warm young lips, they had the strange sweet mystic beauty of a corpse. Iris was not neurotic, but she had a love of beauty: a love so intense that it almost verged on an ache. And mixed with this love was a sense of sorrow: that vague, intangible unhappiness amounting at times almost to a prevision of calamity that is never far distant from the most beautiful of summer days, and that broods like an Image of Pan over the peaceful hills and slumbering valleys and is all the more strongly felt in that it is never defined.

She realised vaguely that she was seeing it all for the last time, and insignificant details impressed her with a curious intensity whilst in the innermost depths of her being a voice said: "Such and such a thing you will remember years afterwards."

How true she afterwards found this. The scent of clover, the song of the lark above the cornfields, the shadow of the clouds idly chasing each other as they darkened momentarily the face of the wind-swept downs: a certain gravel path and the hot scent of geraniums, the vivid scarlet blooms striking as violent a note of colour as the blare of a trumpet and uttering brazen challenge to the vault of the blue remoteness sky. Were not these memories interwoven with schooldays and the age of twelve? And then:

Buttercups, cow-parsley, the far-away voices of children playing in a neighbouring field; the chirping of grasshoppers and a sense of myriad insect life; butterflies, and the cawing of rooks overhead, and with it all a sense of beautiful remoteness, and was she not an infant again?

All her earliest recollections were linked with flowers, and how clearly she remembered them. There was a meadow not far from the house through which a stream ran bordered by willow trees. Bulrushes grew in the midst of the stream and forget-me-nots clustered round the banks. In the spring the field was ablaze with ragged robins, tiny cuckoo flowers and speedwell hid in the grass. Iris would dream away long hours, wondering up at the white clouds, watching the strips of blue through the grey-green leaves of the trees, listening to the song of the birds. It seemed to her that when she lay very still she faded out of herself and became merged in it all; the blue sky, the running water, the trees, they were all herself. The small Iris that was always being scolded by nurse, looked askance at by her elders and generally made to feel superfluous, seemed like a tiny figure seen through the wrong end of a telescope; she was unreal, she was miles away. And the sense of vastness grew and grew until Iris ceased to think at all. She was content merely to feel. She was always happy out of doors. And in March there were beech woods where she discovered the early bluebells, and places where the purple snake's-head grew. Fields, too, that were golden with the marsh marigold, fields that were a-shimmer with the soft blue scabious. And in winter when the snow came and the fields were flooded and the Isis and the Cherwell were frozen hard, she would be transported into a wonderful fairy world of white.

Icicles tinkled from the trees, the reeds in the river made music like the shivering sound of infinitesimal golden bells— the sun like a dull glowing ball of metal peered through the grey clouds, growing larger and larger as it sank gradually below the horizon; faint streaks of orange appeared in the sky, and the great disk disappeared from view like a gorgeous coloured Chinese lantern.

How she loved it all! She would spend whole days romping with her brothers; skating, lighting bonfires on the ice (for they had real winters in those days), playing at Esquimaux and Indians. And how she loved climbing! She could always climb the highest trees—sometimes it was very difficult to get down again—but her balance was extraordinary—she never lost her nerve.

With her brothers and her brothers' friends Iris was a great favourite. Her favourite authors at the time were Fennimore Cooper and Henty. Her favourite indoor door games were *petit chevaux* and chess. There was nothing feminine about her. At the ages of eight she was slender as an elf, had regular features, a mop of brown curly hair, and mischievous hazel eyes, but she was quite unaware of the fact that she was more than usually pretty. When she did realise it in latter years she regarded it as impersonally as she would have done a picture or a piece of statuary. The idea of trading on her looks or trying to score off or humiliate another woman would have been as revolting to her as it would have been inconceivable. She admired her sister where her sister only envied her in return.

Iris was generous. She had a strong sense of fair play and, what is more rare in any girl, a sense of humour. She had a sense of humour, and never having felt jealousy in her life was incapable of understanding in others—she never even suspected it. She put own the behaviour of her elder sister, who for many years made her life intolerable, to a species of insanity. Of repressed complexes she knew nothing, but when she did know she sincerely pitied her. She never retaliated, she just left her alone.

Small wonder was it that if she sometimes failed to understand herself others failed to understand her. Yet surely so it was. For the rest, her tastes were decided.

From her mother she inherited her love of music; from her father her love of poetry; from her Irish grandmother a passion for dancing.

When her mother played Chopin she would go into an adjoining room and dance by herself. The music made pictures for her, she saw landscapes. The Phantasie and the Mazurka in F sharp minor especially appealed to her. In the latter she could visualise the wind. It was a grey wind wailing across wild waste places: there were pine trees in it, and somewhere there was a marsh. In the former there were tree-clad mountains, moonlight and a wonderful cascade. At such times it seemed to her that she left her body and floated upwards with the music, till she became one with the moonlight, the waterfall, the wailing wind, and the sombre gloom of the pines.

In a shower of sparkling drops the music would cease, and Iris would come back to her everyday surroundings with an intolerable aching void that she felt must one day surely kill her.

What it was that she so much wanted she did not know, but she wished to get away from herself, to *be* all that she *felt*, and by a greater expansion of consciousness to lose the sense of her small personal entity. This was how she voiced it in after years.

At the age of ten Iris was sent to a boarding school at Brighton and it was here that they first discovered her "pernicious habit of writing poetry." She was given a long lecture by the dormitory mistress. She was told she was morbid and unnatural and must nor use words of which she couldn't possibly know the meaning, and when she pointed out that the word in question had come into the school lesson, they looked at her queerly. In short, they discovered she was original—at all costs they must crush it out. So they punished her for not joining in games in which she had never been asked to join. If a school-fellow showed a liking for her they always managed to separate them. Iris began to wonder if the curse which had been pronounced on her grandfather by his fellow-Semites when he became a Christian had already began to descend on her. She determined that whatever happened she would hide her emotions.

She did so so successfully that people refused to believe that she ever had any. She was called a "hardened child."

It was about this time that Iris first remembered Uncle John. He had come to meet the train at Victoria Station, and she saw him advancing with springy steps down the platform to meet her. He was dressed in a black braided morning coat and wore dark grey striped trousers, and his top hat was a little on the back of his head. He had just removed a most fragrant Havana cigar from his mouth, and was beaming all over. He looked down at her smiling through half-closed eyelids.

"Well, you Small Thing!" he said.

Iris liked him at once. He had a beautiful voice and the most beautiful hands, and everything he did was right. He was not in the least like her Uncle Osric, who though always joking gave you the impression that he was very bad-tempered indeed underneath and not in the least to be trusted. Uncle John was genuine, Uncle Osric was not.

They had a delightful time for the next few weeks. Uncle John took Iris and her sisters everywhere. To the Exhibition, the Tower, the Zoo; to see *Alice in Wonderland.* Of her father Iris remembered nothing except that he kept them in on beautiful summer afternoons trying to give them Greek lessons, and that he made them go to hear the *Messiah* and the *Elijah* at the Queen's Hall, and that she felt sick with the standing.

Everyone liked Uncle John. He was always good humoured, he had gaiety of heart. His very presence made people feel younger and that life was worth having. He had an inexhaustible fund of stories, and the most delightful laugh. He laughed with his shoulders, Iris remembered, and in speaking of things he always said "one" instead of "I" or "you." He was always ready to play with the Small People, as he affectionately called them. He named them the first day, "Smallness, Tallness and Fatness." Anything under two years old would be an "It" he explained to them; anything smaller still would be an "Itling." They had great fun. He would pretend to be the statue in "Don Juan" and say "*Shake hands*" in a mysterious voice that thrilled them deliciously—a tremendous hug invariably followed.

Sometimes he would be "the man in whom the evil spirit was," and then the formula would be varied by "Who are ye'."

People said that Uncle John was a brilliant conversationalist. He often spoke to her Aunt Laura of the Borgias and Napoleon, and he quoted the "Ancients." Iris always remembered that "the Ancients were very fond of salad." Had not John said so? He had also said on a certain occasion:

"Poor old H. is a worshipper of words."

They had been speaking of her father. This, too, Iris remembered.

It was Uncle John who first took Iris to see her grandfather.

John Sinienski senior was a short man of upright carriage, with remarkably small hands and feet, singularly clear blue eyes, and the most enchanting and childlike smile.

He regaled them, like Melchizedek of old, with and cake and wine. Iris had a small hole in her glove and she hoped that her grandfather would not notice. But nothing escaped his observation. He rang a bell, and the housekeeper was sent for. The glove was mended immediately, and Iris felt positively guilty.

Her grandfather was decidedly autocratic and absolutely without fear or hesitation. At eighty years of age, with one arm held horizontally behind his back, he would walk unaided across the London streets in the midst of the densest and most dangerous traffic. When remonstrated with he would say with authoritative decision:

"It is for them to stop for me, not for me to stop for them," and the remarkable thing is that they always did.

It was during the second year that Iris was at school that her grandfather died, and her Uncle John followed him but a few weeks later. The last time that Iris saw her uncle was when she was returning to Brighton from Victoria, and her uncle as usual (for her father had forgotten all about it) was seeing her off. Just as the train was starting he asked her to kiss him a second time. Iris thought it seemed a little unnecessary as she would be seeing him again in a few months, but she remembered that he gave a little laugh and said:

"One never knows, you Small Thing." She never saw him again.

It was about this time that Iris began to realise a good many things: that her father, for instance, valued books far more than people and was entirely wrapped up in his studies; that he was extraordinarily selfish, and the sort of life her mother had led in consequence.

"If all you children and poor Emily were to die to-morrow Cedric would take the funeral service without shedding a tear, and would go home and eat a good dinner afterwards. The Hamiltons have fishes' blood. Poor dear Emily, if only she had married her Cousin James. James was a *man*." Mrs. Sinienski spoke with the utmost scorn, but Iris felt that she spoke the truth.

It was not long after this that Iris asked her father about Cousin James.

"What was he like?" she said.

"Oh an awfully nice fellow," her father answered. "Mama was engaged to him for nearly a year before she met me."

"Yes, I know," said Iris; "but what was he like to look at?"

"A tall handsome fellow; very proud looking; he always reminded me of an Arab prince," said her father.

Iris wondered why her mother had never married him. She looked at the photograph and came to the conclusion that perhaps her mother had been a little afraid of him.

"Your grandfather," said Cedric, "was of the tribe of Judah, a direct descendant in the royal line from King David—he traced his descent back to King Jehoiachin. Of course," he added, "Sinienski was only an assumed name. Your grandfather was the eldest of several brothers, all of whom converted but they all took different names. He was, I believe, very wealthy and had a good deal of land and possessions; he was disinherited."

Iris was silent for a few minutes, then said at last:

"I always *was* proud of my Oriental blood, now I feel prouder than ever. How wonderful to think that one is a direct descendant of King Solomon!"

"Humph," said her father dryly, "I don't know that that Bathsheba affair was altogether creditable!"

It was after the death of her grandfather that Mrs. Sinienski came to live with them. Iris loved her grandmother. She was a beautiful old lady, tall and slender, with a proud and gracious carriage, sapphire blue eyes and the sweetest smile. Though over seventy she scarcely looked fifty. Often she would talk to Iris while plaiting the child's long thick hair, and Iris loved to listen.

She would tell how when she was a girl they had driven on the coach from Doncaster to London, how it had been snow-ing, and how it had taken them three days. Of her first ball and how she had danced with Count D'Orsay; of the strange things that had happened to her brother, the well-known portrait painter, and how her mother had been besieged during the riots and had married when she was sixteen. She also spoke of her husband's brother Murad, and the strange visitor he had brought with him from the East.

"He was a very good-looking man," she said, "nearly six feet four, and they called him 'handsome Shalaby.' Though staying in Brighton he still would wear his baggy trousers with a wide cummerbund and a bright fez, and he always smoked a hookah in the drawing-room. Once when he had been smoking for several hours, your Cousin James asked him what he thought of Cedric. He continued to smoke for several minutes, then he said: 'He has no salt.' I think he did not speak again for the rest of the evening."

"What happened to Shalaby?" said Iris. The name interested her; it sounded, she thought, like something from the *Arabian Nights*.

"Well," said her grandmother, "it was rather curious; he came to a strange end. He was the head of the tribe, but he was in great favour with the Sultan, and the people feared and hated him. One day he set out with several attendants to go to a distant part of the country: he elected to go on ahead by himself. He was riding a mule and they were going through a narrow pass near the valley of Artas. Shalaby did not return. In the evening men were sent to search for him. They found him in a narrow pass between the rocks. He had fallen from the stirrup and his foot was crushed against the wall. He had been dead for several hours. It was said that certain of the tribesman could have thrown light on the matter, but of course they could never prove anything."

Iris thought it sounded very like the story of Balaam and she always wondered where they had found a mule big enough to support so huge a man. But she knew her grandmother would not have invented the tale.

She enjoyed hearing about these things immensely—it helped her to understand herself a little, and also, if the truth be told, to make excuses for her want of understanding.

How could one expect to feel the same as the stolid Anglo-Saxons around one! It was ridiculous and yet she was always being judged by the Anglo-Saxon standard. In future she would not trouble. She turned then for sympathy and understanding to her Aunt Laura.

Laura was gay, she was beautiful, and Iris, who always loved beautiful things, came completely under the spell of her aunt's fascination. That her father did not approve of this friendship only helped to strengthen It. The vague atmosphere of disapproval which he managed to convey when speaking of her visits to Laura only irritated her. She began almost to dislike her father.

She didn't understand. And Laura in the meantime filled her mind with strange and extravagant ideas. She talked to the child of her mad infatuation for Svaroff, whose letters she would sometimes read to her; she spoke of Ibsen. To Iris, who was ignorant of the most rudimentary facts of existence, who knew not the meaning of marriage, that her aunt was her mother's sister, or why her parents were her parents and nobody else's, it all seemed wonderful as a fairy-tale. That Laura was married and her husband, Colonel Honiton, in India would have meant nothing to her even had she realised it. Laura was romantic and passionate but she was also fastidious, and her long talks and confidences with Iris left the latter as innocent as they found her. But they left her with a very real hatred of conventions and what her aunt called "dull middle-class respectability." She quoted the phase without even knowing what it meant.

"Strike out a line for yourself, child. Don't stick in a groove. Nothing succeeds like success. Don't be afraid to be happy." These were a few of the things that Laura had said. She had also said one day to Iris: "You have a strong personality; people will hate you for it when you are older and do their best to crush it out of you, but don't let them do it."

And then at the age of fourteen Iris had gone on the stage. The play, which was *The Vikings of Helgeland*, had run for a very short time. It was followed by *Much Ado about Nothing*. That was also not a success. At the end of the summer Iris found herself with nothing to do and a very bad attack of scarlet fever. Scarlet fever developed into diphtheria. Diphtheria was followed by influenza, and by the time Iris was better all desire for the stage had left her.

For a long time she was very ill, and then she started writing. Her work, so Hildrebrand, the famous publisher, had said, was altogether above the head of the paying public, "and it may be more difficult for you to step down than others to step up," he had told her. But Iris had no intention of stepping down. Her work quite possibly would never be published but she promised herself it should never be mediocre, and she kept her word.

CHAPTER IV

IT was on a warm June morning exactly three years before this story opens that Iris had first met her husband. She had called at the studio of a friend in New Court in order to return a book. The friend had been out, and from an adjoining studio had walked Eugene John Strickland, a handsome young giant with wonderful grey eyes and Rossetti-like hair. It was simply a recognition: they knew each other from the first. Before he had spoken even, Iris felt she had known him all her life. He told her that Billy had been called out but he wouldn't be long, and asked if she would come in and wait. It was a jolly studio. She sat down in a deep chair and watched him putting the finishing touches to a head.

"I must just finish this, if you don't mind."

Iris thought that he had the most beautiful speaking voice she had ever heard—it awoke in her strange memories that were not altogether of this world.

She watched him painting.

"What jolly hair you've got!" she said suddenly.

He looked up with a smile that was whimsical and wholly delightful.

"If you say that again," he said seriously, "I shall spank you."

"It *is* jolly hair, and you know it is."

He blushed like a girl, then took three strides across the room. He picked her up as though she had been a baby, and placed her upon his knee.

"I told you I should do it," he said, but he didn't spank her. Instead they just talked. It seemed perfectly natural. They must have talked for nearly an hour. Then Iris said she must go, since Billy wasn't coming. He asked when he should see her again, but she said she didn't know.

Thinking it over on the way home, she decided that she would not go again. It was altogether too extraordinary. What would he think of her? And then quite suddenly, without premeditation, she went. He opened the door as though he had been expecting her

"You have come at last," he said. "Why did you stay away so long? I began to think I should have to come and fetch you. I should have come to you had stayed away much longer. It was only the thought of what the Reverend would say to you (she had told him of her people) that made me hesitate at all. I should have faced all the Reverends."

That same morning he proposed to her.

"We'll go to California; you shall get right away from it all. It wants a big strong Blitzen to take care of it."

She had told him of the quarrel with her sister and that she had come to see him because she felt miserable, and when he had spoken of calling on her people she had called him Blitzen.

But she did not take the proposal seriously. She said in three months' time she would let him know. Then for three months he had written to her every day. She had been pleased to get his letters but she had not answered them. She thought that he had acted on impulse and that later he would regret it. The proposal was not definitely referred to, but he seemed to take it for granted that she would come. From time to time he sent her the most beautiful flowers. It was after the arrival of a large box of white tulips enclosing a card with a question mark that Iris went to see him.

The occasional gifts of flowers had made the behaviour of her sister more impossible than ever. Iris decided to go to Blitzen. She could trust him, she told herself; they would live together as friends but of course she wouldn't marry him. It wouldn't be fair to him, she argued. Suppose it were only an infatuation, and he were to tire of her? It would be too awful.

She spoke about it to him in October, but it was not until the following May that she came to him. She still thought that he had acted upon impulse.

The Reverend Cedric Hamilton was away at the time taking a *locum tenens* at the other end of London. The stars were favourable. Iris told her mother that she would be staying with some friends for a while and the address was not asked for. She went from home quite easily. When she next wrote home she was married. But she had not married for several months—she had dreaded the legal bond—she had seen so many unhappy marriages. She dreaded disillusionment.

"What if they too should become humdrum?" The thought was more than she could bear. But Blitzen had reassured her.

"It won't make the slightest difference," he had said, "we shall still be absolutely free, but it saves such a lot of stupid explanations. I can't go about knocking people down."

Blitzen, who was six years older than Iris, dreaded the inevitable gossip that he knew must sooner or later reach her if they continued as they were. She looked such a child. In spite of the fact that she was close on twenty she still wore her hair down; for Blitzen would not hear of her putting it up—and usually they were taken for brother and sister. But Blitzen's mother was making efforts to discover his whereabouts; he would not be able to frustrate her much longer and then . . .

Blitzen refused to allow the train of thought to finish.

"But does it matter what vulgar people say?" she had asked him. "Haven't we the courage of our own convictions?"

"Yes, Kiddie," he had answered. "But it's different somehow for a woman. I can't explain."

Then realising how little her idealism would be understood, his sense of protection had deepened. Never through him, he determined, should she ever have cause to regret her choice. Early that autumn they were married, and meanwhile the companionship was perfect. They had taken a couple of studios on the top storey of an old Adam house in the Adelphia—a delightful old place full of quaint nooks and corners.

They had no servant or charwoman to worry themselves— necessary work was done by a male model whom Blitzen had employed for years. Nothing could have answered better. From the first they revelled in their freedom.

Trying to unravel the mystery of the Universe they would talk until the early hours of the morning. Then, realising that bed was out of the question, they would go for a walk just as the sun was rising. Wandering through the Embankment gardens where the lilac and laburnum were blossoming and the London sparrows chattering, they would watch the dawn spread across the river, till the rays of light resting upon the dome of St. Paul's gilded the cross and fell upon the paws of the Sphinx, and her mysterious smile deepened. Then, going home to breakfast, they would bathe and rest, and afterwards she would pose. Sometimes he would get wonderful ideas, and then she would begin to write and afterwards they would compare notes.

Their tastes were diametrically opposed and they often discussed them. She preferred moonlight to sunlight, green to red, woods and mountains to open spaces, the river to the sea. Blitzen loved above all things the sun, open spaces and the sea. He told her that her point of view was not healthy, that there was no life in the moon and that mystery was never unravelled; she told him that the sunlight *hurt* her, it was "all prickly," and that red made her wish to scream, that as a child she had amused herself for hours looking through a piece of green glass. The Blitzen would laugh, but they never quarrelled. They were too happy.

Sometimes in the early mornings Iris would dance for the sheer joy of living. She would seize an assagai and in a series of quickening circles advance upon the helpless Blitzen. Blitzen pretending to be asleep would suddenly spring up and catch her. Throwing her over his shoulder he would put an end to the impromptu war-dance. They were most delightfully mad. They loved and they were free.

If there was one person in history for whom Iris had always felt antagonism it was St. Paul, whom she considered (though this reflection she made many years later) was hopelessly over-sexed. His admonitions to women particularly enraged her. Why should they be "modest" and "shamefaced." She never felt the slightest discomfiture or guiltiness in the presence of the opposite sex. Women made her feel self-conscious sometimes, and she was more shy with them than she was with men, but that was because they could never get away from sex. Iris had never heard of Weineger much less read a line of him, but she realised this quite early. Most modest persons were singularly immodest, and so-called Puritans were prurient-minded.

She could never see the necessity for conventions between the sexes for the simple reason that she was unaware of the causes for which it existed, and no one had even taken the trouble to explain to her. For an astonishing number of years, therefore, she remained an enigma to herself and others.

When a few days before her marriage she had read for the first time the marriage service, it had so disgusted her that she had thrown down the book and had nor finished reading it. It was barbarous, utterly degrading, she reflected. It placed the union of men and women on a level with the farmyard—companionship was the last thing it mentioned.

She spoke of her nostalgia to Blitzen, who she knew could sympathise. They were married at the Registry Office.

Iris felt intense affection for her husband and a love that amounted to worship, but of love as it is generally understood she knew nothing, and she was absolutely devoid of Jealousy. She couldn't understand it. That two persons could pretend to love each other and yet one of them resent love being shown from outside to the other was utterly despicable; it was also illogical. If one loved another person one surely wanted that person to be happy. Nothing made her feel happier than to hear her husband praised, and had he possessed a dozen wives she would not, she thought, have minded in the least. But she would not have wished to be bored with their company. So few women could talk of the things that interested her.

Indeed, so far did she carry this theory, that feeling there was something she had not given her husband—she tried to get the prettiest models to come to the studio in the hope that he would fall in love with them. She even mentioned this hope to him, but this was more than even Blitzen could understand.

"Sweetheart, do you realise what you are saying?"

"Perfectly," she answered him. "I can't respond to what I suppose is meant by marriage, but I love the Boy more than anything in the world and I want the Boy to be happy."

Then, for the first time, Blitzen realised that that in spite of her advanced ideas she really was a child.

"But the 'Boy' *is* happy," he said.

CHAPTER V

THEIR life together had been one long idyll. Certainly they had had their "ups" and "downs," and they had been more than once in some very tight corners; but always when the mercury had been lowest in the glass it had suddenly risen. Blitzen had received a commission, or some long-standing debt had been paid.

Indeed, they had got so accustomed to the unexpected happening at the last moment, that until affairs were really desperate they didn't anticipate a change for the better, and so it was that at last the inevitable day arrived when the unexpected didn't happen, and they were faced with a blue paper and the unpleasant prospect of uninvited guests, to say nothing of the loss of their goods and chattels.

For the first time in their married life Iris gave way to tears. She couldn't help it. She loved every stick in the place. To her the studios were the symbol of their happiness, and the thought of going elsewhere filled her with a blank dismay. The thing happened after the death of Grimmer, the landlord. Always she had dreaded the visits of old Grimmer—she was really frightened of him: yet beneath his rough exterior he had hidden a kindly heart, as Strickland well knew. Still, his appearance *had* been rather terrifying.

He was nearly ninety years of age, short and thick-set, with a thatch of snow-white hair, white scrubby beard, and bushy overhanging white eyebrows. His eyes, which were grey, deep-set and very keen, almost met above a bridgeless nose. His upper lip was the longest Iris had ever seen in a human countenance. He reminded her of a fierce orang-outang—and his voice, rasping and husky, did not help to dispel this illusion. He always wore a double-breasted seaman's coat with a peaked cap, and a bright blue muffler round his neck.

His trousers, which were grotesquely short through the constant economy of being turned up, exposed to view a pair of very thin ankles encased in white socks, which were all the more noticeable from the fact that the old man wore shoes. He usually carried a short ash stick.

Iris would hear him coming up the stairs long before he reached their landing, for he had a silver tube in his throat, and she would hear the wind whistling through it as he occasionally removed his thumb from the aperture.

But old Grimmer had his own code of dealing with them and he had never yet taken them by surprise. The thing had usually happened in this way. Blitzen, who was supposed to pay each week, would, when the rent had been neglected for some time, receive a note from his landlord couched somewhat as follows:

"Mr. Strickland, Dear Sir,—I must call your most *severe* attention to the fact that the rent is now six weeks overdue, and I must ask for a settlement at your earliest convenience."

If Blitzen could procure the money he would pay at once, pretending that he had been so busy the affair had momentarily escaped his attention. If he could not do so he would say he was expecting a cheque at any moment. It was a simple game of bluff which saved his dignity and put to rest the fears of old Grimmer. For if the latter guessed the state of affairs, as it is probable that he sometimes did, he never let them see it. Once he had said with a grim humour: "That cheque is a long time in coming, Mr. Strickland." But he knew that artists were not like other folk; and clients were very casual when it came to paying for their pictures. Indeed, Blitzen himself had often wondered at the extraordinary slackness in regard to payments that seemed characteristic of the firms who bought his work, but it was not until many months had passed, and both Iris and he had been on the verge of a very literal starvation, that he knew his agent had been systematically cheating him—and then, such were the conditions, that Blitzen had to part with his dress clothes in order to find money to appear at the Court. And it was just at this time that Grimmer had been found dead at the bottom of his kitchen stairs.

The news was brought to Blitzen by the semi-paralysed and mentally deficient son George.

"*I* didn't do it," said the latter, "he *fell* down. Funeral's to be on Wednesday—there ain't going to be no purple nor 'fevvers' nor nuffing. Nice plain car."

They were a queer family. Despite his unattractive appearance old Grimmer had married three times, and had four sons, John, George, William and Arthur. Arthur they had never seen; but John was deaf and suffered from cerebral anaeia, George, was partially paralysed and had a species of locomotor ataxia, William was lame—and (as the milkman had once said to Strickland) "even their cat has no tail!" It was, as a rule, George who brought back the rent book, and on these occasions he usually had a talk with "Boots" the black kitten. For his obvious fondness for animals Iris liked him, but in other respects he made her shiver. The curious mixture of cunning and stupidity, plus the physical disabilities gave him an atmosphere of distinct uncanniness. It was said, such is the strange conceit of men, that he had great belief in his power to charm and thought he was an object of desire to half the girls in London. If ever he met Blitzen in the street he had one invariable greeting. "Keep yourself warm?" he would say. It was half a query and half an admonition;—but it never varied even in the month of August; nor did Blitzen ever quite know what George meant, except that he intended to be friendly. In speaking of George to Iris, Blitzen always called him Dottiville—the name fitted him exactly; the lame one was known as "Hoppiville"; but John was plain John.

Blitzen remembered how once when old Grimmer had wanted John he had banged on the floor with his stick, rasping out in the intervals of knocking, "It's *convenient* to be deaf sometimes." When John, who was close on sixty years of age, had timidly appeared, Blitzen fully expected the old man to set about belabouring his son. "He looked," said Blitzen in telling the story afterwards, "for all the world like an old pirate. I could well imagine him in the old days sailing under the black flag, and wouldn't he just have kept the crew in order!"

"I've done some drawing in my time," he once said to Blitzen, "used to draw a barrow—now I draw dividends," and he laughed harshly at his own joke.

"I used to sleep in the Adelphi arches when I was a lad," he said on another occasion, "and many's the fight I and the 'boys' have had with Charlie the night-watchman."

He spoke, Strickland thought, as though he half regretted those far-off days with all their poverty and hardship.

For old Grimmer was now a very rich man indeed, but he was a genuine miser. In spite of the fact that he owned several streets, besides two houses in the Adelphi, he still went to bed and got up with the birds in order to save candle light; in winter he went without a fire, and he would send one of his sons all the way to Billingsgate Market to save a few pennies on some fish. After his death a large bag of gold had been found under Dottiville's pillow, which was doubtless the origin of the quarrel that had ended in the old man's death; for he had followed out faithfully the example of the miser in the fairy-tales. Yet in his very ruggedness there was something half-attractive; in his own particular way he was absolutely genuine, and affectation would have been a thing quite beyond his comprehension.

It was after the death of old Grimmer that the "ghosts" disappeared. The "ghosts" were two females of uncertain age who lived in the basement of Grimmer's house. They were dressed in black nunlike garments, and had faces like yellow wax. They had never been seen to smile at or speak to anyone, and their footsteps were soundless. Twice a day they both appeared by the railings outside the house, and were seen to glide with a beer jug to the nearest house of refreshment and back. When they got back to the house they seemed literally to disappear into the pavement. Iris had watched them many a time, but always just when they got near to the house something had called her attention away for a moment—the kitten had jumped on to her shoulder, an airship had passed overhead, or Blitzen had possibly spoken. Anyway, she had never seen the "ghosts" either enter or actually leave the house—always they had appeared and disappeared by the railings.

In thinking it over afterwards she wondered whether they were the wraiths of the old man's wives, who were possibly satisfied now that he had come to join them. Be that as it may, she had never heard of any women who lived in the house with Grimmer, nor had Blitzen.

Another strange character who interested them both was the "widower." It was Blitzen who had so named him.

This was a queer creature of about fifty years of age, with a ragged walrus-like moustache, sandy hair, a tall dome-like forehead and nondescript blue eyes. He usually took a bath at 11 a.m., and as he lived on the opposite side of the road, on the floor below and two doors down, Blitzen, who was sketching on the parapet, had not infrequently seen him at his ablutions.

"He crawls on hands and knees to the window, gets into his bath and as often as not starts peeling the potatoes for dinner. I've watched him often," said Blitzen to Iris. "It's the funniest thing imaginable to see him on all-fours dressed in the garments of Nature, when a simple strip of linen at the window would save him all the trouble. Oh, you needn't worry, he can't possibly see me," Blitzen continued. "You see, the parapet entirely screens our window. I know, because I've been in the houses opposite—he probably takes all that trouble on account of the typists next door!"

One day, Blitzen was seized with the true spirit of the gamin. It was just after a late breakfast and he felt ripe for mischief. "Have you ever seen me blow an egg-shell?" he asked Iris.

"No," she said; "what do you mean?"

"I'll show you," he answered; "I've often done it at school."

He picked up an empty egg-shell, and putting the cavity to his mouth, blew out his cheeks as though about to burst a paper bag. Then he slapped the sides of his face, and with a sharp report like the sound of a pistol, the egg-shell shot across the room, out of the window across the street, and straight into the room where the moustached one was bathing. Rolling foolishly, it tumbled all round the bath. Iris was in the studio, so she did not see, but Blitzen, who had hopped on to their window-ledge, said that only May at his best could have done justice to "Widower's" expression. In idiotic amazement he looked up at the sky, from whence he supposed the missile to have fallen, then creeping carefully to the window he dropped the offending egg-shell outside The egg-shell fell on to the head of a passing constable. The constable looked up—and the expression on the two faces was more than even Blitzen could stand. Weak with laughter he disappeared below the parapet, but he never blew another egg-shell.

Yet another oddity was the postman with the flaming red hair, who never wore his hat and who wasted at least twenty minutes each day talking to the maid-servant across the way; and they had strange beings in their own house also.

"One day I shall write it all up," said Blitzen, "but it wouldn't be safe to do so now."

The ground floor was occupied when they first came there by an exquisite youth named Lewis de Willoughby, who looked as though he had stepped straight out of the eighteenth century. He wore a brown skirted coat and carried a thick gold-topped cane, and he was always very debonair indeed. Once Blitzen had come across him in a little general shop buying a three-halfpenny jar of Bovril.

"Awfully convenient, these little places," he had said airily, "especially when one is busy!"

The three-halfpence was probably his last in the world, but de Willoughby played the game bravely.

Once Blitzen heard fearsome screams coming from the ground-floor rooms, the obvious sounds of scuffing and a woman's muffled cries for help. Had de Willoughby gone suddenly mad? he wondered. Was a tragedy being enacted; ought he to interfere?

Just as Blitzen decided that he would have to go down, the door burst open, and in ringing tones he heard de Willoughby's voice. "There, *there* she is, on the *dear old palace roof!*" They were merely rehearsing for the forthcoming show.

Shortly after that de Willoughby left, and his rooms were taken by a youth who had just reached his majority and had come into some money. Van Haage, for so he was named, had the place elaborately polished and painted, and some wonderful bathrooms built out at the back, with frosted glass roofs. He was very proud indeed of the improvements he had made, and insisted on showing Strickland, whom he had waylaid one morning in the hall, all that he had added. The apple of his eye, however, appeared to be the solid silver bedstead! When he took to bathing "lovely ladies" at midnight and there were sounds of Neronian mirth, Hoxton Gunter, the journalist who lived below Blitzen, complained to the landlord, and Van Haage was requested to leave.

Haxton Gunter shared his rooms with a little Scotsman named Anderson, and the latter often came up into Blitzen's studio. He had come originally to borrow a penny when Blitzen had just three farthings. But the borrowing was only a ruse, for the next day Blitzen received a large sack of fruit and vegetables, which the little man begged him to accept, as he and Gunter "couldn't possibly eat the lot themselves, and they would only go bad if kept." They had come from his farm in Surrey, he explained.

The same morning he sent up an enormous bunch of white narcissi and a positive stack of lilac. He thought "the little lady looked as though she liked flowers." When he had been asked in to see their rooms and the wonderful arrangement of the flowers, the friendship was cemented. "He's a real little brick," said Blitzen afterwards. They found that he was brother to "Cynicus" of post-card fame—and he told them all manner of queer stories of the highlands of Scotland, of pacts made with the devil, and how the great grey goat. (Anderson pronounced it "goot") had come to claim the victims.

In the early days of their marriage Blitzen had brought home to Iris a wee black kitten. It was the tiniest thing she had ever seen, and it had an extra toe on each foot. They named it "Boots." Boots was unlike any cat they had had before or since.

When washing it would link together its extra toes and rub its face up and down like a little mouse. It refused to eat unless fed out of Blitzen's hand, and in a number of ways it showed marked originality. The thing that Boots liked best was for Blitzen to roll its body completely up in string, and when it was entirely covered, it would unroll itself, purring proudly.

Whilst Blitzen was painting it would sit on his shoulder like a tiny elemental, and only when the painting was finished would it draw attention to itself. This was done by putting out a soft black paw, gently turning Blitzen's face, and biting the tip of his nose! Once, so quietly did Boots sit, curled under the collar of the Harris tweed, that Blitzen had gone quite a good distance down the Strand before he realised that the little creature was there and then his attention was only drawn to it by the interested expression on the faces of the passers-by, who appeared to be looking with smiling curiosity somewhere in the region of his collar. "Have I forgotten to put on my tie—what is it?" he thought, and then something furry brushed against his chin and ten tiny razor-like claws dug themselves into his shoulders as the little beastie steadied itself. On another occasion it had hung on to his stocking just above his shoe, and beneath the trouser, and wondering what the "bulge" could be he had discovered Boots. It was really most embarrassing, for Boots began to climb "up," and as Blitzen said, "I couldn't undress in the street. I think that people thought my knee was bandaged, and the bandages were coming down. I tried to give that impression." But Boots when reprimanded only purred the louder, and Iris burying her face in its soft black body kissed it again and again. She loved the little creature passionately. When Boots disappeared one morning, shortly after the death of Grimmer, Iris felt that the end had come.

A few months before, Anderson had given them a black-and-white Persian cat, which used to sleep curled up on the head of Boots. The two kittens were great friends, and when the mouse-trap had caught on Boots's tail and the two cats had gone careering wildly over the Adelphi roof, Blitzen had risked his life in a way that to this day makes Iris shiver to think of. In the early hours of the morning in question "Woollie," the Persian cat, had come home alone; but Blitzen, who fancied he heard a crying, had climbed on to the steep roof, clad only in his pyjamas, and, with bare feet, had jumped from one of the houses to the other in the hope of finding it. The distance between the houses was some ten feet or so, but the drop, had he missed his footing, was over a hundred feet, for a deep area was below the ground, and the roofs were at an angle of 75°. "I closed my eyes when I took the return leap," he told Iris—but on that occasion Boots *had* come back, though not with Blitzen. Now it had gone for ever.

To console Iris and also to console the Persian kitten, Blitzen had bought a tortoiseshell kitten named Cairo. It was a half Persian, and when they had it first, was too small to lap; but Woollie had mothered it, and the two had soon become inseparable. And then, one day, Woollie disappeared. Hoxton Gunter and Anderson had to go away, and the blue paper arrived. Looking at a strange magazine, Iris had seen an advertisement of *The Hieroglyph*, the official organ of the Silver Star (a society dealing with the occult), and the editor was Vladimir Svaroff. She had written, and an answer had come; but Blitzen had been strangely averse to her going, and for the first tune in their married life Iris had gone without a word of good-bye! But the *look*?

Strickland was wise enough not to pretend to know women; he did not attempt to fathom the expression, but just sat down to his work.

It would all have to be done over again. His heart was not in it, and all the while the words kept ringing like a death knell in his ears. "Something must be done," and always came the answering echo, "Nothing, nothing can be done."

Restlessly he got up and searched amongst his studies for something that might help him. Now that their happiness seemed about to come to an end, the accuracy with which he had portrayed his wife surprised him. There she was, smiling, thinking, sorrowful, gladsome—every shade of expression he had seen there but one—the expression she had worn as she passed through the doorway. "It was not a look of dislike or disdain exactly—I can't quite make it out," thought Blitzen.

If only he could have got away from the egotistical point of view from which most men view their wives he would have seen that it was merely a look of self-defence, defence of her right, dignity and freedom.

CHAPTER VI

STRICKLAND looked at his wrist-watch reposing in an unused ash-tray amongst the litter of crayons and paints. For some unknown cause it had always refused to go when he wore it, sometimes galloping ahead, sometimes with equal unaccountableness stopping abruptly. "Seven-fifteen." Well, it would be light enough to work for at least another two hours. Lucky it's the summer, he thought; how amused would some of his varied acquaintances be to know that the inimitable Blitzen had not the wherewithal to procure a light. Well, they never need know, he thought. He remembered the classic occasion when Furnival, of the *Record*—Furnival, once a mill hand, and now making some fifty pounds a week—when that ass had come in one evening ostensibly for a few minutes' talk, but in reality to ask for some information which only Blitzen could supply. The said information received, he had risen to go. "Well, it must be nearly eight," he had said, "I must be getting some dinner. I suppose you have had yours." "As a matter of fact," said Blitzen in that elegantly languorous tone not unmixed with humour which was so to unmistakably a part of his personality and which inevitably aroused suspicion and ire in the minds of those about him, "as a matter of fact we haven't yet breakfasted." He yawned ever so slightly and smiled whimsically at Iris. "Lucky devil," had said the friend in a tone of envy, "I wish I had your life. Nothing whatever to do and all your own time in which to do it! Now *I* have to work like a sanguinary black." He had gone out obviously meaning what he had said, and Iris and Blitzen looking at each other had burst into unrestrained laughter, laughter not untinged with a suspicion of hysteria, but it was genuine laughter for all that. Iris had then gone to a little side-table and had patched up the salt-cellar. "Look here, Blitzen, we've still got three grains of salt, we're in plenty. We can't expect the glass to go up when there is still so much in the land of Egypt." She had examined critically the thermometer, and they had laughed again. That, perhaps, had been the nearest approach to disaster they had ever known and she had stood it like a little brick.

What a fool he had been not to explain to her his reasons for objecting to her going. Remembering the contract, he had dreaded to appear jealous—yet that contract had been in reality less than a scrap of paper. No, it had been more than that, he had hated to acquaint her with facts with which he knew she was so far ignorant—to spoil the daring innocence which made her so delightful and which was always appearing in the most unsuspected places. Really, he thought, it had been a curious form of selfishness. She was his, something set apart and flawless. He wouldn't have her vulgarised like other women. Half her charm lay in her spontaneity. Heavens, how retrospective he was getting—quite morbid in fact. Mechanically he picked up a piece of Conte. Why not portray the expression with which she had left the room? It would be something new.

Blitzen's jaw suddenly hardened and a cold light came into his half-closed eyes. The expression was conveyed in all its self-revelation to the paper before him. He looked at it steadily.

"Good God. Could that be Iris?"

There was a light step on the stairs followed by a characteristic rat-tat-tat. Quickly he placed a blank sheet over the tell-tale drawing.

"Come in," he said, in that unemotional tone that is the greatest betrayer of our hidden feelings. "You're rather late, aren't you?"

Iris paused at the door for the fraction of a second, then came gaily in. Her eyes were curiously bright, her step higher than he had known it for months. At a time other than the present this fact would have pleased him, now it but added fuel to his hidden anger. He quickly crossed the room and stood behind his chair, and he noticed the strange aroma of incense, galbanum or was it olibanum that clung about her hair? What on earth could she have been doing? he thought. She laughed happily. "Now, Bunco-Blitzen, say slowly after me, 'I was a *pig* for not wishing you to go.' I've done all that I meant to do. I've had a most wonderful day. Svaroff has taken three of my poems—he wants to see more, and, best of all, a cheque is coming in the morning—so the situation is saved. Aren't you glad?"

Then, as an icy silence greeted her, "Blitzen, what on earth is the matter?"

"What else did you give him?" said Blitzen brutally. It was not so much the simple words as the tone they were expressed in which conveyed the insult. The next moment he could have bitten his tongue off. But the damage had been done. Iris flushed quickly, looked at her husband with unutterable scorn and walked slowly and deliberately into the next room. She closed the door behind her. Well, he thought, she hasn't answered the question. She must be guilty. Why did she colour? It was a pitiful attempt to justify his conduct to himself. But he refused to face the fact squarely. "I'm going out," he called casually; "don't wait in for me—do anything you like."

He went out, hatless, leaving the door open. The minutes sped on to hours. Iris, her little universe shattered to atoms, sat in a species of trance. Blitzen, of all people, her God, her Super-Man in whom she had placed such boundless trust. In

dumb misery she picked up Cairo, the small tortoiseshell kitten. Somehow its soft warm body comforted her. She held it
against her face, softly stroking the electric fur. "You wouldn't
have misunderstood me," she said to herself. "Shall I go
away?" A big tear fell on to the kitten's head—it was followed
quickly by another which fell upon its nose. The little creature
shook itself disdainfully, brushing off the offending drop with
a remonstrating paw. Even Cairo seemed to fail her. Iris put
the kitten down.

She went to bed, but not to sleep.

Hour after hour the events of the day rehearsed themselves
with sickening reiteration. What on earth could it all mean?

Towards the early hours of the morning Blitzen returned.
He came in softly. Iris pretended to be asleep. He noticed the
undried tears still upon her lashes, the utter weariness of her
face. A great longing to take her in his arms seized him. He
would beg her forgiveness, smother her in a thousand kisses.
But no, she hadn't cleared herself. She hadn't answered his
question. She hadn't even reproached him.

Blitzen gave her one more look, made sure she was sleeping, and lay down beside her. He must sleep there or on the
floor. There was nowhere else, besides, she was fast asleep, she
wouldn't know. In a few minutes, from sheer force of habit
his arm had stretched itself across the pillow behind her head.
His own head was a few inches below hers. Wearily he closed
his eyes the better to think, at the same time trying not to
think. A scalding tear fell upon his neck. Remorse changed to
a definite cruelty. "Self-accusation," he said to himself, "but
she hasn't told me yet."

In the morning Blitzen rose early as was his usual custom,
and entered the studio to allow Iris to wash and dress. When
she left the room he in turn took possession. Neither of them
had spoken. Returning after some twenty minutes, immac-
ulately garbed and shaved, "I'm going out," he told her. "It's

time, in fact, we went our separate ways. You'll find all you need here for the moment. We may have to settle a few things later. I think there's a letter for you."

Before she could recover from her astonishment he had again hurried out. But a steady walk of some two hours had brought him to his senses. How perfectly irrational it was! He must be suffering from some obscure form of indigestion! Hadn't they arranged from the very beginning that they were free to do as they liked? That, surely, had been the very basis of their happiness, yet here at the first suggestion that it was being put into practice, he was behaving like some rotten little suburbanite. His behaviour was little short of swinish. He knew that Iris would never go home. She had no money. Was he not going out of his way to fling her into the arms of Svaroff? What a blind, hopeless fool he had just been. He would go back and discuss the matter calmly with her. He would admit that he had lost his temper. He was beginning to feel quite magnanimous.

And meanwhile Iris, too, had had time to think. After the first few minutes of utter bewilderment caused Blitzen's going, she had thought calmly and dispassionately and with a certain cold, clear logic.

Yes. Men were on a decidedly lower rung of the evolutionary ladder than were women—much lower. Really, she supposed, one ought to pity them. Pity might be akin to love and no doubt often was; at present, however, her pity leaned decidedly towards contempt. It was Blitzen's own fault entirely: He had himself shattered the wonderful image of himself that she in her adoration of him had set up and that she had wholeheartedly worshipped. Even if the quarrel were to be patched up and her forgiveness were to be asked ever so humbly, she knew she could never feel quite the same again. The whole thing had been in such execrable taste. That, it was, that jarred so horribly, far more, in fact, than the injustice.

After all, she was used to injustice. She had had little else all her life—but vulgarity, she simply couldn't and would not stand it. She thought of a certain occasion when Blitzen had come home in the early hours of the morning. "Beashtly drunk," as he had been careful to explain to her, and "don't come near me, Kiddie." True, he had been terribly penitent later in the day and had given her a careful catalogue of all his doings. But she had never asked him a single question, nor had she dreamed of so doing. She had felt genuinely sorry for "the perfectly rotten head" that had been the natural consequence of the debauch.

"Just think of it, Kiddie, thirteen absinthes straight off," he had told her, "and then old Denis Vivian carted me off to his studio in New Court where we drank some weird concoction made of Angelica. God! That was stuff if you like! I'll do some magnificent drawing when my hand is a little more steady."

He had done some really fine work, and she hadn't complained of his "night out."

Things like that had happened several times, yet she had only stayed out a few hours longer than he expected and there was all this ridiculous fuss; that he knew of the harmless kiss she had taken for granted, forgetting maybe that she had not yet told him. She looked at the table and the seven sovereigns he had thrown down. She wondered vaguely where he had got them and whether he had paid the rent. That, after all, had always been his business and she was not going to interfere now. But she would die rather than touch a penny of his money. What on earth did he take her for? Her thought reverted swiftly to Svaroff. How charmingly he had smiled when she had kissed him. How perfectly he had understood. Here, she thought, was the very perfection of breeding. Svaroff, in his own way, had just as much genius as Blitzen. Blitzen had been a beast.

She remembered the letter that he had flung down upon the old gate-legged table, and she walked wearily across the room to pick it up. Had it come to this? Must he write the things he had not the courage to say? She looked at the envelope.

Blitzen's writing most obviously, but the letter bore the S.W. postmark, and had been posted shortly after midnight, also the seal bore the rayed triangle of *The Hieroglyph*. Vaguely wondering, she tore it open. It was from Svaroff and was accompanied by a small cheque. How amazingly like Blitzen's was the handwriting!

"DEAR MISS HAMILTON"—the letter ran—"I am called away to Paris for a few days, but on my return next Friday shall look forward to seeing you and as many of your friends as you care to bring. We shall give further information concerning the symposium later on. It may be necessary for you to fast for a few hours beforehand, but that, I fancy, you will not mind. I enclose a cheque for the verses. If you think it too little, please remember that our contributors are not paid, ever—you will be the very first. It was so nice to see you. Don't forget that long poem.—

"Yours sincerely, VLADIMIR S."

She put the letter down, and lay back in the low chair beside the fireplace. In a few moments she was asleep and dreaming of Svaroff—a vague and curious dream in which she had gone to the offices of *The Hieroglyph* against her promise, and had been the victim in some strange and unholy rite. She woke with a start, yawning exaggeratedly as Blitzen entered.

"I'm so sorry," he said, "that I made such a fool of myself. I'm also sorry that in consequence I should temporarily have forgotten the laws of common politeness." He spoke with constraint and almost as though he had rehearsed the words. Iris had an overwhelming desire to burst out laughing, but she knew that were she to do so it would be fatal. She nearly found herself saying, "Don't mention it," in the approved shop-girl fashion, but she pulled herself up just in time and said instead; "It is quite all right." Her voice created a polite but definite barrier. Then, as he walked to the window, "Have you had breakfast?" she added.

"No," he answered, "I don't want any." Then, by way of explanation, "I've been smoking too much."

As an afterthought he added, "Have you had yours?"

"No," said Iris, "but I've not been smoking; I've been thinking. I think I'll go out, but first you had better read this."

She handed him the note from Svaroff. Blitzen took it grudgingly and with obvious aversion, but a glance at the contents riveted his attention.

"Fellow seems to have copied my hand," he said dryly; "what's the idea?"

"How could he," said Iris; "he's never seen your writing."

"True, I forgot that," said Blitzen.

He read the note and was silent.

"Well," said Iris, "why not come to the symposium? We shall learn more about it, and you'll see that he's quite harmless." She smiled vaguely, looking into the distance.

"He'll be harmless when I've done with him," said Blitzen grimly.

So passed a day that was utterly futile for them both. Both were horribly polite and both horribly distant. Only Iris felt the full humour of the situation. She went to bed early feeling tired. Blitzen had again gone out.

Meanwhile, after the fashion of the movies, let us revert to the evening before, to the offices of *The Hieroglyph*, and to its two strange occupants.

In the large front room, lit only by the light of the crescent moon, was Svaroff. He was seated at the large table before a strange book. He had been reading for several hours previously but was not now reading. He was dressed in a blue snake-embroidered robe that set off to perfection his smooth athletic figure. The air about him was filled with a sweet and penetrating odour, as of ambergris and myrrh combined with camphor. He seemed lost in thought. At times he looked expectantly towards the door as though about to welcome some unseen guest, at times he seemed to listen intently. Then he again concentrated on the page before him. The book was a narrow one with black covers, on the outside of which was a square in red letters— SATOR, AREPO, TENET, OPERA, ROTAS. So read the words whether looked at horizontally from right to left at the bottom or from left to right at the top, also whether looked at from north to south or from south to north.

In Svaroff's right hand was a leaden-coloured cylindrical rod about half an inch in diameter and some ten inches in length. The rod was hollow and weighted at the end with mercury, the end at the moment was resting beneath his palm. "Queer," he said to himself, "it's never failed before. She ought to have been here by now." He turned the pages, switching on a heavily shaded electric reading lamp as he did so. A strange glint came into his eyes—the Chinese mask had descended.

A slight fusillade upon the door—one knock followed twice by three, was repeated several times. It was then varied by three knocks followed by four. Then, as Svaroff appeared oblivious, the door opened and Newton entered.

He took in the situation at a glance.

"I say, Guru, why not chuck it? You know she's not that sort, and besides, you'll be rottenly tired by to-morrow."

"Perchance she sleepeth, or is on a journey," murmured Svaroff softly, then he turned quickly to face the intruder. "Did I ask you to interfere, you son of a he-goat by a bastard she-mule? No? Well, then, don't. As to 'not being that sort,' we are not all on the qliphothic level of your beastly libidinous self. The girl has genius; she'll be invaluable. God in heaven! Do you imagine that if I wanted a whore I'd have to indulge in *this*?" Svaroff spoke with an almost brutal savagery. "What's come over you, Newton?"

"Nothing," replied the other, "only I'm glad that it's all right and that you're not monkeying about."

"Why?" said Svaroff, and fixed him with a blank stare. Then as a sudden thought occurred to him, "What about the Brixton Flapper? I'm afraid you've no sense of the fitness of things."

"Have you?" said Newton, and vanished into the next room before Svaroff could reply.

Svaroff again read the page that explained failure. Could it be that that was the barrier? No, he would never believe that. There was only attraction or the reverse. Love didn't exist, love as usually understood. Somehow she had seemed sexless, yet strangely tantalising. He thought of the kiss and his flesh tingled queerly.

Was it possible that for two years she had lived with Strickland and had never . . .

Well, he had heard of such things, but if it were so, this would be the first authentic case he had come across. How could one ever be sure? Most men couldn't, of course. But Svaroff had one infallible test which he divulged to none.

He thought of that amusing satire by Swift, the test of the lions. Would there be one who would pass the trial in the whole of London? She might, yes. His thoughts wandered on.

Certainly she was no prude—her chastity seemed as that of a child, yet she was surely as old as Eve.

His thought travelled from her to Tommy Fanshawe. Tommy, who dressed almost like a boy, had a deep contralto voice, wore her hair short, and played the violin. There was a girl who had always intrigued him; in a way he linked her up with Iris. He found himself in imagination writing a letter that might have been addressed to either:

"DEAR BOY OF THRACE"—so ran the epistola—"Arcadian greetings and all Panic pleasances to you. I am so glad to be *en rapport* once more. I, too, hate the bloody proletariat and long for the intelligence of Greece. It would be nice to lie on hot sand with naked body bathed in the sun as God Pan piped. But if one were to do this by the Round Pond I expect 'a burly arm in a white-braided blue coat-sleeve' would interfere!" Svaroff, with closed eyes, smiled at his own thoughts in the darkness. "Don't you understand, though, you little shepherd,"—the letter continued,—"that it is impossible to be natural in our circumscribed society. Despite this let us hold Greek converse ere long—we could search for Pan in the gardens or I could meet you where you will. I wish my poor dead friend Oscar could join us and inspire our Greek musings—you would have liked him even as I did. It was good to hear from the little shepherd.

"Arcadian Greetings to the Boy, from the Man—

"VLADIMIR."

The cylindrical rod clattered noisily on to the table. He pulled himself up with a shock. Most definitely he had been dreaming. This would never do. He remembered suddenly that he had not yet sent that letter he had promised. He scribbled a few lines and wrote out a cheque. Searching for an envelope, he directed it and then called for Newton.

"Are you dressed? Well, stick on any old thing. This letter must go at once. What? You've gone to bed? V.H.O. Newton."

Newton, a mackintosh over his green pyjamas, went out with the letter, and Svaroff, getting himself out of the blue embroidered robe, put on some black monkish garment. He curled himself up in a sleeping bag upon the floor, and in a few moments was once more dreaming, a faint smile upon his lips. Seen thus in repose, his features bore an astonishing resemblance to those of the sleeping cupid at the British Museum. Young he looked, and most amazingly innocent.

Newton, returning a few minutes later, looked into at the doorway. He closed the door very quietly.

"Good old Guru," he said softly, then he too lay down in the adjoining room.

All the world seemed to sleep.

Only the moon seemed waking as she travelled across the sky to meet the dawn.

Outside, in the deserted street, a sleek black cat stretched itself, then lay down again in the shadow of the kerb to await once more the advent of the early morning sparrows.

Verily, as Voronoff would have said, "Quod est superius sicut est infer ius."

CHAPTER VII

FOR a better understanding of the actions of Svaroff it might be as well at this juncture to say somewhat of his antecedents, to give some slight account of his childhood and of the years which followed. For reasons, which are obvious, we must of necessity draw a veil over much.

Vladimir Semeonovitch, son of Wassili Semeonovitch was a strict adherent of the sect of the Oukobors, that strange little-known community of pious souls which seems in many ways to be an offshoot from the religious life of the Middle Ages, and which has a life and character specifically its own. It has been thought by some, including the present writer, that the sect had its original roots in a branch of the Albigenses with whom its heresies have much in common—but that is a thesis the truth of which future historians must settle for themselves.

Wassili, a grand old man and father of the community, died a few months after the arrival of himself and family in Saskatchewan, and was buried with full honours and according to their ancient rite. Gregor, his grandson, having arrived at years of discretion, after the days of mourning were accomplished, quarrelled with his father Vladimir, with whom he had never been on the best of terms and disappearing one fine morning from the community was never seen or heard of by them again.

He came to New York and, after an interval of some eight months, using once more the family name of Svaroff, he married Anna, the only daughter of a rich Quaker of semi-Irish descent.

The father of Anna, a widower, died shortly after his daughter's marriage, and having left to her and her son, should she have one, his by no means inconsiderable fortune, Anna as the result of a prophetic dream journeyed with her husband Gregor to England. There, five months later, having found the house of her dreams in one of the southern counties, she gave birth to a son. She named him Vladimir after the saint, and not after his grandfather, for that had been part of the dream, and from his earliest years Anna cherished great hopes of the infant. Certainly if one may judge from his early portraits Vladimir was an attractive child and it is small wonder if his mother worshipped him, and also if after the manner of most mothers she did her best to spoil him. But admitting this to be the case, the antidote was supplied by his father at frequent intervals and in no small closes.

Gregor was a man of strong principles, courageous and fanatical, and above all a prohibitionist. He prohibited most things. He prohibited intoxicating liquors, he prohibited cards, he prohibited theatres, he prohibited games on Sunday, and most especially he prohibited companionship of the opposite sex.

He would not have his son spoilt by girls, no, not even in the nursery. Thinking it over in later life Vladimir often wondered how his father had ever brought himself to marry, but undoubtedly his mother was a pretty woman, and even the best of men are not consistent. He was content to leave it at that.

For the rest Gregor adhered to the habits of his ancestral faith. He was a vegetarian, he forbade the use of leather in any form, even shoe leather being forbidden, and for his wife there must be neither silk, fur nor feathers. Since he did not believe in the domestication of animals and at the time of which we write motor-cars had not come into use, the family travelled but little, for horses were obviously taboo.

So little Vladimir was dressed for the most part in homespuns; in the garden or house he seldom wore shoes, and for the street he wore rope-sandals.

Religious instruction played a great part in his early upbringing. There were family prayers night and morning, prayer meetings on Sunday and prayer meetings most other days of the week. The most ordinary events of the day were regarded by Gregor and his wife as a special dispensation of Providence and as a mark of special favour to themselves. They spoke of Providence rather as though He were a wealthy and well-disposed cousin. Quite early in life Vladimir had his own opinion about this mysterious personage.

It was a most unnatural upbringing for any child, and the wonder is that Vladimir survived it as long as he did, for, boarding school being out of the question, he was educated at home, first by his mother and afterwards by a tutor from Oxford. The tutor was a mild-mannered man, of exceptional intelligence and with an easy temper. The wonder is that he, too, survived, but that is another story and does not enter into this history.

When Vladimir was nearing his twelfth birthday, Gregor made the acquaintance of a Polish Rabbi, a convert to Christianity; and the meeting with this unusual man had upon Gregor an almost magical effect. He became for the first time quite human in his life. He also became very thoughtful.

He talked with the ex-Rabbi for hours on end, usually in Russian, with here or there a word of Hebrew or medieval Latin. Sometimes the talk was in English. Vladimir coming in one afternoon caught the words Chassidim and Qabala. He was puzzled, and a few days afterwards asked his father what it all meant? Who was the strange guest and what was the Qabala? "All in good time, Vladimir," was the answer, "you are not yet twelve; we have both of us much to learn." The latter half of the sentence was made almost to himself, but Vladimir heard it distinctly; and then, three weeks later Gregor was dead. He had grazed his ankle whilst out on a climbing expedition with his son—he had refused to see a doctor—blood-poisoning had set in, and two days later he was dead.

For a time Vladimir was inconsolable. But the memory of boyhood is mercifully short, and six months afterwards, freed to a great extent from parental control, he was becoming a danger to himself and others. He was also becoming possessed of strange ideas.

One day when his conduct had been particularly perverse Anna had taken him to task, pointing out what must be the inevitable result of such behaviour, and begging him to desist. Vladimir listened in silence, then—"But whatever could you have been doing, Mother, to produce such a son?" Anna actually blushed. Then, before she could recover from her astonishment, "Perhaps he disguised himself as an Angel of Light," he added cheerfully.

But this was more than even the best of mothers could be expected to stand. "Vladimir, whatever are you saying?" she said hurriedly; "pray speak respectfully of your father." "I am," came the immediate response, "I'm thinking of that verse in Genesis which says, 'There were giants on the earth in those days.' Rabbi Elhanan says father was a man of God. I believe in heredity—I'm going to be a GIANT."

Anna gasped, and Vladimir, whistling to his dog, joined his newly arrived cousin Erskine on the lawn outside, and disappeared for the remainder of the day.

Was her son abnormally innocent or abnormally precocious? Anna decided that he must be the former, but he was obviously reaching a difficult age, and the problem of his future education seemed bristling with difficulties. She wished for Gregor as never before.

It was the season of the summer holidays, and from the date of the conversation referred to, Vladimir continued to absent himself from the house for hours at a time, sometimes he appeared for meals, sometimes he did not. But always he was at home by dusk, and he slept soundly. If his clothes were more than usually muddy—well, it was the holidays, and she must not be over-inquisitive. With Erskine he could not come to harm. So she waited. But the air of mystery which surrounded him grew and grew, and then one day the problem solved itself in an unexpected manner.

She received one afternoon a visit from one of the neighbouring farmers. He was a disagreeable man at the best of times, and now, purple with rage, he was threatening her with a legal action for damage done to his estate. The stream which ran through his field, and which was essential for the working of his mill, had been diverted from its course, and her son Vladimir was responsible for the same—or so he said. Anna almost laughed; it was too absurd and of course it could not be true; all the same she was not quite comfortable in her mind, and she asked the man how he knew this.

"Because I caught him at it, the Son of Belial," said the irate farmer, "and there was another, a taller one with him. But ask him for yourself, Madam, he is bound to be in before many minutes. I can wait and I will."

And then Vladimir came in with Erskine, and the whole story came out. The man had been surly—he had objected to them fishing in his stream, he had said that they were trespassing. Well, Vladimir had decided that if the stream ran through the common field they would *not* be trespassing. So with the help of Erskine he had dug a tunnel, and by means of many logs and stones they had diverted the course of the water. It had taken them over four weeks, and they had all but accomplished it—the water was already running away to the new ground, when, unfortunately for them, the trick had been discovered.

"There. You hear him for yourself, the brazen young scamp! With your permission, Madam," said the man, taking a cow-hide whip from his coat pocket, "I'll give him a taste of *this*."

Anna was most indignant. She quickly sent Vladimir indoors. "Indeed you will not," she said; "my son has never touched leather in his life, and leather shall never touch him," and then she reasoned with the man for the best part of an hour. Whether it was her reasoning or the gold which left her hands, peace was at last restored, and Vladimir promising not to repeat the offence, the farmer went away . . .

A year after this, whilst experimenting with high explosives, Vladimir blew up the hut in which he was working and was himself rendered unconscious for several days. The result was five weeks in hospital and a scar which he carried for the rest of his days. But there was a yet further result. The doctor insisted on a meat diet, on sensible shoes, and on one or two other little trifles. He must be obeyed, he said, or he would throw up the case. So Anna capitulated, and from that day forth Vladimir led a comparatively normal existence.

Five years later he went to Oxford, and a year after that had been sent down for persistent contempt of the authorities and for less pleasant charges.

After that he threw over the traces completely, and appears to have dabbled in anything and everything. For a time he joined the Church of Rome—then he left that community and commenced to make a special study of all the heresies of the Middle Ages. He learnt all that he could about the Albigenses and the Christian Gnostics. He studied Buddhism and he became interested in magic. He travelled to China, India and Tibet. He went to Mexico and Russia, to Spain and

Egypt. Finally, he settled again in England, and endeavoured "to attain to the knowledge and conversation of the Holy Guardian Angel, according to the Book of the Sacred Magick of Abra-Melin, the Mage."

It was just about this time that he had met Laura. That he was in love with her there seems to be little doubt, but Abra-Melin and Laura could not be linked together, and Vladimir made the great mistake of trying to link them.

He took a lonely house in the Scottish Highlands and with three dogs for companions—a bulldog, an Alsatian and a Great Dane—he began the great experiment. He fasted for long intervals, he spoke to none, he stayed up at night, especially when the moon was full, and at dawn he went with one or other of his four-footed companions for long walks on the hills. If the simple inhabitants crossed themselves when they met him, Vladimir was not displeased, for he probably was a striking figure, and he knew it; but when the Alsatian took to tearing sheep and the bulldog attacked the post man, when there were strange and unaccountable noises at nights, and the local inhabitants could not sleep, the entire populace went in a body to the nearest magistrate and shortly after Vladimir found himself once more in London.

He had obviously not attained to the knowledge and conversation for which he had set out, but he had attained a reputation for dealings with the Evil one, and the reputation remained for an unpleasantly long time.

After this Vladimir had taken to mountaineering and to big game shooting; he had further investigated the religions of strange lands; he had written a number of books; and he had experimented with drugs. Through the latter he believed he would discover the Great Secret; different drugs had different effects—he had already discovered that much.

With the latest drug, a sedative tonic from Mexico, he had hopes of penetrating the future and of over-coming time and space. What might be the physical effects of such an apotheosis he did not trouble to think, for in that case the physical, as commonly understood, would be superseded, and in any case there were plenty of persons who would risk the experiment. So Vladimir looked forward calmly to the future, and the meeting with Iris gave him an added interest.

CHAPTER VIII

THE week that followed was for Iris and Blitzen the reverse of pleasant. Blitzen was definitely sulky and Iris for many days had been in a state of repressed irritation. She wished above all things to go again to *The Hieroglyph*. Not that she was in love with Svaroff, not in the least she told herself—she would like to have seen again that strangely decorative room, to have felt again its strange and fascinating atmosphere, and to have talked again with Svaroff. How intensely alive he was! Beside him Blitzen seemed as one three-quarters dead, and he was not making himself more attractive by this constant exhibition of bad temper. She tried to imagine how she would have behaved had the situation been reversed and Blitzen had gone to the studio of some very nice and fascinating girl. Most probably, she told herself, she would have said nothing—pride would have kept her silent. But had she been unable to preserve that silence, she would have asked him quite nicely if he preferred the girl to herself. In the event of his saying "Yes," of course he would have been free to go, but if he had said "No," then she would have asked him quite simply not to go again if he wished to please her, or if he did go to at least take her with him. Yes, that is how she would have behaved.

And meanwhile a strange thing was happening. Between Iris and Blitzen a barrier was growing up that assumed at times an almost tangible shape. Iris mentally called it "The Black

Shadow," for that is how she visualised it. It was something cold and relentless, a separate entity daily growing stronger, and driving them apart. Was Blitzen also aware of its presence? A week ago she could have asked him, and no doubt he would have told her and put her mind at rest. But with affairs in their present state he would probably raise his eyebrows and suggest that she paid a visit to the doctor. No, it was no use asking Blitzen.

Had her love of the past been just a glamour? Had she as usual only worshipped her own ideal? All she wanted to do was to sleep and sleep and sleep. To forget everything. That is what she wished. A postman's double knock roused her from her lethargy and she went down to the front door to take in the letter. It was a largish envelope, and the sight of the rayed triangle made her heart beat strangely. Why should the mere sight of a letter so affect her? Was it the strange elusive perfume faintly medicinal but wholly delightful that once again was frightening her? But she must go upstairs at once or Blitzen would be wondering. At present he was shaving, and the kettle would soon be boiling for their morning coffee. She went upstairs, tearing open the envelope as she did so. What jolly-looking blue paper was her first thought. Her second was a quotation from Edgar Allan Poe, "Over the mountains of the moon, through the valley of the Shadow, ride, ride, the Shade replied, if you seek for Eldorado." Yes, it must certainly be that strange incense. She would ask Svaroff about it. She would like to have some. It transported one straight away into the world of dreams. And such delightful dreams. Mysterious realms where were moonbeams, shadows—water-lilies, and blue lagoons, mountains, Aeolian harps, and through it all the voice of some Mighty Being telling of things before the Dawn of Time. "The Image of a Voice," "The Shape which shape had none." Where had she heard of these things? Blitzen entered the studio and she handed him the letter. "Are we to go?" she asked. "It's not until eight o clock this evening, and evening dress is optional. The minimum fast is three hours beforehand, but five or eight hours would be better. I shall make it the latter as I'm never too sure of my 'tummy.' I want to go." The words had slipped out almost before she could realise it. The note of entreaty was unmistakable, but it was quite unintentional. Blitzen looked at her quickly, then, taking the letter, moved across to the other side of the room, so that for a moment his back was to her and he faced the windows. He raised the paper seemingly to examine the type more closely, but in doing so managed to pass the sheet below his nostrils. A puzzled look came into his face. "What could the fellow be playing at? Was it to be a drug party?" Well, at the moment he badly wanted some inspiration. If there were no harm in it, it would be amusing, and in any case he could always write it up for the *Rostrum* or some such rag! On the whole, thought Blitzen, he might as well go.

He turned to Iris. "Very well," he said, "we'll go. But there's no sense in fasting a day beforehand; we're not exactly going to Midnight Mass! Take my advice and have a good meal at least five hours before we start. Meanwhile, what about some breakfast?" He seated himself at the table and poured out coffee. Already there was a subtle alteration in his manner. The Shadow was there, but he was trying to cloak it.

"If only he could realise that he has been mistaken, everything may yet come right," thought Iris. But she decided not to force the situation. "I'm so glad," she said in answer to his remarks. "I've an idea that it'll be awfully interesting." Blitzen looked at her musingly but said nothing.

For the morning and greater part of the afternoon he worked steadily at his drawing. Then, for a couple of hours he read Baudelaire and de Quincey, whilst Iris rested in the big arm-chair. At seven o'clock he dressed himself most carefully and Iris did the same. Eight o' clock found them at the foot of the stairs which led to the offices of *The Hieroglyph*.

"I rather think," said Blitzen, as they mounted the stairs together, "that this is an experiment. It will serve them jolly well right if we tell them nothing. Keep close to me and whatever you do don't go to sleep. If you feel yourself growing sleepy use your will power."

Iris promised.

And now they had reached the fateful landing. The place was dimly lit, and Iris saw what at first she took to be a huge figure of St. Michael. It was a tall man garbed in a monk's robe of scarlet. Through the drawn cowl the blue eyes gleamed strangely. The hands of the figure rested upon a gigantic, two edged sword which gleamed bright as silver in the semi-darkness. The figure eyed them in silence then, suddenly raising the sword as though to strike or warn them back, it swiftly altered the direction of the weapon and pointed it at the door on their right. The door opened as if by magic, and in a veritable blaze of light they came face to face with Svaroff. He appeared at first sight to be almost nine feet high. He was dressed in a long black Tau-shaped robe of some soft cloth material which hung in the most delightful folds and which was bordered at neck and hem with a broad band of doth of gold. A large gold cross was embroidered upon the garment back and front. His powerful neck bared to the base, gleaming above this priest-like garment, gave to the onlooker the impression of an almost superhuman strength. It suggested a granite column. Iris thought of Egyptian Gods and wondered whether Blitzen had noticed the resemblance.

The two men looked at each other with interest.

Iris sensed immediately intense antagonism on the part of Svaroff and admiration on the part of Blitzen. No word of greeting was exchanged, but Svaroff turning to the table beside him poured out some dark brownish-looking liquid into a little glass phial. He held the phial out to Iris. "Drink!" was all he said.

Iris automatically passed the glass to Blitzen, but Svaroff stayed her hand. He looked again at the latter as though taking his measure, then, "It's not enough for him," he said by way of explanation. "Will it make me sleep?" said Iris. The odour of the stuff was certainly not inviting, it suggested bad apples and laudanum, and for the fraction of a second she hesitated. "On the contrary," said Svaroff, "you will wake up as you have never waked before." There was a curious glint in his eyes, and he spoke with a peculiar drawl that had in it somewhat of menace. It made her think of a purring tiger that might suddenly snarl, but he was obviously enjoying himself. Iris drank the contents and handed the glass to Svaroff. For a few seconds she was conscious of a perfectly terrible sensation. It was as though a powerful motor-car had somehow got inside her body and the engines were working at top speed. Svaroff glanced at her obliquely, then poured out a double quantity of the liquid for Blitzen. As the latter drank it, "You will find plenty of cushions and smokes in the next room," he said. "It is best to keep quite quiet. Take things easy, later you may have something to report," and he turned to speak to some new arrival.

At this juncture Newton, barefooted and dressed in the white robe of a Neophyte, appeared from the further room and took Iris and Blitzen through another door on their left. He pointed to some cushions close to the wall and near to the door by which they had entered, at the same time placing beside them a stone jar of Turkish cigarettes; then he went out again. The room was heavy with the haze of smoke and filled with the low murmur of many voices; except for the very dim light of a swinging censer they were in complete darkness, but as their eyes became accustomed to the gloom they could see here and there men and women in evening dress reclining against the walls.

Most of them appeared to be smoking, and all of them were talking. In the centre of the room was a square altar. Somewhere in the infinite distance as it seemed, a tom-tom was faintly throbbing, the strange rhythm rising and falling. There was a curious tenseness in the air.

Iris took Blitzen's hand in the darkness and he returned the slight pressure. How thankful she felt. The Black Shadow had departed.

"What do you think of him?" she said. "He's a tremendously powerful fellow," he answered in a tone of admiration. "I should have all my work cut out to tackle him, and he's a splendidly modelled head, almost Roman. There's something a little queer about the eyes, almost a squint I should say, but the mouth is definitely beautiful. It's exactly like your own, Kiddie. But we'd better not talk." They lapsed into the friendly silence of perfect companionship.

From time to time a black-robed figure paused beside them. "Anything to report?" it asked; and "Nothing" they both answered, and then a queer thing began to happen.

Time seemed at a standstill, or rather it was unwinding backwards: they were going back through the ages. That is how it seemed to Blitzen. Bronze Age, Stone Age, Glacial Age-dancing figures brandishing stone-knives, flints, clubs, antlers of animals, every kind of uncouth weapon, they were coming from a distance leaping down a narrow defile upon him. Again and again he kept them back by the effort of his will—but at every new approach they seemed to come nearer. Could he continue to keep them off? So long as he realised them for what they were—yes. He turned to Iris, "How are you feeling, Kiddie?" he whispered. "Rather transatlantic," she answered, "I seem to get nothing but water-lilies and stars—but I've got the last line for my sonnet."

And now it seemed that a number of tom-toms were playing, the music was becoming wildly barbaric; there was a patter of bare feet, a swish of robes, and Newton in a rhythmic dance was whirling round the altar. Faster and faster he went as though pursued by the very furies of Hell, and beside him was dancing another figure, a phantom shadow of himself. Suddenly he crashed to the ground and lay motionless in a huddled heap beside the altar, but the phantom figure continued the dance for several minutes longer, then it flickered out and vanished like the flame of a candle.

"Did you notice?" whispered Blitzen. "Yes," Iris answered. The tom-toms were still faintly throbbing, otherwise the stillness was almost oppressive. Suddenly a rich contralto voice broke the silence. "I wish they'd bring us some whiskies and sodas," it said; "I'm going home." There was a sound of several persons rising, and a tall girl in company with an older woman and a man in evening dress moved towards the door.

"Is that you, Tommy?" said Iris. "Who is it?" came back the answer in a tone of surprise. "Iris—Iris Hamilton." "Good Lord, fancy meeting you," was the reply; "but you always were a weird little thing." The girl laughed pleasantly.

"Must you go, Rachel?" said Svaroff addressing the older woman; "we've not yet had the invocation." "Yes, we've to get to Eastbourne. But I'll see you during the week." They went out. "Hadn't you better leave the door open and let out some of this smoke," said Newton, who had seemingly recovered and Svaroff held open the door. "I've not seen Tommy for several years," said Iris, "we acted in a pageant when I was at school. I'm getting a bit stiff," and she rose to her feet, stretching her arms as she did so.

"Why not sit here," said a voice that had not yet spoken, and a youth in a scarlet robe indicated the tall padded fender-rail. He held in his hands a tom-tom which, from time to time, he thrummed softly. Was it St. Michael? She didn't like his mouth, but he had pleasant, careless, laughing eyes. Blitzen rose with her, and the three of them sat upon the fender-rail—

the tall youth upon the right of Iris and Blitzen upon her left. "How are you feeling?" he asked her. "Pretty awful," she answered, "but my head was never clearer. I feel as though my brain had been washed. I could read the thoughts of everyone in this room if I wished to." "That would be interesting," he replied, but she did not offer to enlighten him. "How much did you have?" he asked. Blitzen answered for her. "About one hundred and eighty," he said, "but I had two hundred and fifty. I particularly noticed the marking on the glass." "I suppose you've been here pretty often," said the youth.

"No," said Iris, "it's our first initiation."

"Well," he volunteered, "it's a pretty stiff dose for a first kick-off. I've been several times—it's quite good fun. But if anything should do really wrong, Dr. Olaffson can give the antidote." He indicated as he spoke a tall dark man standing by the doorway. Then he handed the tom-tom to Iris. "Play this," he said, "it will take your mind off." As he spoke several other persons went out.

Then the door closed and Svaroff came up to them.

"Brother Capricornus, what is the hour?" he said solemnly.

"It is the hour before the dawn when the stars take council together," answered the other.

"Well, hadn't we better get on with it?" said Svaroff; "the profane ones no longer disturb the sanctity of our peace and Anubis guardeth the portal." "Even as you will, Great Magus," said the youth, and leaving the fender-rail he joined the Master. They moved off together.

There was intense silence, then a bell sounded. The sound had a most curious effect upon the nerves; it was an intensely fine tingling sound, much like the bell at the elevation of the Host, and although not loud, there were eight octaves which echoed round the walls of the room, each octave growing finer and more penetrating. Iris found her flesh becoming goosey. Then there was the flickering of a sword in the darkness, the swish of heavy robes, and Svaroff began to intone in some strange tongue. He moved in turn to the four corners of the room, starting at the north and going round by east, south and west.

Once more facing the north he intoned anew tracing upon the darkness with the point of his sword some geometrical figure. It seemed to Iris that the room became many degrees colder, the blackness palpable. Then, through a silence which could be felt, there was a distant rumbling and a strange vibration of the floor as when the bass of an organ is playing or some distant locomotive passing—a column of greenish smoke was rising from the ground, a crocodile-headed god was faintly visible.

Her hand was upon the collar of Blitzen's coat—for safety's sake he had advised her to keep it there. Was it her disordered imagination or was the coat moving towards her?

A heavy body slid behind her, there was a crash as the coat wrenched itself away from her grasp, and with a dull thud Blitzen fell. His head struck the steel fire-irons and he lay motionless. The lights went up even before she had time to scream, and Svaroff came over, looking with a curious mask-like expression at the fallen figure, which had every appearance of death. "You devil, you have killed him," she said. He did not answer. Then to her great relief and the obvious relief of Svaroff, Blitzen spoke. "What's all the fuss about?" he said; "I suppose I must have fallen asleep." Before Iris could speak, Dr. Olaffson and the tall youth had escorted Blitzen out. "Leave him alone for a few minutes," said the youth; "he'll be all right." Then Newton came up to her. "He's pouring water over his wrists," he said in a tone of wonder, "and he wants to know the time. He says the fire-irons brought him round. Lucky he's got thick hair." And then Iris was seized with a deadly nausea. Dr. Olaffson came up and gave her a white powder, and the next thing she remembered was lying back in a chair in the inner room and Svaroff pouring her out some tea. In doing so she spilt some on her wrist and immediately wiped it off with a blue silk handkerchief. "I'm so sorry," he said. "It didn't hurt," said Iris. "I wondered if you would feel it," was the somewhat cryptic answer. "Oh yes, I felt it," she said, "but it didn't hurt." She lay back in the chair and allowed her thoughts to drift. How entirely one she felt with these people. It seemed that she must have been there since the very dawn of time. With the exception of the tall youth and Dr. Olaffson, the remainder of the guests had gone. Blitzen was still studying his watch when the latter re-entered the room and asked the time. "Three-thirty," said Blitzen. "But it must be more," said the other, "I've been in the next room for at least an hour."

"When did you light that cigarette?" said Blitzen.

"By Jove, you must be right," said the doctor, "but it is the longest cigarette I've ever smoked in my life." Newton and Svaroff laughed. "He's not had any," said the latter, "it's the fumes, but it's given him 'time-extension' for all that. I once remember writing a letter with a pen that was a mile long; and, needless to say, I covered leagues of paper. Each letter took an hour to form. It was quite a lengthy business I can assure you." And then Blitzen rose to go. "It has been most enjoyable," he said "and we must have given a lot of trouble, but we really ought to be going now. We have to get to Barnes."

"Why not stay to 'breaker'," said Newton. "The night is yet young and you won't be working on Sunday."

"Thanks mostly awfully," said Blitzen, "but we really can't."

Svaroff shook hands. "I'll be interested to know how you get on," he said.

How fresh it was outside of the rooms they had left after the heat and smoke. The morning air seemed like iced wine, the earth newly created. As together they crossed the street they laughed for very joie de vivre. Life was just a glorious game and they had discovered the Universal Joke.

An old beggar man was crouching in a door way—he seemed like a beautiful picture by Rembrandt. A bird flying across the street gave them infinite joy. And what colour there was in everything. Never before had Iris realised how beautiful was the world. Everything was harmonious. There were glorious gold and purple shadows, and the most ordinarily inharmonious sounds now fitted in to a wonderful orchestra whose symphony filled the earth. How marvellous it was! Why was anyone ever unhappy? For the first time in her life Iris felt that she really loved the world—that she loved everyone. "Oh, Blitzen, it's good to be alive," she said.

"Rather, Kiddie," he answered enthusiastically.

Gaily they stepped out together. A passing constable eyed them curiously, then smiled in sympathy. "Love's young dream," he said, addressing a perky sparrow. "Well, we all of us has it. Good luck to them!" And he looked with admiration at Blitzen's broad shoulders and careless stride, and at the slender figure of Iris with her leopard-skin cap, and her dusky curls floating in the wind.

The clock was striking a quarter to six as they reached the beginning of Castlenau Mansions and knocked at the flat of Blitzen's mother. "Who is it?" said a frightened voice. "Me," said Blitzen ungrammatically. There was a slight pause; then a drawing of bolts and bars, and Blitzen's mother in the daintiest of morning wraps stood before them. "Whatever has happened?" she said in a voice of alarm. "Is Iris ill?" "No," said Iris, coming forward. Then she looked at Blitzen. Blitzen looked at his mother and back again at Iris and suddenly he and Iris began to laugh. They laughed continuously, holding on to the door post. "I'm awfully sorry, Mater," he at last managed to gasp out, "but we have just discovered the Universal Joke."

Blitzen's mother looked at him severely. "Really Eugene, I'm surprised at you," she said. "Whatever you do yourself, you should have some consideration for your wife. Have you no sense of responsibility? She's little more than a child, Come in, both of you. You had better go to bed. But first I'll make you some strong black coffee." And Mrs. Strickland, opening the door of the sitting room, left them together.

Blitzen looked solemnly at Iris. "I honestly believe that Mater thinks we are drunk." he said. "I'm afraid she does," said Iris. They laughed again.

CHAPTER IX

THE drug that Iris and Blitzen had taken was one which, besides giving an expansion of consciousness, and in the jargon of the mystics "loosening the girders of the soul," was also a strong aphrodisiac. It had this further peculiarity that it invariably heightened the chief characteristic of the person who had taken it. In the make-up of the average young man or woman, sex looms pretty largely, however much they may seek to deny it—hence had Iris and Blitzen been at all average, it is not difficult to see what would have happened. Each would have been attracted to the person around whom their thoughts had been centering of late, and the censor being withdrawn (as in dreams) they would have blindly succumbed to that attraction. Had Jealousy been in the foreground, jealousy would have been given full scope; quarrels would have followed, hopeless misunderstandings have been intensified. But as we have said before, neither Iris nor Blitzen were average. In the former as in the latter, love of truth and love of beauty prevailed. The disappearance of the Black Shadow testified to the first, and a realisation of universal harmony to the second.

Above all things Iris loved music and colour; rhythm of form and rhythm of movement. Circumstances had prevented her from learning to play either the piano or the violin, but she knew exactly how compositions ought to be rendered and could she have been given three wishes as in the fairy-tale, the first of these would have been for power to play with her hands as she already played with her brain. Only two persons had she known in her life who could do this—the great Paderewski and her own mother. She did not hesitate to link them together—she had heard the same pieces played by them both, and she knew. When she thought of how the almost divine genius of her mother had been swamped by the selfish egotism of her father, she hated the latter anew. It had, of course, been jealousy on his part—she saw that plainly now. But the just anger that she felt at the realisation of this was swept away on the crest of a glorious wave of sound, and, like a swimmer in sight of the happy isles, she plunged anew, drowning herself in this sea of light and rhythm and beauty. This ecstasy lasted for the best part of a week.

As for Blitzen he, too, had an expansion of his consciousness, though on a slightly lower rung of the ladder. Lying awake in the early hours of that Sunday morning he painted on the ceiling with the longest of long brushes scenes that befitted the dreams of the poets of all the ages, but he knew the brush to be illusionary and he longed for it to be real. For the time, however, harmony was restored.

But to return for a moment to Castlenau Mansions and the well-meant advice of Blitzen's mother. As a result of the mild lecture that both of them had received, they had become wildly hilarious and happily inconsequent, and after a number of suitable excuses followed by a short sleep, they had returned at a respectable hour to the Adelphi. Iris had some hazy recollections of having been attended to at Svaroff's by some rather nice girl whom she had not thanked nor subsequently seen. She felt distinctly uncomfortable about it, for the girl (not a servant, by the way) had been most considerate and sympathetic. At the dictation of Blitzen, therefore, she wrote a short note to Svaroff, again thanking him for the enjoyable evening before and apologising for her omission.

"After this," said Blitzen, "we'll really have to drop them. It was certainly amusing, but we can't afford to know them. You must see that surely, Kiddie? We should soon be placed in a hopelessly false position."

"I suppose so," Iris said, but there was little conviction in her tone. Why was it, she thought, that in regard to *The Hieroglyph* Blitzen seemed determined always to look on the gloomy side of everything? Personally she thought it would be delightful to continue to know them. However, she would not argue with him, the fatalistic side of her was coming uppermost. If it was to be it would be. When Blitzen asked her not to write to Svaroff again, she gave her promise quite naturally.

Two days after the events referred to, a letter arrived for Iris.

It was written in the strangest and most spidery of scrawls and was worded as follows:

"DEAR MISS STRICKLAND, —Salutation, and thanks much for screed. We are glad you survived the fearsome ordeal, and trust that all is well with thee and thine. As to the persons who were kind in their attentions, believe me they simply don't exist! Thine, in the Mysteries,

"BENJAMIN N.

"*P.S.*—When will you come again?"

"What an awful fist!" was Blitzen's comment. "He must have made another night of it, judging by the writing. But he probably means well. Of the two, Svaroff is by far the better man. But don't forget, Kiddie, you gave me your promise. You'll keep it?"

"Of course I will," she made answer.

They'll have to write to me about the proofs was her secret thought. By that time, perhaps, Blitzen will see things in their proper light. Outwardly she appeared to dismiss the subject from her mind. A week passed and then a fortnight, and still no word from Svaroff. Iris began bitterly to regret her easily given promise, but she had not the slightest intention of breaking it. Keeping her word was one of the few things upon which she really prided herself, that, and telling the truth. Often these causes of her pride had landed her in the most inconvenient of situations, but somehow she had always felt that the inconvenience was more than compensated for by the justification of her will power. Now, for the first time, she was beginning to doubt this.

At the end of three weeks the old tug-of-war had commenced anew; at the end of four it was becoming definitely painful; at the end of five, to her great relief, the wished-for letter arrived. Blitzen was out at the time and she read it hastily. Only a few lines, but how they brightened the recently dulled horizon!

"DEAR MISS HAMILTON,—Are we never to see you again? There's tea here any time you care to call—Yours truly,
VLADIMIR S."

In a few happily chosen words she answered the letter, posting it immediately lest she should weaken in her decision. She glanced at the dock as she left the study—a quarter to two it said. With any luck he should get the letter by tea-time, and, who knows, perhaps to-morrow she would see him. It was the first time she could remember that she had ever broken a promise, but now she felt that it was justified. Blitzen had no right to have extracted it—it was almost as though he could not trust her—but of course she would tell him when he came.

At four o'clock he came in with some rejected sketches, looking white and worried.

She told him at once, even before he had time to cross the threshold, but this time he showed no anger, perhaps he looked a little tired—it was difficult to say what he felt. She almost wished that he had shown some annoyance, his failure to do so made her feel, somehow, mean.

"I know," he said quietly, almost tonelessly; "what is more, I can tell you when you posted it. Nearing two o'clock, was it not? Perhaps I should say a quarter to two? I knew at once that you had written the letter, and I knew that you would send it. I was at Billy's and I couldn't tell you not to."

"But, Blitzen, no harm is done. You know you can trust me."

"I know."

Blitzen held her at arm's length and looked deep into her eyes. His own held infiniteness, tenderness and sorrow. "No harm is done—perhaps—but, Kiddie, you've broken your word."

For the third time in her married life Iris shed tears. She was tired, she was puzzled, yet she was strangely happy.

"Blitzen, everything will be all right, I promise you," she said, then pulled herself up as though guilty of a falsehood, and blushed. But this time Blitzen understood. He smiled suddenly, almost radiantly. "Come, Kiddie, no use crying over posted letters. Shall we go to Kew? I've not been for ages and the flowers are gorgeous now, especially the roses. Stick on your leopard-skin and the tweeds—we've got five hours at least."

They went out together. If the image of Svaroff appeared from time to time it was definitely at a distance. The day being Tuesday, the Gardens were mainly deserted, and Iris and Blitzen surrendered themselves unreservedly to the beauty around them. Seated beneath a flowering lime tree whose branches swept the ground, they gazed through lazy, half-closed eyelids at the narrowing vistas beyond them, noting with pleasure the dark green of the fir trees showing almost inky black against the deep blue of the sky, the exquisite fairy green of the larches, the wax-like buds of the oleanders. They breathed in the scent of roses, heliotrope and syringa, listening the while to the cello-like droning of the bees and the sharper chirp of the crickets. After a while Blitzen stretched himself full length, and Iris drew his head into her lap. She commenced to stroke his hair, moving her fingers with the lightest of light touches across his temple and behind his ears, lightly raising his hat and letting it fall again, noting with appreciative eye the gleams of gold and the Rossetti-like waves above the brow, the full contour of his throat, the long, well-set eyes and close-set ears, the subtle lines of the chiselled, faintly humorous mouth. Of a truth there were few persons as comely as Blitzen. Why could she not be entirely happy?

"What a wonderfully magnetic touch you have, Kiddie," he said.

"Have I?" she answered. "Laura used to say so, so did the girls at school. They were always asking me to stroke them. Some people don't like their heads to be touched, but one finds as a rule that they are invariably conceited and nearly always selfish. Don't you think so?"

"I do," said Blitzen, "but I didn't realise you were so observant. I can think of quite a number of men who hate to have their heads touched, and they are certainly as you have said. One might almost divide the sex into the touchables and the untouchables. I agree with you that the former are far more pleasanter. Do you realise, Kiddie, that you haven't kissed me for weeks?" he added.

"Haven't I?" She bent down, lightly brushing his eyebrows with her lips. "Close your eyes, Blitzen." He did so obediently. She kissed his closed eyelids, following up the kiss with a flutter of her eyelashes across his mouth. It was what she called butterfly kisses.

109

Blitzen looked absurdly happy. For the moment he made her think of a great big Newfoundland puppy. Suddenly she felt that whatever the calendar might say she was in reality years and years older than he; she felt she was his mother. Why was it, she wondered, that nice men always looked slightly foolish and utterly bewildered when one kissed them. If they didn't, they were definitely dangerous. The most dangerous type of man was the man who laughed when he kissed you. He was invariably sadistic. Then there was the type of man who looked arrogant and slightly ferocious: she thought of her cousin David. He, too, was dangerous, but not nearly so attractive as the sadist. There was a fourth type, the man who looked pleasantly amused—he was almost sure to be interesting and could be, one felt certain, an excellent companion. It was to the category of the fourth that she relegated Svaroff.

"How did she know these things?" you may ask. The answer is a simple one. Through the medium that she used for the writing of poems—in a word, through intuition.

"Blitzen," she said, "I promised to go to tea with Svaroff to-morrow. Do you mind? Or if you do, won't you come too?"

"I wish you hadn't," he said. "As to my coming, I shouldn't dream of it."

"But you said yourself that Svaroff was all right."

"He is," said Blitzen. "It isn't Svaroff that I distrust, but the sort of people you are likely to meet at his rooms."

"But, Blitzen, I am not a child."

"You are not," he said decisively. "I sometimes doubt if you have ever left the cradle much less the nursery. The trouble is that you will insist on judging people by your own standard. Given a pair of fine eyes and a pleasing voice or carriage, and you straightway endow the owner of them with all the virtues of the Knights of the Round Table, with not a few special excellences of your own making thrown in. Beauty or attractiveness means in nine cases out of ten absolutely nothing;

I wish you could be made to realise this. But seemingly you can't. What is the logical result? The image invariably tumbles, and one of these days it will crush you, perhaps maim you in its fall; and what will the Blitzen do then, poor thing?" he finished mockingly, to hide his rather too obvious emotion.

"But surely everyone judges others by the standard of themselves," she answered. "How else can one judge?"

"Of course they do," he replied, "and in the case of 'everyone' it pans out pretty fairly. They know what other persons will do and the reasons why they do them, so the contest works out fairly. But the reasons you have for doing things are not the same as those of the crowd. That is where you get misunderstood, and why you are always getting hurt. Listen to the wise old Blitzen who really loves it and understands it, and don't go running after strange gods; no, not even after the gods of *The Hieroglyph*. Promise?"

"Of course," she answered.

"H.B. and no L.P.?" he asked.

"What does that signify?" she said, smiling.

"Honour bright and no leg-pull," he said.

She laughed. "You're nearly as bad as Newton. But I promise."

"But what did you mean about the persons I should meet at Svaroff's? I didn't notice anyone."

"Didn't you? Well, I think someone noticed you. That boy in scarlet, for example. Take my word for it, he's a thorough degenerate with quite a lot of the Sadist in him. Sadism is never good in anyone, but it is especially bad in anyone so young. He couldn't have been more than twenty. He was watching you just like a vivisectionist."

"He didn't attract me in the slightest," said Iris, "and even if he had I loathe scarlet; besides, he wasn't a bit sympathetic about you. What strange ideas you have, Blitzen."

They stood up.

"Have I? Well, I'm intensely relieved, anyway. Oh! Kiddie!" and Blitzen suddenly picked her up as in the days of the old assegai dances. He glanced swiftly to the right and left. Nobody was in sight. Holding her firmly in one arm he brought her head down to the level of his own. Then he kissed her on the mouth. As he placed her once more on the ground they laughed simultaneously.

Suddenly Blitzen looked at his wrist-watch.

"Do you realise, Kiddie, that we must have been here nearly four hours? I believe I'm getting hungry."

"I don't believe it, I know it," she answered.

"Let us go to Antonio's," said Blitzen.

They left the Gardens, ending up the evening at the little Soho restaurant that was their own special discovery. Later they slept the sleep of the young, the tired and the very happy.

At the offices of *The Hieroglyph*, meanwhile, the masochism of the sub-editor had nothing further to wish for; even Svaroff got a little tired of exploiting the thickness of the shell that hedged his minion about.

"Newton, you nauseate me," he said.

"Well, why do you keep me?" was the answer.

It was the last word that either addressed to the other that day.

CHAPTER X

ON the following afternoon Iris called to relieve the monotony. She was met by Newton with a mighty flourish and low salaams.

"Hail! fairest lady, Keeper of the Stars. Hast any new Lyrics from Lesbos?" he queried.

"What does he mean?" said Iris, turning to Svaroff.

The latter looked at his sub-editor with open contempt.

"I don't think he knows himself," he answered.

"By the way," he added, "this is just idle curiosity. Are you tremendously fond of girls and women?"

"Good lord, no," she said; "in fact, generally speaking I loathe them. Why do you ask me?"

Svaroff looked triumphantly at Newton, as much as to say "I told you so," but Newton was seemingly quite unabashed.

"Why do you write love poems to them then?" he asked her. Iris looked utterly amazed.

"But I don't," she said; "it's all purely imaginary. One can't very well write poems to a man—I couldn't, at all events. So I just imagine myself a man and write as I imagine he would feel if writing to myself. I choose myself because I know myself best. But, of course, I don't really feel these things; if I did I shouldn't dream of writing about them. I've never written about anything that I've felt. I couldn't; it would be a sort of mental prostitution and in the very worst of taste. I've never even described a landscape that I've seen. It seems to me that only inasmuch as a thing is imaginary is it at all real and lasting. It seems to me that there are universal types. Am I talking nonsense?" she added quickly.

"Not at all," said Svaroff. "Have you read much Blake?" he added.

"No; why?" she answered.

"Only that you seemed to echo his arguments, that is all."

"I'm afraid," said Iris, "that I've never even heard of him. Ought I to have? It's very strange, but I'm always being told that ideas I thought were uniquely my own were really those of somebody else, but usually they belong to Plato and a lot of other persons beginning with a P."

"What? Plotinus, Porphery and Pythagorus?" said Svaroff.

"Yes," she answered. "But however did you know? I think Laura must have been right. You must be a magician."

He smiled.

"Nothing magical about it—it is just a matter of simple deduction. But it's curious the drug should have had no effect. Other persons wrote me reams and reams, and such piffle, most of it. Did you really get Nothing?"

"Of course not," she answered. "We were both of us gloriously happy for one thing, and I knew heaps and heaps of things. I'm afraid I've forgotten most of them now, but perhaps they'll appear later in some poem."

"That's quite possible," he said.

Then she told him about the music and their walk to Barnes.

"And Strickland? What did he get?" was the next question.

"Oh, Blitzen? He got colours chiefly and pictures, I think."

"I see," said Svaroff. "But I wish he'd have written. When in a state of exaltation one sees with the eyes of the angels. Later one cannot always recall the vision.

"So *that* was Blitzen," he continued. "Somehow I took him for your brother, an older brother," he added quickly. "Are you *really* married?"

"Of course. Why?"

"It seems strange, that is all." Then he quickly and deftly changed the subject.

"Have you written any more verse?" he asked.

"Yes," she said, and she showed him *The Skull amongst the Roses* and *The Maelstrom*. Svaroff read the first named poem in silence—he seemed obviously impressed. Then he read the second; which we quote in full:

THE MAELSTROM

Beyond that outer space which bounds the blue,
Beyond the confines of the furthest star,
Beyond all thought and sight, where comets bar the light,
But myriad motes the sunlight filters through!
Vaster than Time or Space, madly the planets race,
From ever widening circles drawn afar
As drifting spar,
Down to the whirling centre: there anew
To be cast forth, till haply lost to view
In That One Eye; which is the vortex.
Narrow the circles to resurging fire!
Stars battle blindly in that dim abyss.
See in the whirling tide, as one vast suicide,
Creation stagger! Yet the one desire,
Ever insatiate, must darkly gravitate
To that deep centre, till it comes to this:
Failing, we miss.
Missing, by that same failure we acquire
One chance the more,—so vainly we aspire
To gain our final goal,—perfection.

So far is comprehended. But one Eye
Of the All-Seeing holds our Universe.
Great though to Man the Storm, 'tis but a shadow form
Slow-passing in that centre. How descry
Of that deep Eye, the Soul, the structure of the Whole,
The meaning of the Maelstrom, or that terse
Tremendous curse
By some called Destiny! The Eternal "Why?"
Mayhap is answered when Infinity
Becomes at last the Finite, and—the End.

"Definitely good," he said. "How did you come to write them?"

"Oh, I had the idea for them for a long time past, but I suddenly felt that my brain had been washed and anything I wanted to do I could do. It was the same as when I was a child at school. Anything I wanted to do then I could always do. The trouble now is that I can't want to do things. I get tired of everything, quite often of living." She laughed inconsequently, but her eyes were wistful. He looked at her gravely and with seeming sympathy. How easy he was to talk to, she thought. No adopting of superior airs, or making one feel a fool.

"When did you last have a holiday?" he said simply.

"About four years ago," she answered, "and of course I've been ill a lot."

"You ought to get away," he said. "Have you ever been to Eastbourne?"

"No," said Iris.

Then in answer to her questioning look, "My mother lives there," he said. "You'll have to meet her.

"But before you do we must enrol you as chief citizen of the 'Republic of Genius.' What do you say, Newton?"

"Rather," answered the latter.

Svaroff with a mother! How incongruous it seemed. Somehow he had appeared to her as a being set apart. She could not imagine him with any relations. She linked him in her mind with Margrave and Zanoni, and found in speaking of that in speaking of them he shared her appreciation for a "strange story," and of much of the work of Lord Lytton.

"What about that tea?" he said; "whilst you are getting it I'll explain to Miss Hamilton about the Great Scheme. It is only fitting that she should be the first to know of it."

In a few minutes Newton came back, but with rather a blank look upon his face. He said a few words to Svaroff that Iris couldn't catch, but she saw the quick look of annoyance that flashed across the face of the latter.

"Fortnum's haven't sent? How is that?" he asked. Then, "Did you remember to phone them?" he added.

"No. I thought they knew," said Newton.

"How should they know?" said the other; "are they clairvoyant? Phone at once, say that it is most important, and keep out of my vision for a little while."

Newton took the portable telephone in to the next room and Svaroff turned with a word of apology to Iris.

"I hope you're not frightful thirsty for a few minutes," he said. "We appear to have got a few messages mixed up. But you see now; the wisdom of such things as V.H.O.?"

Iris smiled.

For a second or two both were both silent. Then, "Has it ever occurred to you to try to problem of genius?" he said.

"No," she answered, "but I have often thought about inspiration and what it stands for."

"Well, how would you describe it?" he asked her.

"I think that it is contacting Divinity," she replied. "One touches the fringe of something very much greater than one's normal self, and one brings one's knowledge back."

"Exactly. But *how* does one 'contact Divinity'?—to use your own phraseology. In what state is the consciousness at the time of such contact?" he continued.

"I should say," she replied, "to use a musical simile, that one was the equivalent of an octave higher, perhaps several octaves higher, and that one was sensitive to a wider range of vibrations. Isn't that it?"

"You have partly answered my question," he said, "but not entirely. I will try to put it more easily. When, for example, you describe a storm, a particular tree or a wild animal, shall we say, and you do not copy from the original, how do you do it?"

"Oh! I see what you mean," she said; "it's quite simple— one just *becomes* that thing for the time being, then one writes as one feels. I suppose really it's an intense form of concentration; one shuts out everything else, otherwise of course one couldn't do it."

"Humph!" said Svaroff. He looked at her meditatively.

"Well, if it's so simple, why can't you always do it—why could you do it more easily as a child than now?"

He waited for her answer with considerable interest.

"Because, for one thing," said Iris, "I find it so much more difficult to get away from myself now than I did years ago. Then the higher vibrations were more real to me than the everyday ones; then I could get away from the things I hated whenever I wished by simply shutting them out, and I always did so whenever I was alone. I had a rotten time at school," she spoke almost fiercely, "but I always made up for it at night," she added with a laugh. "They couldn't prevent me from going where I wished then; so I went everywhere and did everything. I quite outdid the *Arabian Nights*. I expect now, if I ever went to the East, I should be horribly disappointed."

"You would," said Svaroff with decision. "But after you had the drug didn't you get some of that early state back?" he asked.

"Not exactly," she replied. "You see, after the drug it was so very much better. I felt *so well*. It was like being an Archangel or a god—I felt that for the first time I had found my real self, and the real self was—"she hesitated for the fraction of a second, and then said the words boldly—"the real self, was *God!*"

"The Reverend would have a fit if he heard me," she added, laughing.

"The real self is the real self," said Svaroff, "and I see that you do understand. But what if by following out certain instructions and by cultivating the will one could contact the higher state whenever one wished. Wouldn't it be worth it?"

"Rather," she said enthusiastically.

"Well, one can," said Svaroff. "Genius is another name for Divinity. Divinity another name for genius. Provided they proceed along the lines laid down for them, that I shall lay down, the most mediocre talent can develop into genius, and the genius become a god. I'm not joking," he said, as he noted her look of amazement. "Look at Newton for example. He did the rottenest work imaginable when he first encountered me, and now it is at least passable." Then, as the subject under discussion entered the room, "When he takes the trouble to remember, it is good. Are Fortnum's sending?" he said.

"Yes. The goods will be here in about ten minutes, and the kettle takes two to boil. I'll go and fill it." Newton went out again.

"To proceed with what we were saying—the genius can become a god—but the fool will only become a greater fool. That is, and always will be, the great difficulty. The majority of persons are fools, and the conceit of the fool out-tops all other concept. I shall hold out to them a mirror. They will see only their own ugly faces, and in their mad fury, monkey-like, they will break the mirror and try to destroy the holder of it. But the wise ones will see a beauteous image, and they will worship. Yes. We all do the Narcissus stunt sooner or later, but not until we have embraced him and lost our own identity do we ever realise that he is *not* and that *we are*, that both of us are

One." He smiled suddenly and charmingly, and immediately his face looked ten years younger.

"What a solemn little sibyl it looks," he said.

"Won't you smoke?" He handed her his monogrammed cigarette-case in which were two long rows of fat Turkish cigarettes, and as she took one out he lighted a match. What a delightful aroma they had, and how very nice his hands were—just like her Uncle John's, she thought. She lit the cigarette, smiling lazily into his eyes.

He returned the smile with just a ghost of mischief.

"Won't you do it again?" he said.

She shook her head. "I don't see the necessity," she answered.

"No? Perhaps not," he replied. "But if we only did the things that were necessary what a very dull place this world would be. But I never ask for anything twice," he said.

"Neither do I," said Iris, and at this juncture Newton came in with the tea.

Over tea, Iris resumed the discussion.

"Would Blitzen do better drawings? Would he be happier?" she said.

"Of course," said Svaroff

"Well, then, I'll tell him. May I?" she asked.

"Naturally. The more the merrier. But we shan't have too many. What the mob want is something for nothing. They'd like to sneak into heaven by a back door or through the pantry window if the place of their dreams possesses the equivalent of such exits and entrances. But in this instance they'll have to work and they won't like it. That is why we are in no danger of being overcrowded. I shall plant a ladder and put their feet on the first rung of it—they will have to do the rest. Well here's to the Republic of Genius and to the future of its foremost citizen." He raised his teacup, smiling at Iris over the golden tail of the raised peacock.

"All hail," said Newton.

There was a timid knocking at the door and Svaroff looked at his sub-editor.

"Who on earth can that be?" he said. "Better say I am out." Newton went to the door and came back.

"He's heard you talking and he says he wrote you he was coming. His name is Barlow—he's a medium or something."

Svaroff looked profoundly bored. "Very well, tell him to come in," he said.

A little man looking like a retired grocer, dressed in a black-tailed coat and with a black tie, entered the room hesitatingly. He carried a shiny top-hat in his right hand which he uneasily transferred to his left on meeting the blank stare of Svaroff.

"Yes?" said the latter. "You wrote to me? So many people do that. What do you expect of me? Do you want me to procure you a love philtre or produce the Devil from my waistcoat pocket?" He spoke in an even tone, but his look was miles away; he looked through and beyond the little man and in some strange way completely over his head.

Iris felt very sorry for Mr. Barlow. He looked so completely crushed and he was obviously not used to feeling so. Probably in his own little circle he was quite a personage.

He looked nervously at Iris and Newton.

"You can have nothing to say that cannot be said before my friends," said Svaroff, "and I can assure you they won't be interested. Well?" His note was challenging and slightly mocking. Not once had he removed the blank stare that was so utterly disconcerting to his unwelcome visitor.

The little man appeared to make a superhuman effort, then he spoke quickly and in a low tone—his gaze shifted constantly away from the face of Svaroff and back to it again; he made Iris think of a trapped rabbit. She caught the words, "séance, entity, evil obsession." The look of boredom on the face of Svaroff openly increased.

The little man appeared to be making some request, and Iris purposely transferred her gaze to the window. When she looked round again he was saying goodbye to Svaroff.

"It has been *so* nice to see you," said the latter, still keeping his blank stare and speaking in the stereotyped tones of convention.

The medium held out his hand which Svaroff took limply, still keeping his far-away gaze on the other's face. Then he dropped the hand, looked at his own, and absent-mindedly wiped it on the seat of his trousers.

"Good-bye," he said.

Mr. Barlow literally wilted through the doorway. Svaroff smiled with a look of infantile innocence.

"Poor devil," said Newton.

"I don't think he'll come again," said Svaroff musingly.

"I should think not," said Iris. "If it is not a rude question, who was he?"

"Oh, one of those Spiritualists," he answered; "they bring in their train all the foul larvae of the pit. Whew! Open the window, Newton. I want some fresh air." And Svaroff leaned his head out of the window and breathed deeply. Then he turned round and looked inquiringly at Iris, who had risen.

"Must you go?" he said.

"Yes," she answered. "After this I shall be almost afraid to shake hands with you."

"I'm sure you needn't be. Why?" he asked.

Then he seemed to realise something, and laughed, throwing his head back. Suddenly his face became profoundly serious.

"It really has been awfully nice seeing you," he said. "I really mean it. You will come again soon, won't you? We shall soon be having another symposium. Come to it, and bring the 'Boy'."

"I will if I can," said Iris.

Later that evening she recounted the day's doings to Blitzen, telling him of the Great Scheme and not forgetting the episode of the medium.

"Poor devil," he said, echoing the words of Newton. "Only I can quite understand Svaroff's behaviour. If he didn't choke them off he'd be inundated with such people, and God only knows what they'd be seeing. The Apocalypse unveiled wouldn't be in it. But I'd have liked to see it if only from the viewpoint of a comic drawing—*Absent-minded host*: 'So glad you are going!' What?" He laughed happily.

"He wants me to do a book," said Iris, "and I rather think he wants you to illustrate one. Would you if he did? You'd have *carte blanche* for your imagination, I fancy, and he wouldn't interfere; he's too much of an artist. I think he quite likes you," she added.

"I'm not so sure about that," said Blitzen; "but now that I've met the man I take back a great deal that I'd previously thought of him. As far as we personally are concerned we have nothing to complain of. Perhaps the experiment was a little unwise, but after all, we took the stuff of our own free will. I hate people who do silly things and then directly they come to harm throw the blame on somebody else. What Svaroff actually does is to hold up a mirror. Most people aren't too pleasant to look at, and so we get hyena howls and worse. I understand the man entirely. In a way he is like my *alter ego*, the other side of me," he added quickly. "I believe I could say for certain what he would do under a given set of circumstances."

"And could he tell what you would?" said Iris interestedly.

"No. That's the curious part about it all," said Blitzen. "I don't feel that he could, but he would trust me to do the right thing, anyway," he added.

"*Curiouser and curiouser*," said Iris.

"What is?" said Blitzen.

"Everything," she replied.

She picked up the small kitten. "Cairo looks as if he knew everything in the world," she said. "How many fat mouses has it eaten to-day? It feels like a small dromedary!"

"Ask it?" said Blitzen.

For answer Cairo purred lustily.

CHAPTER XI

FOR the next few days Iris worked on her book of poems. Thanks to the almost magical power of encouragement she accomplished in a short time more than she had done for years, and both she and Blitzen were pleased with the result.

"Didn't I tell you, Kiddie, that you could do absolutely anything you wished?" he told her, smiling. "I only wish I had half your brains. It's a wonderful small child. That Svaroff has been the first to recognise your genius is no small feather in his cap. It will certainly be accounted unto him for righteousness. If the man had not the undeniable charm which he has I should still always feel that I owed him thanks if only for that one thing alone."

"I'm glad you like the 'pomes,'" Iris replied, "but it's all nonsense about my having brains; you've ten times the intelligence that I have. No, don't interrupt me," she continued, as he demurred; "the trouble with the old Blitzen is that it's far too modest. It does magnificent work and is quite unaware of the fact that it is magnificent. Now I always know when I do good work and am not ashamed to say so. That's the difference between us. I could no more sit down and do a thing to order, as you often do, than I could jump over the moon. It's Blitzen who is the genius. And for anyone to say otherwise is rank heresy."

"And she says she isn't modest," said Blitzen, addressing the ceiling.

"They said at school," replied Iris, "that pride was my besetting sin, and they spent most of their time in trying to make me humble. Not only was I never praised for anything I did, but they even tried to make me appear ugly. One term they cut my hair short, just like a convict's, really because it was thick and curly, but ostensibly because I wouldn't keep it tidy, which for them meant screwing it back behind the ears and dragging it back from the forehead like a charity girl. 'Before honour is humility' was even pasted across the fly-leaf of our prizes. Had I stayed there for any length of time I should certainly have outrivalled Lucifer, but fortunately, whilst still in the lower school, I was expelled for smoking and for throwing religious doubt on the faith of my companions."

"What an awful place," said Blitzen. "They ought to have had me to deal with. But to have got expelled, especially for the last-named offence, is quite in the approved tradition. You're in excellent company, Kiddie-wee."

"Am I?" said Iris. "In what way?"

"Well, wasn't Shelley expelled?" replied Blitzen.

"Was he? and for the same reason?" came back the answer.

"How can you say I am clever when I don't even know things like that—things that everyone ought to know. But I never heard of Shelley until a few years ago. I suppose at school they thought he was wicked They made us learn Keat's 'Ode to a Nightgalle' at the second school I went to, and that line about a Grecian Urn, but I've never read a line of Keats since, and I don't mean to."

"Why ever not?" said Blitzen.

"Because," Iris replied, "I made a vow not to when I was just fourteen. A friend of the Reverend's said at that time that my work was extraordinarily Keatsian. I asked who Keats was, and when I was told, vowed I would never read a line of him until I had established myself."

"Well, you can break the vow now."

"Why?"

"Well, isn't it obvious?"

Iris laughed.

Yes, thought Blitzen, she was certainly a never-ending source of surprises

At the end of the week came an invitation from *The Hieroglyph*. It was on grey paper, not censed, they noted, and the type was black.

"For the invocation of Saturn," read out Blitzen. "I wonder what strange brew they'll give us this time. I see it's to be at eight o'clock as before, but he would prefer we come earlier to avoid the *profanum vulgus*. He's added a foot note to that effect. Well, there'll be no difficulty as far as I'm concerned," he added.

"I suppose he's remembered that I hated crowds," Iris remarked. "What is the time now? About four-thirty? Well, we've nearly three hours to prepare ourselves for the ordeal. The invocation of Saturn sounds a bit Lethean, but it's sure to be interesting, and we've the Lord's Day in which to recover."

She smiled mischievously.

"Sixteen men on the dead man's chest—
Yo ho ho, and a bottle of rum!"

she sang with gusto.

"Drink and the Devil had done for the rest—
Yo ho ho, and a bottle of rum!"

Blitzen finished. "Well, there's nothing like anticipation. If hope deferred maketh the heart sick, hope realised sometimes maketh the tummy squirm. What?"

"You were just as bad," said Iris.

"I know. It was only a gentle reminder."

They smiled at their mutual reminiscences.

At seven-forty they were ascending once more the stairs which led to the offices of *The Hieroglyph*. No stately St. Michael greeted their arrival; they were accosted instead by a squat figure garbed in black, whose monk's cowl was drawn across the face, covering seemingly even the eyes. We say "seemingly," for the eyes of the figure were large, black and lustreless, which doubtless caused the momentary illusion. After a moment's dramatic pause, during which they were subjected to a challenging scrutiny, the figure seemed satisfied, for it raised a short red-hilted sword, and with a gesture which was intended to be dignified, waved them to the entrance.

"Pass," it said, or rather barked, for the voice was harsh and guttural.

The door opened as before, and they saw in the distance Svaroff. He also was robed in black, and was barefooted. Then the door of the room of assembly opened. Newton came out and instinctively both stepped backwards.

"Ye gods! Whatever is it?" said Iris in a tense whisper.

"Satanic, most certainly," was Blitzen's reply.

They were met by an appalling odour like a third class continental train—stale garlic, unwashed humanity and all the intensified effluvia of the Arabs' seventh hell.

"It's quite all right," said Newton cheerfully. "It's only the Pan incense which has got mixed up with that of Saturn. This ought to lay flat even the bravest of the suburbanites. Don't you think so, Guru?"

"So there's method in your madness?" said Blitzen, raising his eyebrows with a quizzical smile.

Newton bowed at the implied compliment.

"Don't you believe him," said Svaroff. "It's just his damned carelessness, and it's just like him to profit by it. He has all the combined cunning of the ten lost tribes, besides the special attributes of his own chosen one. But he has his uses, at times, nevertheless, and to-night he has proved it. Get some cigarettes," he said, and as Newton re-entered the large room from which clouds of evil-smelling smoke were still issuing, Svaroff turned once more to Blitzen and Iris.

"Once you're smoking you won't notice it," he said.

"Pan incense," he explained to them, "is the nearest approach one can get to a very aged goat; Saturn—well, we'll leave that to the imagination." Then, as Newton returned with the cigarettes, "The fact is that to-night we're expecting some members of the Press, for whom I have no special liking. They'll be anticipating the Lord knows what, and verily they shall not be disappointed.

"Oh, I shall give them their money's worth," he said, as Blitzen cocked an eyebrow; "have no fear of that! Sundry knockings, ritual they won't understand—plenty of abracadabra, *and* the incense. Yes. That ought to do it. I don't think, somehow, they'll be too anxious to come again," he finished dreamily and with a far-away look in his eyes.

Iris thought of Mr. Barlow, and both she and Blitzen smiled.

"But before the fun starts we had best partake of the water of Lethe," Svaroff continued.

"No. It won't make you sleep," he said, turning to Iris, "and the only things you will forget are the things best forgotten. *It's my own invention*, a nectar of the Gods, and not for the imbibing of the herd. So we house it right royally. Newton, the goblets."

Newton returned in a few minutes with three Jade goblets and a wonderful jade bowl filled with greenish golden liquor.

"Since the other had no effect, try this," he said.

He dipped two of the goblets into the bowl, then handed them simultaneously to Iris and Blitzen.

"But aren't you joining us?" said the latter.

"Not at this stage of the journey," was the dramatic answer, followed by just the ghost of a smile, "though we all travel the same road sooner or later," he added quickly.

Then, "*Salve atque vale*," and he left the room.

"*Ave Cæsar, Imperator*," murmured Newton below his breath.

They drank, and neither Iris nor Blitzen fell down dead—though had this happened it would not altogether have surprised the former. But Blitzen had understood the smile. This little byplay was for the entertainment of Iris.

His liking for Svaroff increased.

"What is it?" he asked, as the latter re-entered the room. "It's uncommonly potent stuff, it seems like everything desirable in turn."

"Isn't it a cocktail?" Iris asked.

"Thou hast said," was the answer. "It's base is liqueur-brandy and there's a touch of Vodka, also Vermouth and a good many other things. But these secrets are not for the profane. Perhaps, when you are *one of us*, who knows?" He smiled mysteriously.

Quite a likeable sort of Casanova, was Blitzen's mental comment.

They continued to talk for several minutes, then,

"*Ave soror*," said a voice, and in the doorway, stood the tall youth whom Iris knew as "St. Michael." He nodded, smiling carelessly at them both. "You'll have to hurry up, Vincent," said Svaroff, "if you're not to shock the profane ones with your evening dress. You'll find all you need in my room, and call out for anything you don't. How's poor old Ivan?" he added in a low voice.

"Looking pretty glum," was the answer. "I should say he wanted a drink."

"Verily he shall have one," said Svaroff.

He knocked three times on the floor with a black baton.

"Brother Warden without, enter the Sacred Presence; we have need of thee," he called in a loud and authoritative voice.

The black-robed figure without entered with alacrity.

"The bowl of libation—a foretaste," said Svaroff, and passed to him the half-filled third goblet. Then, seeing that he glanced at Iris and Blitzen, "In the realm of Saturn all names are forgotten; but we shall meet anon. Drink, brother," he said.

Ivan drank.

And now a girl with a violin-case, and a younger and shorter girl with her hair in a pigtail, appeared together. "The dressing-room is on the left, Newton's room," he explained to the taller girl. "You've only got ten minutes."

"That's all right," came the answer; "you know I'm used to quick changes."

"True, I'd forgotten," Svaroff said; then he turned to speak to Vincent, who had entered the room dressed in a black robe, similar to his own.

"Musical comedy," was Blitzen's comment; "but she has quite a nice face."

"Isn't the little one pretty?" said Iris.

"Not a patch on the tall one," Blitzen replied. "I wouldn't trust her round the corner. Now that girl with the fiddle has some character. Mark my words and see if I don't prove right. The other——" but whatever Blitzen had been about to say he checked himself abruptly, and glanced across at Svaroff.

"It's quite clear is it not?" the latter was saying to Ivan. "I have my back to the crowd. I drink, I pass the bowl—I collapse, a victim to the Gods; *You* drink, *you* collapse. The 'slave of the temple' and the 'guardian of the Flame' rush in together. The guardian of the Flame falls wailing upon the dead body of the Master of the Temple. The slave draws a veil across the mysteries: the play is finished."

"Quite clear," said Ivan, and he returned to his post of Warden Without.

The two girls entered together—the taller one similarly garbed to Svaroff, but the shorter girl, like Newton, dressed in white. She looked remarkably well, with her long black hair hanging loose upon her shoulders and a fillet of silver leaves around her head. Her cheeks, which were deadly pale, were in striking contrast to her mouth which showed a vivid splash of scarlet against the white. Her dark shadowed eyes rivalled the blackness of her hair.

To the inexperienced eyes of Iris she seemed a Vestal Virgin incarnate, but Blitzen had far other ideas, for she had most definitely looked at him with a lingering glance from beneath her long lashes, and—well, she didn't appeal to him.

"I should advise you to take your places," said Svaroff. "For the present, farewell," and Newton piloted Iris and Blitzen into the front room.

Since the strange liquor they had drunk and the excellent cigarettes with which they were still provided, they quite failed to notice the Pan-cum Saturn aroma, but that the fast-arriving guests had not been similarly provided for was evident from the scraps of dialogue which reached them through the closed doors.

"If you fear to enter, there is still time to turn back," came the harsh voice of Ivan.

"For those who endure there remains the water of Lethe—but from the realm of Saturn only the dead may be carried out."

"Is this a practical joke?" queried a laughing voice.

"Enter and see," replied Ivan.

"Well, Norman," said the voice which had just spoken, "if you can stick it, I suppose I can, *but never again.*"

Two young men entered, hastily lighting cigarettes. Then a man and a girl, then more and more men.

At last the door for the guests closed and there entered by the other door the Vestal Virgin, followed by black-robed attendants. The room was plunged into semi-darkness against which the white face and whiter robe stood out eerily. She began to chant some weird dirge in an effective low-pitched voice, of which the chief refrain appeared to be, "Woe is me, my God, woe is me, for all my song is as the sound of the sea, which lappeth against the dead shore in the darkness," or words to that effect, for though the simile constantly varied, the theme was ever the same. Scarcely had the voice died away than the violin commenced to play Tchaikovsky's "Chanson Triste," and the girl most certainly *could* play. But these things were merely the preliminaries which took the place of the voluntary in church.

They had, it appeared, the desired effect, for the intermittent whispering which had preceded them, quieted down, and a profound silence reigned. This was the signal for the entry of Svaroff.

The room was arranged as on the occasion of their previous visit, save that on the floor was a carpet of black-and-white squares to emulate the floor of a temple. This carpet covered the half of the room farthest from the guests, and continued for about a yard beyond the altar which, as before, occupied the centre of the room. On either side of the altar were long black curtains hanging from ceiling to floor, so arranged as to draw back silently. The electric switches which controlled the entire lighting were beside the fireplace just behind where Blitzen was sitting. He had noted these facts with an appreciative eye almost as soon as he had entered. Now, with the other guests he awaited the denouement.

The door on his left opened, there was a blaze of light which plunged the audience into greater darkness, and Svaroff, sword in hand, entered. He was preceded by Newton carrying the jade bowl, and followed by Ivan and Vincent carrying swords also. By some curious trick of the light, Svaroff seemed preternaturally tall and imposing, and even Ivan seemed to have grown in stature, but Newton appeared what he was— the slave of the temple. Svaroff walked majestically to the north side of the altar, then, "*Procul, O Procul, este profani,*" he exclaimed. The door behind them closed and once more they were in semi-darkness. Thereupon, sword in hand, and tracing strange figures upon the four cardinal points, Svaroff circumambulated deosil chanting barbarous words of power in an unknown tongue. It seemed that the atmosphere lightened a little, and in place of the ghastly aroma before mentioned there was a slight scent of cedar wood. That, thought Blitzen, was quite a good idea; seemingly the Guru had in some measure repented him of the evil he had planned.

"What is he doing?" whispered a voice.

"The banishing ritual of the pentagram," answered another voice which they recognised as that of Norman.

But seemingly he had not finished, for yet again he circumambulated, making yet other signs and sounds. They caught the words, "Isis, Virgo Mighty Mother, Scorpo Apophis, Destroyer," then a phrase which they could not catch, then: "Yod, Nun, Resh, Yod." The scent of cedar wood became mingled with that of myrrh.

"Well, I'm blest," whispered the voice of Norman (he was evidently quite close to them). "He means to do it thoroughly. He's banishing again. Well, he's certainly got rid of Hell's kitchen. Now we can breathe in safety," and he did so audibly.

But we shall not weary the reader with a full account of the evening's doings. Suffice it to say there were various question and answers, knockings of three and counter knockings, searchings for a lost God, suitable poems by Swinburne and Baudelaire interspersed with Russian dirges excellently executed. At last came the great moment.

"Brother Capricornus, what is the hour?" asked Svaroff in solemn tones.

"It is the hour of the triumph of Set," answered Vincent impressively.

"Let us depart," said Svaroff.

Newton, kneeling before the altar, offered the jade bowl, and Svaroff, raising it aloft, drank deeply. When, horror of horrors, "De owl have hoot, de bat have flapped her wings. Pass de bowels of libation," came the guttural voice of Ivan.

One cannot altogether blame Svaroff; the liquor went the wrong way! Quickly Newton retrieved the bowl, but disaster seemed imminent. Not for nothing had Svaroff practised Hatha Yoga, and now that practice stood him in good stead. But it was an awful moment. He did not utter a sound but the muscles of his neck began to swell and the veins on his forehead stood out. He seemed in imminent danger of apoplexy. Newton looked terrified. With quick presence of mind Blitzen switched off the lights and the room was plunged in complete darkness. Swiftly he stepped to the side of Svaroff. "Say when by a knock," he said in a low voice, and he returned to his stand by the fireplace.

After what seemed an eternity, but was in reality but a minute and a half, there was the faintest of faint knocks. Blitzen half lighted the room, and Svaroff, bowl in hand, was still standing beside the altar. He drew himself up to his full height and with a lordly gesture passed the bowl to Ivan; then, hand to throat, without a sound he fell backwards across the altar.

Blitzen switched on the lights full. To all appearance Svaroff was dead.

A shuddering gasp broke from the guests. It was the best piece of acting Svaroff had ever accomplished, and even Blitzen had his doubts. But Ivan was not to be outdone. He looked at the Master with despairing eyes, drank also, handed the bowl to Newton, and hand to side fell with a heavy thud across the carpet. His groaning was genuine, for he hurt himself rather badly in the fall.

There were frightened whispers amongst the guests. "I tell you it wasn't acting. I saw his neck—no man could have acted it. And look at the other, the stuff was poisoned. Oh, my God! What shall we do?"

"Let me out—let me out," and a terrified man rushed wildly to the door. He was followed by several others. Blitzen wisely let them out and partially lowered the light.

Ivan was still writhing upon the carpet.

"The Guardian of the Flame" rushed to the altar and flung herself with a despairing cry upon the body of the Master. The curtains fell. From an infinite distance it seemed, yet growing nearer, came the lament for the death of Asa. The wailing sounds fell shuddering upon the still air, which was heavy with the scent of death, with cedar and with myrrh.

"Go!" said Vincent in authoritative tones, and he pointed to the open door. Then as the guests seemed frightened and uncertain what to do, "Go! The Master has departed—it is finished." He spoke with suppressed impatience.

After quick and undecided looks they began to file out, at first slowly, then in more and more haste. Only one man remained, the man named Norman, and he walked with Iris and Blitzen into the inner room.

In a few moments Svaroff joined them, preceded by Newton still carrying the jade bowl. "You have endured to the end. Drink of the water of Lethe," he said, and he handed the bowl to Norman.

"Of a truth it was well and bravely done," said the other, and he drank. Then, "What a tale for the *Record!* I too must depart or I shan't get the copy in." And he went out.

"So that explains it," said Blitzen. "He was a journalist?"

"Yes," said Svaroff; "I've known Norman for years. As journalists go he isn't so bad, but I've no great opinion of the species." He turned to Blitzen with a look of genuine admiration.

"Strickland, you're a man of resource; you're a man of genius. You should have been a Bismarck! I wish that Newton could be made to take lessons from you—but at the crucial moment he will always fail one."

"Hang it all, I was holding the bowl!" said Newton in an aggrieved tone.

"Yes," said Svaroff. "But it might well have been '*Turn down an empty glass.*' You didn't think of that? Did you? No. I thought not."

Then turning once more to Iris and Blitzen he asked them to stay to breakfast. "I'm off to the Sahara on Thursday next," he said, "and I haven't too much time, but I've a proposition to make which I think may interest you. You're the very man I've been looking for, Strickland. But of this more anon. Where are Ivan and the girls?" he added.

"In the next room," said Newton. "Ivan thinks he has hurt himself."

"Well, perhaps he has," was the answer. "He fell with quite a good thud."

"Poor old Ivan! And he doesn't see the joke even now! I shall take to him the water of Lethe with an extra dash of Vodka—that should help him to recover. But get those girls off or they'll miss their trains. We can't afford to have irate parents bombarding our premises. V.H.O., Newton."

"It shall be done," said Newton, and in a few seconds he returned, escorting the younger girl. The other followed with an amused smile.

"It went off quite well, did it not?" she asked.

"Excellently," Svaroff answered, "but it's time that good little girls were in bed. You'll see her home, won't you?"

"Of course," she answered.

But the younger girl objected.

"I won't deny that I'm good," she said primly and with downcast eyes, "but I'm certainly not little. I'm quite big enough to stay up late, if I want to." she added petulantly.

"I should be inclined to reverse the statement," said Svaroff, but fortunately he spoke in Latin.

"Is that another of those classic quotations?" She retorted. "I hate them. They're always full of *double entendres.*"

There was a general laugh in which Blitzen and Iris joined, also Vincent, who had re-entered dressed for the street.

"I'll see you off," he said, "if you'll be really quick. But I've got to get back to Oxford, so there's no time to lose."

In a surprisingly short time the two girls were ready, and the three of them went off together. Svaroff glanced in the direction of Newton.

"Off on another astral journey?" he inquired. In his eyes was the faint flicker of a smile.

"No," said the other. "I was only feeling a little tired."

"Ah. I'm not surprised," was the answer. "You ought to keep earlier hours."

CHAPTER XII

A FEW minutes later Ivan walked in looking somewhat green about the gills, and having been congratulated on his fine performance and condoled with on the score of his accident, he was introduced to Iris and Blitzen.

He looked at Iris solemnly, then, bringing his heels together with a click and bending in half from the waist, "Ya lublu vas, moya Krasatka," he said.

Svaroff looked at him sideways with an expression it was quite impossible to fathom.

"Since you know a little English, why not speak it," he said, "or have the waters of Lethe done their work too thoroughly?"

"I was merely saying 'How do you do' in my native tongue," said Ivan.

"Oh, were you?" remarked Svaroff with a smile; "then it is I who have forgotten."

"What do you mean?" said Ivan testily.

"Only this," was the answer, "that your sense of humour has a tendency to develop at the wrong time and in the wrong places."

This little criticism was delivered with a good humoured laugh that should have disarmed the words of their sting, but Ivan, for reasons best known to himself, chose to take offence. He bowed to the room in general and without a word of good-bye to Svaroff walked out. A minute later they heard the hall door dose with a bang.

Newton laughed impishly. But Iris looked uncomfortable and Blitzen smiled a polite inquiry.

"Don't let it worry you," said Svaroff. "Ivan can't afford to quarrel with me, and he won't. In a few days, when the Vodka has worked itself off, he will be here to express his sorrow."

"What does he do?" asked Iris.

"Writes," was the answer—"prose, and not at all bad stuff either. But the trouble with Ivan is that he has too great a fondness for the nectar of the gods, especially my version of it. It's very foolish of him, because he is quite ruining his eyesight, and in time the stuff will ruin his brain. You are all witnesses that I said nothing to-night to which any reasonable man could object, yet you saw how he behaved! Still, all things work together for good, for those who know how to make them," he added cheerfully, "and I could scarcely have discussed the matter I have at heart with Ivan in the room.

"Miss Hamilton looks tired," he said, looking across at Iris, "would you not like Newton to show you your room? For it will be your room very shortly if things work out as we wish. You're not in a great hurry, Strickland? Well, then, I'll explain."

Iris went out with Newton and Svaroff turned to Blitzen.

"I understand," he said, "that you would not temporarily be averse to a change of residence?

"It is like this. I have to go away. The rent here is paid up to January. If it suited you and you could sub-let your place for a while, I should be delighted if you could come here and guard the fort in my absence.

"All my tradesmen are at your disposal, and for the time of residence you may regard the place and all in it entirely as your own. All I should want would be news from time to time and the keeping off of the ultra-inquisitive.

"Then, but only if you have time, there is a book I would like illustrated—some magical diagrams—but we can make arrangements about that later. What do you say?

"There are three days in which to decide if you cannot do so now. Just think it over."

"I don't think there will be any difficulty about it," said Blitzen. "I may be able to let you know the day after tomorrow. Will that do?"

"Excellently," was the reply. "What about Newton?" "Oh, he'll be coming with me. We're going to regions where it won't matter if he doesn't wash or shave for a week; he'll be as happy as a child making mud-pies. I shall do the banishing ritual each night with this. He held up a little bottle of patent insect-destroyer. "For if we chance upon the spot where there has been a late Arab encampment there'll be quite a lot to banish—big Qliphoth, little Qliphoth, and so *ad infinitum*. Yes. That's the worst of travel, but we can't have it all ways."

Three days later, Iris and Blitzen, with Cairo in his special travelling trunk, were ensconced at *The Hieroglyph*, their rooms being let for the time to some artist friends.

Before going away Svaroff went further into the matter he had discussed with Iris. He explained to her and to Blitzen all about Indian Yoga, and gave them useful tests and practices for the development of the will. Finally he presented them with numbers 1 to 3 of *The Hieroglyph*.

"If you manage to get through those before I get back, you won't have done so badly," he said. "But don't overdo things. The trouble with most people is that they become fearfully enthusiastic at first, and after a little while give the thing up entirely, because they don't become Mahatmas or magicians or whatever it is that they expect to become. As I've said before, it all depends upon *yourself*. And it's not a bad idea to keep a diary of events, not only for the analysis of the mind, but also for keeping one up to the mark. It's amazing what a number of things will present themselves as excuses for your not doing what you have set out to do. Try it and see."

"It sounds," said Blitzen, "rather like the exercises of St. Ignatius, only treated from the scientific point of view."

"Ah," said Svaroff. "So you've tried them have you? If the question is not indiscreet, what was the result and how far did you go?"

"Not very far," said Blitzen. "I got most horribly depressed—suicidally so. I think that they start at the wrong end. They should allow man to realise his divinity first, afterwards he will be strong enough to sustain the burden of his manhood. It is no use stressing the fact that we are miserable worms and then expecting us to aspire to Godhead. The psychology is all wrong. I'm convinced of it. I have travelled quite a long way, but I've never done it through the help of an inferiority complex. No, and I never shall. Lucifer was an angel of light—the greatest of the angels. Once an angel always an angel. There can be no good or bad about it. Such petty distinctions are for the *slave* minds of mortals. *Odi profanum vulgus.* Yes, *et arceo.*" He spoke with a scorn that was virulent.

Svaroff looked at him with interest. "What made you leave," he said, "and how long ago was it?"

"When I was sixteen," was the answer, "but I'd rather not talk about it—I was profoundly disillusioned. Still, of the creeds, I think it is the only one worth considering—it is the only one I could ever tolerate."

"I agree," said Svaroff.

For a while the two men were silent, each wrapped in his own thoughts. At last:

"Well, I'm glad that that was your creed," said Svaroff. "When one does not get bigotry there is always a definite poise and balance about the Roman Church's adherents—and, thank God, they are not afraid of beauty and do not overstress the sins of the body to the entire exclusion of the sins of the soul. Every harlot was a virgin once and every virgin may well become a harlot when the opportunity arises. But for the mean man and the smug man there is neither hope here nor hereafter. Their god is director-in-chief of the co-operative stores, and they look to him always to give them overweight and sometimes unlimited credit as well."

He laughed, lighted a cigarette, and going over to the big table, commenced to write.

Strickland getting up also, accidentally shook the table.

"I'm awfully sorry," he said.

"Not at all," said Svaroff. "Do it again!" and he went on writing.

Strickland looked at him quizzically.

"No, I mean it. Go on shaking the table, shake it harder. Yes, that's better; I'll tell you when to stop."

For the space of some five minutes Blitzen continued to shake the table whilst Svaroff continued to write, a smile of quiet amusement upon his face. At last:

"I think that will do," he said, and put down the pen, at the same time handing over for inspection the letter he had just written.

To all appearances it was the writing of an old, old man or one in the last stages of neurasthenia. It was to a well-known firm of solicitors and was worded as follows:

"DEAR BLANK,—I am ordered away by my doctor to the south of France for several months, for four or five, it may be. Absolute quiet is essential. As soon as I am able I will inform you as to my progress—at present I am in a state of complete collapse due to overwork and worry. Matters must wait over until my return. It is unavoidable.—Yours sincerely,

"VLADIMIR SVAROFF."

"How's that?" he said.

"Excellent," replied Blitzen. "You're a genius."

"Yes," was the answer, "I've had serious suspicions to that effect myself before now."

The two men smiled in mutual admiration.

"Post that the day after to-morrow," said Svaroff. "I'm ill—I've gone away to recover—there can be nothing of importance requiring immediate attention. I leave everything in your hands. Open all my letters, even those that seem as well as those that are marked private. I leave it to your discretion how to deal with them. If anything very unforeseen should happen, of course, acquaint me with the fact and I will post on instructions—but I don't somehow think that anything will."

"It's very flattering to be the repository of so much trust," said Blitzen. "But are you being altogether wise?"

"You're not Newton," was the answer. "If you were, perhaps not. But I know N. and I know you and I'm not in the least likely to get you mixed."

"Well, good-bye, and all good luck to you."

"Good-bye, I. H. and S.," said Newton. "By Jove! that's a happy combination! Together you should do some quite good salvage work! Eh! Guru?"

"At times," said Svaroff slowly, turning to his sub-editor, "you have definite flashes of wit; I hadn't noticed that before. Not only *will* they, but they have already! Even *you* show signs of improvement Newton."

He ran lightly down the stairs, turning to wave to them once more before getting into the waiting taxi.

Newton followed, looking like a happy but dishevelled elemental. They drove off.

Iris and Blitzen smilingly returned to the big front room. Iris seated herself in the sun chamber.

"Mark my words," said Blitzen, "he'll be back in less than three months, and he'll walk in one morning quite unannounced. I know the man far better than he knows himself." He laughed amusedly.

"I shouldn't be surprised," said Iris; "it was just the sort of thing he used to do with Laura."

Cairo, tail very much in air, was walking round and round the altar, purring loudly.

"The little creature seems definitely to like its new surroundings, does it not?" she remarked.

"Very definitely," said Blitzen. "It's most curious. It's almost as though the little beastie could see something, and whatever it saw it liked. Cairo, come here," he called.

But Cairo took a flying leap, and landing upon the head of the monstrous leopard, began to play with its paws. "I think I'll sketch it," said Blitzen, and he commenced to do so. Iris, taking down number one of *The Hieroglyph*, was soon immersed in its pages. She read without a break until lunchtime.

Then Blitzen took the book away from her and insisted on her going for a walk.

"What did V.S. tell you," he reminded her. "Aren't you being in rather much of a hurry? Not to make good use of this glorious weather is a positive sin. Let us go out and feed the gulls. If you've never seen them in Kensington Gardens—it's a sight worth remembering. Somehow," he added, "it always makes me think of a Hans Andersen story come to life. What would the little beastie make of them, I wonder?"

"I wonder, too," said Iris.

CHAPTER XIII

"ARE you surprised that they are referred to as 'the vermin of the Press'? Look at this," and Iris held out to Blitzen a copy of *The Record*.

It was the Sunday following the events related in the foregoing chapter, and seeing some sensational headlines about an amazing orgy in a West End flat, she had bought a copy of the paper.

To her astonishment she found it was a garbled account of the invocation of Saturn of the week before, so garbled that it was scarcely recognisable. There were deliberate falsifications—the obvious symbolism of the whole performance had been overlooked, and foul innuendoes were scattered copiously throughout the narration.

Iris read it, an expression of cold contempt upon her face; then she put the paper down.

"Blitzen, you've a good memory, especially for time and figures—for how long was the light switched off?"

"For about a minute, or at most a minute and a half," was the answer.

"I thought so. Just listen to this." And again picking up the paper, with an expression of disgust that she made no effort to conceal, Iris read out the following extracts:

"For the space of half an hour the room was plunged in Cimmerian darkness, during which, behind the carefully arranged curtains, the handsome young Neophyte was initiated into the Mysteries by the Master of the Temple—the nature of those mysteries it is not difficult to imagine."

"If the room was in darkness, how could they possibly see?" commented Iris. She continued reading a good deal more to the same effect. Then followed paragraphs of pious disapproval. But this was not all. There were faked photographs, calculated to stimulate the jaded appetites of Mayfair and to provoke the smug puritanism of suburbia.

She turned to an earlier page. It contained an account of the pretty little flapper who, as Vestal Virgin in company with a number of youths, as scantily dressed as herself, had opened the proceedings in a room specially darkened for the occasion. The fact that amongst the performers were the scions of several of England's oldest and most illustrious houses did not detract from the spiciness of the tale.

The liqueur of which they had both partaken: (and concerning which they were in a position to judge) was referred to as a dangerous narcotic, calculated to induce drug-forming habits.

"It was time"—the writer continued—"that we awakened to the dangerous degeneracy in our midst." And so on, *ad nauseam*.

"Poor old Guru! It's a damned shame."

"And to think that that fellow Norman professed to be a friend. Upon my soul, I honestly believe that in order to get a story some of these creatures would violate the corpse of their own mother. Anything for sensation. We live in an age of hopeless vulgarity, and that is the truth, Kiddie-wee."

In writing to Svaroff he touched as lightly as possible upon the subject, and received in return this characteristic reply:

"My friend lifted up his heel against me and lo and behold! I saw that it was the hoof of an ass! R.I.P."

Iris and Blitzen laughed.

"All the same," said the latter, "I am sorry that it has happened. That fool Norman has started the ball rolling—it will gather both momentum and size, and God alone knows where it will end. It is all very well for V. S. to treat the matter with contempt, but there is such a thing as underestimating one's enemies, especially their malevolence. When will he learn sense? Never, I fear, and if he did, would he possess half his charm?" Blitzen felt that most definitely he would not.

About a fortnight later they received a most amusing letter from Svaroff:

"Newton"—it said—"has created quite a sensation here. He preceded me into the Hotel at Biskra like this." (Followed thereon a most life-like sketch of the said Newton, head shaved as smooth as a billiard ball save for one long lock which stood out from the centre of the forehead like a curled ram's horn.) "The natives"—continued the letter—"are convinced that he is a very holy man. At present I shall not disillusion either them or him. These things have their proper evaluation in the Scheme of Things. My love to you both, and don't forget to send, *les dernieres nouvelles*.—Yours as ever, V. S."

"And to think that in many quarters he is regarded as a villain. Isn't it idiotic?"

"Absolutely," agreed Iris.

By this time she had read through number one of *The Hieroglyph* and a considerable portion of number two, and was enthusiastically practising Yoga. Being abnormally sensitive to pain, it goes without saying that after the fashion of all beginners, she adopted the most difficult poses for Pranayama and tried the most strenuous of the breathing exercises. Before five days were over she found she could keep for hours a pose that originally had been unendurable for two consecutive seconds. It was then that queer things began to happen. She found, for example, as the weeks went by, that by holding her breath and seemingly stopping the beating of her heart she could leave her body at will and travel to strange regions beyond the earth.

Her consciousness seemed to become as smoke, and she felt herself being drawn through the back of her skull. That is how she tried to explain the phenomenon to Blitzen. Once free of the physical body the sensation was extremely pleasant, and she rose as high as she could—the higher she rose the stronger and freer she became. On returning she always wrote an account of what she had seen and done.

On one occasion she decided to go to one of the planets, and after travelling a tremendous height above the earth and its surrounding atmosphere, found herself stopped by a dark thunder-cloud. She called a certain name the requisite number of times and the cloud parted. Before her appeared what at first seemed a wonderful ivory statue of the most perfect athlete, the muscles rippling down the magnificent limbs. She could not see the face clearly; it was lost in a blaze of light,— *but it was very terrible*, and the whole figure seemed literally bristling with wrath. The left arm was raised in a menacing manner, and carried what she supposed was a species of scimitar, but at first it seemed more like a gigantic quill or palm branch.

Behind the white figure, a little to the left, was a black angel equally beautiful in demoniac fashion, and vaguely seen were several other heads, all very frightful.

The white figure literally scorched her eyes to look at, and whilst she was gazing in ignorance and defiance, it suddenly lunged forward and brought its arm down. A streak of lightning seemed to strike her eyes, and for several seconds she felt as if blinded—then she was back in her body again, but not before she had seen an immense figure standing with its arms extended in cruciform fashion. The black angel (an extremely handsome Arab type) remained for several seconds after she had been struck, and the demon heads were the last to go. She watched them slowly fade against the blank wall, on the left-hand side of her bed. As the last head vanished the clock struck two.

On another occasion, after a number of strange happenings, she came to an immense wall built of reddish-looking bricks. With some difficulty she rose upwards and arrived at the top. There was a species of tablet set into it after the fashion of a coat-of-arms, and she tried to understand it. The squares were black and white and there was a species of fleur-de-lys.

She stayed a long while trying to decipher the tablet, and then realising she ought not to remain stationary, she rose above the wall. It surrounded a city which was enveloped in a dark-grey shadow. A hill loomed through the darkness and dully silhouetted at its base were two black Calvary crosses; a third was in the centre at its summit, the three forming a triangle. As she looked, the cross which formed the apex of the triangle seemed to come downwards and the others to go upwards, so that it formed some symbol. At the foot of the hill were many white stones, some with inscriptions, and she realised that it was a cemetery.

"It almost seems to me, Kiddie," said Blitzen, when she recounted these things, "as though something were trying to warn you of disaster, or telling you to leave such experiments alone. Anyway, you can't say that they are cheerful or that they leave you feeling physically fitter," and Iris was forced to admit that he was right. Thereafter she made a definite effort to stop such journeys, and to a great extent she succeeded.

Early in October she had one more experience which is perhaps worth recording. She wakened one morning from a very vivid dream to the strains of a military band. So real was the music that she remained listening to it for fully five minutes after she had wakened, and Blitzen had some difficulty in convincing her that no band was or had been playing. The dream had been of a deserted village, an old horse-pond, and charred and blackened trees. A few houses with broken windows, smashed doors and walls which were not all standing, looked upon this desolate scene; in one of the houses the staircase was plainly visible, a few pictures still hung upon the wall and a framed certificate. As she gazed in wonderment, men, obviously soldiers, began to march by in a blue-green uniform. She had never seen the uniform before and in describing it to Blitzen asked him if it were German or Russian.

"The kind of blue you speak of sounds more like French," he told her; "the Uhlans would be more like this," and he illustrated the difference on the margin of the sketch upon which he was working then with another and cleaner brush obliterated the spots of blue. From discussing the ever-fascinating subject of dreams they soon got to the still more fascinating subject of Vladimir Svaroff. The man had become for the two of them the pivot around which their thoughts centre, and they never tired of speculation about him. What he would do under this that or the other circumstance; how grossly he was misunderstood by the mob and worse still by his fellow artists, who should have had more intelligence: the perverse whimsicality of his humour; his rare and wonderful appreciation of some little act of kindness, and his childlike trustfulness. This last-named quality going, as it did, hand in hand with an almost uncanny intelligence and a profound knowledge of the more unsavoury facts of life, was to Blitzen a never-end source of wonderment. From time to time as he moved about Svaroff had written to them—always amusingly; now they had not heard for over a fortnight and were awaiting with interest the new address. As they sat together over breakfast a few days later, they were still discussing him.

"How V. S. can be such an amazingly bad judge of human nature, or rather I should say of individuals, passes my comprehension," said Blitzen. "I could see at a glance the sort of person that Norman was, and Ivan was quite easy to sum up: one had no need to see either of them a second time to come to a just conclusion; yet V. S., who has known them both for years, was apparently quite unaware of the innate unscrupulousness of them both, and he seems to be in the same state of blissful ignorance in regard to nine-tenths of his so-called friends, who, when they are not vicious spongers, are rather dangerous fools."

"Why? Has Ivan turned against him also?" said Iris.

"Yes," Blitzen answered. "He called last week when you were out, and under some very thin pretext tried to get hold of a mass of the Guru's correspondence. I need hardly say that he did not succeed.

"He then said that Svaroff had fled the country and would never come back, and talked a great deal of rubbish along the lines of Norman's article. Finally, he suggested buying up at a ridiculously low figure the remaining stock of *The Hieroglyph*, which includes, as you know, all of Svaroff's earlier work besides the magazine itself. He looked very much surprised when I all but showed him the door. Svaroff is well rid of him and I have said as much."

"But what an extraordinary thing," said Iris; "he himself took part in the show there was all that ridiculous fuss about. What on earth does it all mean?"

"Sheer funk," said Blitzen; "that and an overdose of cunning and stupidity. He thinks that Svaroff went away in order to avoid exposure, and that it will be an excellent opportunity for Ivan to reign in his stead; whereas we know that he has gone for an experimental holiday and that he went before he knew anything of these newspaper calumnies—yes, and he will come back again just when it suits his purpose and *malgre* all the newspapers in the world."

"He will, children," said a voice that they both knew, and turning quickly in surprise, for they had been seated in the "sun chamber," Iris and Blitzen saw standing in the opposite doorway the subject of their discussion. He looked remarkably fit and well, and was bronzed a deep copper hue.

He was smiling quietly to himself at the shock he had all but given them, and he looked like a happy and mischievous schoolboy. He was wearing a species of hiking kit and a light knapsack was swung across his shoulders. In his right hand he carried a strangely carved ivory cane, up the stem of which twin serpents climbed and twisted, their crossed heads meeting at the top. After a moment's hesitation he allowed Iris to examine it, smiling enigmatically at her admiration and evident curiosity.

"No, there's probably not another in the world." he told her, "or if there is, I've never seen it. This has cost more lives than one, and it may guard more lives than one yet." He spoke apparently in all seriousness, but they could never be sure that he was not joking.

"I mean it," he said, and for a moment the blank look came down upon his face. Then it lifted and he smilingly greeted the small kitten, who, seated upon the head of the alligator and playing with the leopard's paws, which hung over the long, low chair, he had momentarily mistaken for an elemental.

The little creature at the sound of his voice went to meet him, tail very erect and body quivering from stem to stern.

"Well, little thing!" There was a magnetic caressing quality in his tones that evidently matched the magnetism of his touch, for Cairo responded ecstatically, purring like a roll of small kettle-drums, as it walked round and round his shoulders rubbing its head against his chin. Svaroff laughed, looking across at Iris, then whispered mysteriously into Cairo's ear.

"What are you telling him?" she asked.

"The latest news from Egypt," was the answer.

There was a moment's pause, then, "Let me take your impedimenta," said Blitzen, and he helped Svaroff to remove the knapsack. The two men took stock of each other once more.

"You're looking awfully fit."

"Yes, and I feel it," was the reply. "I enjoyed every moment of the time, yet it's good to be back in England once again; there are always advantages and disadvantages to everything.

"We went," he continued, "right out of the beaten track—it was necessary for the work in hand but that, of course, meant an absence of baths and such—like amenities of civilisation. It's astonishing how one appreciates such things when one can no longer procure them."

"I imagine so," said Blitzen.

"Was the experiment successful?" Iris asked.

"It was," he told her, "and what is more, I've had a considerable look into the future. Things are going to be pretty bad all over the world before long, but especially so in France and England. You, Strickland," he said, turning to Blitzen, "have Mars strongly aspected in your horoscope and Jupiter is well placed, but I don't like the aspect of Uranus and Saturn, especially for the years 1914 and 1915. You have Uranus in the seventh house, which always foreshadows the violently unexpected."

"And Iris has it in the second," said Blitzen.

"Ah! I should have guessed as much!" said Svaroff.

For a moment he looked very serious, then he suddenly plunged into an amusing story about Newton and his various adventures as a Holy Man. Before five minutes had passed, the three of them were laughing heartily, all sinister prognostications forgotten.

"Where is Newton now?" Iris asked.

"Waiting for his hyacinthine locks to grow," was the answer, and remembering the sketch, Iris and Blitzen laughed again.

✳

Alone in the inner room with Blitzen, Svaroff's serious look returned.

"What does it really mean?" he said, repeating the former's question. "WAR, and war on a colossal scale, too! I have work to do, work that must be done, but it will require at least a five years' preparation. I must get away from here and if possible before nine months are over. But, *nous verrons*." Then, "Tell me all the sad news," he said.

CHAPTER XIV

BLITZEN told him.

"Ah! well, *quien sabe*? Perhaps it is all for the best. At least we know where we stand. Christ had but twelve disciples, and of those not all were honest. In the hour of His supreme trial all deserted Him. If I can rely even upon three I shall be lucky."

"You can rely upon two," said Blitzen.

Svaroff looked at him gravely. Then, "I believe you," he said.

Later in the day he spoke of some work he wanted done, and explained to Blitzen about the Elemental Tablets.

"It is not a matter I would entrust to anyone—there are apt to be results. I should be especially on my guard when painting the Fire Tablet. You smoke, so does I. H. Well, be careful, that is all."

"What do you mean?" said Blitzen.

"Wait and see," was the answer, "but don't say that I didn't warn you."

In the weeks which followed, Blitzen had cause to remember these words.

He was not a careless person; neither was Iris. Realizing that their goods were not insured, and that most of them would be irreplaceable, they had never run foolish risks. Cigarette ends were always stamped out, a guard was placed over the fire, and all reasonable precautions were taken. Yet, despite all this, fires were constantly occurring.

Blitzen painted the Tablets in a small, almost empty studio he had hired for the occasion. The canvasses were large and, moreover, he wanted privacy, for the work needed intense concentration. Each Tablet consisted of forty-nine squares by forty-nine, each square being again sub-divided into black and the three primary colours, and upon each colour was superimposed a strange letter. Each square was therefore different, yet in some curious way the dominant note of the Tablet prevailed, and that of the Fire Tablet was a vivid scarlet.

Before he had finished it, the thing seemed definitely alive, flashing and moving in a way that was almost terrifying, and do what he could, fires seemed unavoidable. One day the hot tobacco from his momentarily removed pipe fell upon the rush matting at his feet, and, immersed in the work, his trouser-ends were singeing before he discovered the accident. On another occasion, a coal flew out of the grate and set fire to some papers, and he had considerable difficulty in saving them from destruction. By the time the Tablet was finished every imaginable form of accidental fire had occurred even Cairo sharing in the honour. For one cold morning, sitting by the fender, the little beastie's tail had caught fire and by the time Iris had caught it, a considerable portion of the fur was missing.

Iris, herself, though in no way connected with the work, had a narrow escape also, and one that might have proved fatal.

Passing a road-engine one day where the street was being tarred, a hot spark had blown from the smoking chimney, and, catching her extremely light and billowy hair, had set fire to it.

With quick presence of mind, a passing stranger had enveloped her head in his mackintosh and no real harm had followed; but it had been an unnerving moment. Blitzen was extremely glad when the four Tablets were finished. There had been accidents with them all, both of air, water and earth, but the fire tablet had been the worst.

"I think," said Svaroff, "until they are needed for their destination, we will have them under lock and key," and he made arrangements with a large London storehouse to house them in a special room—steel-lined and with steel doors. Thereafter the three of them walked in safety.

By the following December, Iris had published her book of poems. The work had created a stir, and definite attempts had been made in certain quarters to "lionise" her. But Iris refused to be "on show"—she refused to give her opinion upon subjects of which she was ignorant, and she remained her simple self. This did not suit the showmen who, in the amazingly precocious "married child," had hoped to start a new centre of interest and of fashionable insincerity. Where she should have made friends, all unwittingly Iris made enemies. In future, decided the critics, her work shall be ignored. Blissfully ignorant of it all, Iris went on writing.

In the spring she went to stay with Svaroff's mother, and in so doing, made acquaintance with yet another side of the Guru's character. To hear Vladimir being chided by his mother like a very small and naughty boy, and to see him calmly accepting the situation, was both humorous and quaint.

That Madame Svaroff adored her son there could be no question; that she equally believed him to be entirely given over to the Evil One was beyond question likewise. She prayed for him without ceasing, but she refused to have in her rooms a single article of his personal belongings—even his pipe and a few books being banished to the attics.

She recognised the sterling qualities of Strickland, admitted his "good influence," and trusted that he would be the means of "saving her son" before it was too late; but she had a definite sense of humour with all her "religion," and in this trait one could see the unmistakable likeness of mother to son. Once, they were told, when Vladimir was masquerading under some high-flown title, she had discovered his address and had sent in her card to him as "The Countess of Cosmos." It was a characteristic move of the old lady, that showed both originality and wit. What Vladimir did on that famous occasion the historian has not seen fit to divulge, but we rather suspect that, being very young, he lost his temper. That the old lady won seems evident from the damning fact that the title was dropped!

In the summer, Blitzen was asked to interview Rachel, Svaroff's one-time wife, and it was then that they learned about his divorce and the youthful cause of it. Blitzen had also to interview the "cause." It needed considerable tact, but he managed the situation with remarkable skill not telling a single lie in the process, and remaining excellent friends with them both.

"After this," said Svaroff with a humorous twinkle in his eye, "Machiavelli must take a back seat, likewise Casanova. You're a marvel with women, Strickland; how on earth do you do it? You must know the devil of a lot about them."

"Well," said Blitzen, with a slow smile, "I married Iris Hamilton, didn't I?"

"Yes," came the answer. "You must have had a difficult nut to crack there."

"I've never tried to crack it," said Blitzen.

"Ah," said Svaroff, and he looked profoundly wise

Yet, in reality, the matter was extremely simple. Iris loved her husband, therefore she trusted him implicitly. They lived under the same roof, they had much in common, but that was no reason why she should in any way consider him her property or resent the attentions to him of other women or his attentions to them. In fact, the reverse was the case. She was genuinely pleased that he was so popular. When women asked her, as they occasionally did, whether she minded this, that or the other, she was always astonished. Mind? Of course not! Why on earth should she? The questioners became puzzled in turn; sometimes they were definitely uncomfortable. They went away convinced that one of two things was the truth. Either Iris didn't care for her husband in the slightest or else she had the most extraordinary ideas on the subject of morals. According to the temperament of the questioner, whether jealous or libidinous, so their ideas leaned to one or the other extreme. But to the truth, which should have been so plainly obvious, they remained blind to the end.

Was it for this reason, the inability of the average man or woman to see her that truth was said to reside at the bottom of a deep well? In after years, Iris seriously asked herself this question. She felt that it must be so. To all the worth-while things of life, most men and women, and not a few children, seemed as blind as bats or moles to the sunshine. The longer she lived the more she realised this, and more and more she was thrown back upon herself.

And, meanwhile, the year sped on to its close.

Before the year had finished, Iris had become seriously ill. She was rushed into a nursing home and operated on in haste. The surgeon who performed the operation (a man with a Dutch name, who had been a surgeon in the Boer War) said that, scientifically, she had no business to be alive, adding that it was a record case; but why he said this, Iris was not sufficiently interested to inquire. All she knew was that she was very tired of existence and "wanted to go."

"But they're not going to let you off so easily," Blitzen told her; "you've got lots more to go through."

Thereupon Iris had smiled—afterwards she began to get better. But it had been a very close shave, far closer than Blitzen cared to realise. He must get her away. Above all things from the atmosphere of *The Hieroglyph*. Svaroff, who had been abroad the time of the trouble, had been quite sympathetic, still, on this one point Blitzen was firm. He handed in his resignation and in the following spring the two of them went to live with Blitzen's mother, who had removed to the N. W. of London.

Early in the summer they learned through the medium of a well-known London daily of the suicide of the Flapper. She had married soon after the "rites"; she had left her husband to live with Newton. The husband had brought a divorce, and on the eve of it, Newton had fled to the Continent. The Flapper was a neurotic little thing, with free love ideas, which, unlike Iris, she had put into practice. She did not care to face the exposure of Courts. On the morning of the trial, she had shot herself in a Chelsea studio, and a few weeks later, Newton had written a satirical poem on the subject!

Iris and Blitzen were disgusted, and even Svaroff who afterwards discussed the matter with them, spoke out plainly. "It was the action," he said, "of a thorough-paced little skunk; he might at least have helped her to face the music! Well, I am glad that he was not still in my employment. It's more than a year since he left."

"Yes, it must be," said Blitzen. "How time flies!"

There was one very queer thing in connection with the tragedy. On that very morning, Iris had dreamed of the Flapper. That she had walked into the office of *The Hieroglyph* wearing a certain dress which was strange to Iris, and had walked to the book-case and taken down a book, the third on the left-hand on the second shelf. It was in that selfsame dress that her dead body had been found, the revolver by her side. They had had nothing in common, but Iris was sorry.

As to Svaroff, from time to time he sent Blitzen drawings for some magical work he wanted done to scale, and more than once he definitely asked him if he would not come back, a very great concession on the part of the Guru, who "never asked for anything twice," but Blitzen refused.

There was no quarrel—anything Svaroff wanted done he would be pleased to do, if it came within his province, but he could not go back. He and Iris had their own lives to live. Only now that they had got away, did they realise the slow process of disintegration to which they had been slowly succumbing.

Everything for the last two years had been Svaroff. Nothing had existed for them except as it bore relationship to him; all their time had been taken up in thinking and in working for him—as separate entities they had almost ceased to exist. "And yet, when it suits his purpose, Svaroff will cast me off, just like an old glove. Not that I in anyway blame him—it is the nature of the man—but I don't intend to give him that opportunity." So Blitzen had voiced the situation to Iris, and she had fully agreed with him.

In the fresh garden atmosphere of Hampstead with more than five miles between the Guru and themselves, it was almost as though they were freed from the shadowy tentacles of some giant octopus. Iris, who had been ethereal in her slightness, weighing in the heaviest of her winter clothes, less than seven stone—now began visibly to improve. Life was again beginning for them; they planned for the early autumn a tramping tour. They would walk across the moors from Wensleydale to Windermerre, for Blitzen's sister lived in Yorkshire. It would take them three weeks. If necessary, in the warm August nights, they would sleep in the heather wrapped in a large Burberry and Blitzen's Highland Plaid— for Blitzen's grandmother had been of the House of Argyll.

On August 4th war was declared.

On August 8th Blitzen had joined up—and it was in the ranks of a London regiment shortly bound St. Albans.

The news came as a terrible shock to Iris. He had joined without first telling her—perhaps on a sudden impulse, and with the wish to help her cousin Audley who for some time past had been going to the dogs and whom both he and she genuinely liked. But he ought to have warned her. She would never have stood in his way, even in so decisive a matter as this. Freedom, absolute and unconditional, had been the basis of their union, and she would never go back on it.

Without analysing, for she dared not, she realised it was the beginning of the end. "But, Kiddie, we shan't be going abroad; it's only for home defence." And Audley reiterated the statement, obviously believing it to be true. Iris knew they were both mistaken.

Well, the die had been cast; she refused to think further. She would hope for the best. Outwardly she appeared to enthuse and be amused, just as Blitzen's military duties varied. If she could do nothing else, she could at least appear cheerful. He would need all his courage before many moons were over, so too would she. In the feverish activity of the days that followed, she had little time for repining.

In the third week of September, Svaroff called to fetch some sketches and to say good-bye. As usual, when on the eve of a journey, he was gay and inconsequent.

He looked at Blitzen almost affectionately.

"In some ways," he said, "I wish I hadn't to go; I wish you were coming with me, Strickland. When shall we three meet again?"

"Never," said Iris. Then wished a thousand times that she had not said it.

Svaroff looked at her swiftly, and keenly, taking in Blitzen with the glance.

"I mean," said Iris, "I shall be kicking up the daisies before then." But she knew that she spoke falsely. She hoped that the ghastly intuition which had followed on the carelessly spoken word, had at least, not reached one of them. Svaroff hoped so too. He broke quickly into an awkward silence.

"Good-bye, Strickland," he said shaking Blitzen warmly by the hand and giving him the strongest of Masonic grips. "God alone knows where I am going or whether I shall ever get there, but if you can ever find the time to write to me I shall be glad to hear how you are getting on. A letter care of Lloyds will always find me."

"Thanks," said Blitzen, "but I don't expect be much time for letter writing. Good-bye."

They shook hands and Svaroff ran quickly down the long flight of steps. At the garden gate he turned to wave to them once more. A moment later he was gone.

Iris rushed to her husband and flung two thin little arms round his neck.

"Oh, Blitzen! All I want is *you*," she said.

"And I you, Kiddie," he answered. There was a queer catch in his voice as he returned the hug with interest.

A few minutes later, Audley joined them, and out on the lawn the two of them spent considerable time cleaning up their buttons, contrasting the comparative inefficiencies of their kit and wondering how they could wangle something better out of the Quartermaster-Sergeant. It was a happy and hopeful trio.

Now that they were both in uniform, Iris was struck by the amazing likeness of her cousin to Blitzen.

"Yes, we're usually taken for brothers," Audley told her. "Sometimes it's rather convenient for me, but I don't know that it would be safe to reverse the statement."

"Why not?" said Blitzen. "There's nothing I can do which you can't, if you wish to. For one thing, we're going to get our stripes together, later we may get our swords. Why not?"

Audley smiled with humorous shy sympathy. He had a very charming smile and eyes that any girl might have envied. He looked across at some rose bushes.

"What a glorious-looking creature," he exclaimed, and following the direction of his glance she saw a magnificent blue Persian cat with amber-coloured eyes. Audley picked up the cat, and for the rest of the evening seemed perfectly happy caressing it. Afterwards, she remembered the little incident which so plainly pointed to the contrast in character and temperament between the two men.

CHAPTER XV

THE regiment was now stationed at Hatfield, a few miles from St. Albans. The weather was almost tropical, and Iris and her sister, who had managed to secure a week's holiday, took rooms at the house of the head gardener of Lord C.

The Lodge was a delightful place with a charming flower garden back and front, surrounded on all sides by the Park, and within easy walking distance of Hatfield House.

They spent most of time out-of-doors, when possible, with Blitzen and Audley, at other times watching the numerous parades in Hatfield Park.

It was difficult to realise that all this preparation was for war. It seemed far more like picnicking on a gigantic scale, and the cheerful temper of officers and men added to the illusion.

One morning, when they were sitting under some trees, for the sun was extremely hot, a very youthful officer rode up to them.

"What are you doing this morning?" he asked with a friendly smile, preparing seemly to dismount.

"Watching my husband parade," replied Iris promptly.

"And who is your husband?" he asked quizzically, obviously not believing her, for she still looked almost a child.

"Corporal Strickland," she answered.

He looked surprised, and at the same time relieved. Then, "Good," he ejaculated. He turned to her sister.

"And you?" he queried.

"Watching other people's husbands parade," she replied cheekily.

He laughed. "I say, hard lines, hard lines for us both. What?"

Iris had a sudden thought. "Are we trespassing?" she asked.

"As a matter of fact, you are," he said; then as she prepared to rise, "no, don't move, you look so awfully jolly seated there, and, I should say, jolly comfortable too. It's quite all right, if anyone says anything, you are friends of mine—Lieutenant Peters—but I'll see that they don't. Good-bye."

He saluted and cantered off.

"What a nice boy," said Iris and Irene together.

They, subsequently found that he was in charge of Blitzen's platoon and whenever it was possible he made things easy for them.

Once when Blitzen failed to respond to an order—"What's up, Strickland?" he asked. "Thinking of those ladies you were with this morning?"

But Blitzen was quite equal to the occasion.

"Why? Would you like me to introduce you?" he asked.

"Rather," was the response.

Later in the day, Blitzen, in company with Peters, walked up to Iris and Irene.

"Lieutenant Peters," he said, then turning to them both, "My wife, my wife's sister."

Lieutenant Peters blushed. Then, "I think we have met before," he said, and Iris explained about their trespassing and what had happened.

When, shortly afterwards, Peters was transferred elsewhere, they were all sorry. There was a freshness and spontaneity about the boy that was extremely taking. He was just down from Oxford and stood out in pleasing contrast to some of the odious little counter-jumpers that they were to meet with later.

By November the regiment had been transferred to Braintree, and rumour had it that any day or hour they might now be yet further transferred to Flanders.

During the intervening months, Iris had seen but little of her husband, and once only, when desperately ill, had he been allowed leave. Always he seemed to be taking duty for some one or other of the men or N.C.O.s who had "fallen sick." That he was sick himself counted seemingly for little, and on one occasion he was carrying out his usual duties with a temperature of 102 °, and during that same fortnight lost two stone in weight. Iris thought it far more likely he would lose his life in England than in France, and wondered if even in the trenches life could possibly be more full of dirt and discomfort than it was in Braintree and St. Albans. The men of Blitzen's regiment were alive with vermin when they joined up, most of them stank, and they had no proper sleeping accommodation. For weeks the men were crowded into an empty schoolhouse where they slept on the floor, one man's boots sticking into another man's neck or belly, as the case might be, and vermin could be seen crawling on ceiling and floors.

In the vain endeavour to keep himself clean, Blitzen would walk about all night, whenever possible keeping out-of-doors, though the temperature was many degrees below zero! When in desperation the men mutinied, they got half-rations and double work, and were told, in regard to the vermin, "It was nothing to what they would get in the trenches."

"Quite possibly," thought Iris, but she devoutly hoped that the young bounder who passed the remark, and who was most comfortably housed himself, would meet with a speedy and unpleasant dispatch when he got to France, and have his full share of the said vermin beforehand. One thing she specially noticed, and it made her furious, as she was powerless to help in any way. Men like Blitzen and Audley and one or two others similarly placed, who would above all have appreciated something approaching clean surroundings, were always put into the filthiest billets and given, whenever possible, the filthiest work: cleaning "dixies," scrubbing loathsome outhouses and so on. It almost seemed as though the persons responsible for this were satisfying their own class hatred and inferiority complexes. Occasionally the officers were gentlemen, and then, of course, it made all the difference in the world to Blitzen and those like him. But, alas, they were few and far between.

With alarming rapidity the days sped by, and a couple of days before Christmas Audley and Blitzen got leave for the last time.

They spent Christmas Day with Iris and her Aunt Laura, and not until Blitzen rose suddenly, at Laura's request, to fetch something from the adjoining room, did they realise that he was the thirteenth. Audley assured Iris that he too had risen, and really there was nothing in these superstitions—but the little incident had cast a chill over more than one of the party.

Later in the evening, when they were pulling crackers which contained jewellery and patriotic mottos, Blitzen got a "diamond" and "ruby" cross with the words, "It is a good and noble thing for a man to lay down his life for his country," and Iris got a signet ring with a blank shield.

Blitzen laughingly tossed over the cross, saying that "he never wore jewellery," and Iris wondered, "What particular brand of idiot could have been responsible for the mottoes: Obviously some fool entirely devoid either of sensitiveness or a sense of humour. It was damnable that such imbecilities should be permitted." But again the incident was forgotten and before long gaiety was restored. They played charades, there was singing, and afterwards the folding doors were thrown back the furniture placed against the walls, and they danced.

Everyone was at their liveliest and the dance in full swing when a loud "telegram" knock sounded on the front door. There was the fraction of a second's pause and the knock was repeated even more imperiously.

The music ceased—alarmed looks took the place of smiling as the maid entered, handing papers to Blitzen and Audley.

"Report at headquarters at once," read out the later, adding immediately, "I'm hanged if I will. It's a mistake, it must be. You, at all events, old man, haven't had a day's leave for months, and quite probably this is our last. We were to have had a week at least. How are they to know it has reached us? Take no notice," and everyone present gave the same advice.

"No, we can't do that," Blitzen answered. "It is probably a test for discipline, and I must say it seems pretty rotten putting it over on Christmas Day. But we *must* play the game. Come on, A. *Au revoir*, everyone," and with a smiling good-bye to his hostess he made for the door!

"Don't worry, Kiddie-wee," he whispered to Iris; "we're sure to get our leave made up."

Little did he know the ways of the army.

It was a terrible night, pouring torrents and very cold. But they were fortunate in commandeering a taxi and in due course arrived at St. Albans in the early hours of the morning.

Seemingly they were the only men of the regiment who had answered the call.

"Official blunder," was the trite explanation given them.

"Then I suppose we can finish our leave?" suggested Audley. But this, it appeared, was out of the question. The order had not been officially countermanded or some such "red-tape," and they were obliged to stay on. Nor, most amazing of all, was that curtailed leave ever made up to them nor the men who had ignored the summons ever punished.

170

"The trouble with Blitzen is that he's a damned sight too honest. It doesn't pay in the army."

Thus the verdict of Audley, and Iris, when she heard of the matter, fully agreed.

It had all seemed unreal as a play, it still seemed unreal—and would go on seeming unreal to the end of the chapter.

During the weeks which followed,Iris lived as one in a dream, writing whenever possible to Blitzen, and whenever possible going to see him; but he had little time these days to spare for her. Always he seemed to be doing the work of someone else. Indeed, since he had been made Lance-Corporal, he seemed to be doing the work of three. Those in authority had found he was reliable, that he had initiative, and they took full advantage of the fact.

As for Audley, he lost his stripe soon after the Christmas incident. Possibly he was thoroughly disillusioned—anyway he saw no fun in doing double or treble the work and having quite disproportionate responsibilities for the very trifling difference in pay. No. He preferred to be a private. He admired Blitzen tremendously, he was a splendid chap, but he, Audley, was not cut out for a hero.

And nothing that Blitzen could say or do would alter his decision.

He got into trouble and finally was transferred to another regiment.

Two friends of theirs, journalists, left at the same time for the O.T.C. Blitzen was absolutely alone. Perhaps it was as well that his many and onerous duties left him little time for reflection. But always he found time to write to Iris, and his letters, written mostly when he should have been sleeping, are amongst the most interesting and instructive that the War has given us.

Two letters, written 16th and 17th February, and a further letter written 25th February, give a good idea of the conditions of the time.

"DEAR OLD KIDDIE-WEE,—I am glad that your letter seemed more cheerful, also that you are having a little respite from the 'Gloom.' I heard to-day our leave starts from Monday, but it is not certain yet. Do not send me any cash until late Monday night and then to my private address. I cursed all the gods that are so good to me on Saturday. We started out to the ranges, three and a half miles, at 7 a.m. It was the coldest morning we have had yet and blowing a hurricane. So bad was the weather that they sent a messenger back stating that on account of the snow and wind, firing was impossible. We waited there on the hilltop for two hours and then extended out and started picking up all the paper and orange peel that had been left over from Friday's Field Day. I got back literally soaked. The water had come right through top coat, tunic, and shirt and vest. I just had time to clean my rifle, bayonet and boots, etc., and out again on a 24-hour guard—where you are not allowed to take off either coat or equipment!! Still, I feel none the worse for it.

"Evidence seems to point to our going away very soon, and except for your dear old sake, I shall be very glad. Even if I do not come down during the week, it is possible I may get a week-end pass next week.

"Thank Mme. G. for her kind thoughts, etc.

"Must close now. I still have no news.

"BLITZEN."

"17th February, ST. ALBANS.

"DEAR OLD SWEETHEART,—If you address your letters to me at the above address as a civilian they will reach me quickly. I wrote to you while on guard, but did not post it, as I thought I could give you more definite news about my forthcoming leave to-day. I hope to have at least five days in

Town within the next fortnight, provided we do not go away. I was in hopes I could come this week, but only ten per cent are allowed absence at the same period.

"I don't know how it is, but my shooting has been right 'off' these last two days. My eyesight fails me over three hundred yards—hence more expense in getting glasses.

"I am very tired to-night as I got no extra time off for my 24-hour guard, so I am very egotistical. In other words, I cannot express myself in cushkoo lingo, but I am awfully 'bucked' that you are feeling happier and weller.

"Dear old thing, I wonder if we will ever be able to settle down again and have a place of our own once more? I can hardly fancy mixing up paint and worrying my head over tones and the wonderful colours of its snakey 'bodie'! Do you remember the yellow screen and the blue Chinese trousers, with two plaits and a bit of gorse? Do you also remember what a big part that little bit of flower played in my little life, you bad, bad girl? Still, it is all over now, a different future lies before me; cold and wet, disease and death. I wonder if I shall survive? You, too, will have your part to play, so after all, if to play our separate parts well is made our common cause, we shall still be linked as close as ever. I think, perhaps, yours will be the hardest to play, but stick to the old Blitzen, dear, and we will come through all right. Existence doesn't end with this rotten life, and I feel sure we can help one another if one or both get knocked out. I heard on good authority the German war would be finished by August next; but *that* won't be the end, in my opinion.

"I must close now, dear one. Thank Mme G. for me for her kindness to you.—All my love,

"BLITZEN.

"*P.S.*—I was going to enclose my Sunday's letter, but I have mislaid it."

Seemingly, however, he found it in time, for the two letters arrived together.

On 25th February arrived another long letter:

"DEAR OLD GIRL,—I was so glad to get your two cheerful letters, also contents. I would have written before, but the Col. has had the rats badly, so it has been drill, drill, drill, until my voice is cracked with shouting, and I have cursed that little bit of ribbon on my arm. I have just heard that my name has been sent in again (the third time) for promotion, but whether I get it or not is another matter.

"I am awfully anxious about your welfare after you have left Number 75. Dear old thing, I would hardly have you otherwise, but it seems so hard on you to have to rely so much upon others." (Then followed some advice as to the best course to adopt.)

"Don't forget all the best you have learnt from S.," the letter continued. "You know better than I the responsibilities and obligations that are yours. You have nothing now to worry or depress you but the feeding and housing of your poor troublesome 'bodie': Knowing how you are influenced by your immediate surroundings, try to make them such as to influence you in the direction you wish your path to lead. For some reason you have reverted (or *appear* to have reverted) to Malkuth (?). If this is so it is a good start, as you know for the first time *where you are*. Of course you may be in Kether, but I think not, as I miss the exaltation!! Dear Waif, how I am talking out of sheer—what? Joking apart, you really have arrived at a time that you must prove to yourself your own potency. This surely should be your first undertaking. First take into consideration those local conditions which are beyond your power to alter or neglect. These are such that your natural poetic and aesthetic leanings are out of place.

"Aesthetic art for the moment is dead. All is now sorrow, hate, and the other attributions of Mars. To combat this just now would be beyond your strength. Therefore, for the time being, you must swim with the tide until you have recuperated enough strength to swim up-stream, collecting the lesser lights as you go. How are you going to do this? I have neither the brains nor time to think, but *you* have both and must teach me. I would suggest that you first get with someone who has already been swirled about a bit in the said stream, and learn to swim a bit from them; then, as time goes on, you can indulge in a few antics—a few fancy strokes (i.e. swimming with your legs perpendicular in the air, etc.). By this method you will, I assure you, attract attention, and you will then have your first small following to tow up-stream.

"What will happen as the War progresses, or immediately after the War, I do not quite know. I should say a feverish return to commercialism, out of which, of course, will spring art. Before art, however, will come the great reforms (esoteric), which will soon be expressed in the art to follow. Remember, war is always re-generate, so that art will also be re-generate—personally I should say through some regenerated form of Religion. . . . All these things, as I say, are beyond your control, but you have all your time to yourself to investigate them. We are living in the most *historical period* the *world* has *ever known*, and you are allowing it to slip through your fingers and taking Russian lessons!!! Try and get back your old wide outlook, dear Heart, and you will soon begin to grow and find your feet.

"I must close now. Write me soon.—All my love,

"BLITZEN."

"*2nd March.*

"SWEETHEART,—Please note I am no longer Lance-Corporal, the Lance is now dropped. I am so sorry I could not let you know before Saturday, but at the last moment a corporal went sick and I had to take his place for company

175

orderly corporal. That means going stark raving mad for a week. I gave Audley a telegram and cash on Saturday, but he said to-day he was unable to send it. On Friday last I rose at 4.30 a.m. and was off my feet exactly 45 minutes between that time and 12.15!! Up again next morning at 6 a.m.

"I shall probably be down on Sunday next for the day, if I am not on guard. . . ."

On 4th March he wrote again:

"SWEETHEART,—The great day is quickly approaching. We have had every mortal bit of kit inspected—all men on leave have been recalled, medical inspection, teeth, etc., all on top of one another. We might be moved on Saturday next to Winchester. Anyway, orders have come through that we shall be there on the 18th. The Brigadier has already gone to France, so we shall not be very long in following his footsteps. It will be hard lines if I cannot see you before I go. . . . I hope to arrange for you to come to St. Albans—only God knows where you can put up; all the houses are full of soldiers.

"Personally, I don't think we will cross the water until the end of the month, but one never knows what is likely to happen now.

"I must mount guard now. Try and think of some way we can meet. Will write again if I have time."

Another letter followed quickly.

"We undoubtedly start on Saturday next, and nobody knows where we are going . . . go to the above address, you can then see us off on Saturday.

"All my love, dear heart.—Your old, old

"BLITZEN."

CHAPTER XVI

IRIS came up. Where she billeted mattered little, but see Blitzen she must. The constantly promised leave had been put off as usual and now he was going away. She came up on the 5th, and on the 8th the regiment would be starting. Between that time and the time of leaving she saw him to speak to for perhaps five minutes.

He came in dead tired, flung himself down in the hearth-rug and asked to be waked in twenty minutes, then he would have time in which to talk, maybe. Iris and his mother watched him sleeping. How unutterably weary he looked. They decided that sleep was at the moment more important than all else—he must sleep as long as possible. They wouldn't wake him. But, as though conscious of their intention, he waked himself at the appointed hour.

He stood up and stretched himself, then held out his arms for Iris. He said nothing, but Iris felt a sudden excess of strength. It seemed as something God-given. She knew now that she could face anything. She knew now what it was that had enabled the martyrs of old to go cheerfully to the stake and worse. Thank Heaven she was not going to disgrace him, to make things more difficult for them both. She had dreaded, above all, this minute, and miracle of miracles, it was without terrors.

Even so, she had time to feel sorry for Blitzen's mother. It must be dreadful to be a mother. To see all that you love irrevocably tied to someone else; to feel that no matter how skilfully camouflaged, one has now taken a second seat. Poor Mater thought Iris. She looked across at her, praying inwardly that all would be well, and Blitzen's mother smiled bravely back. She, too, had felt the influx. Thank God.

A peaked cap thrust itself in at the doorway.

"You're wanted, Strickland."

"Damn," said Blitzen under his breath. "Quick! Two little sticky arms," he whispered, and Iris reached up. He gave her a swift hug, lifting her off her feet as he did so. Again that marvellous influx. She knew now for certain that it was Heavensent.

"Shall I see you again?" she asked.

"God only knows," he answered. Then, "Yes, it will be managed somehow if I commit murder to do it."

The regiment set out between three and four in the early hours of the morning. The town seemed mostly asleep, but Iris had discovered the whereabouts of Blitzen. She walked quietly up and slipped her hand into his.

There was so much that ought to be said, and now she would never say it. Perhaps, after all, silence was best. They understood each other entirely. Words—what need had they of words? Again that strange dream-feeling descended upon her. It was a curious pageant in which she and these others were taking part. She was abnormally sensitive. She felt the sneering, semi-resentful attitude of the soldier behind her. Perhaps he didn't believe in love; perhaps he wished that his girl had waited to see him off. It was unpleasant that he was feeling like this. Or was it again that vile class-hatred that she sensed?

A sharp staccato command like the crack of a pistol shot, and they were marching. In five minutes and they had left the town behind were on the open road. Tramp, tramp, tramp, tramp—tramp, tramp, tramp, tramp. Where Iris heard that sound before when it had so terrified her? With amazing clearness, she remembered.

She was a small child of three, sleeping alone in a big room at the top of their old house in the Isle of Wight. It was her heart that was pounding but this, of course, she did not know. She thought of men coming nearer and nearer. Dark-bearded men with hidden faces. What were they were going to do? Nearer and nearer they came; they were approaching the window—a sudden swirl, then she felt herself spin through the air, then merciful blackness wrapped her round. Night after night it had happened, but she had never cried out. Strange that she should think of it now.

It was a glorious night, a pale yellow moon sinking behind the trees, and she could see dimly stretching out before and behind, the long, black, snake-like line of men with their bayonets fixed. The moon shone on the fixed bayonets, turning them to silver.

"What a marvellous lithograph it would make," she said.

"Magnificent," Blitzen answered.

Again a command.

They swung into a quick march, and one or two other civilians who were marching alongside dropped out.

"Can you stick the pace?" whispered Blitzen.

"Yes," she answered. But it was all she could do to manage it.

At the first picket, two miles or so from St. Albans, she left him—drifted away into the night. How she got back she never knew. The road had grown darker and darker. There were deep ditches on either side. Artillery rolled and rumbled. At any moment the horses might be upon her—the soldiers challenging her. She had to walk warily, and it was well that it was so.

Tramp, tramp, tramp, tramp. Would the sound never end? Iris heard it that night, the next night, and for many nights to come. It followed her even in her dreams.

Two days later she received a postcard:

"Arrived at Southampton about 12.40. Will embark to-night for unknown destination. All well and going strong. . . Will write from other side as soon as allowed."

Unlike her other letters the card was stamped "On Active Service."

For the first time things were becoming real.

The letters of Blitzen, written under all and every condition and never intended for publication, have already travelled to more than one continent and have published in more than one language, and how they came to be so is a story in itself that has been dealt with. But as was inevitable during the War, much was left out and much was too private a nature to make publication desirable. The latter still holds good, but the former may now be dispensed with, and we shall give as many letters as will throw light on our story.

"Dear Heart"—he wrote on the March—"We arrived at some place in France, safe and sound. Our departure was as dramatic as the burial of Sir John Moore. We left Southampton about 9 p.m. Not a wave of a hand, or an echo of a cheer, or a laugh or a sigh, to denote anything happening of any interest to anyone. We disembarked with the same lack of interest—except a few remarks concerning some nurses who were looking out of a window of the Hospital. Although it was 9 a.m. the streets of the town were almost deserted, and the few we passed gave but a cursory glance and went their way. The dominant note of the local attire is black, and after the crowded gaiety of London, Desolation seems to reign. We are under canvas some distance from the town and we shift to-morrow. I am writing this in a small cafe where the boys are struggling with bad English and worse French to get grub.

"Will write again soon.—All my love,

"Blitzen."

Iris was struck by the amazing smallness of the writing. Almost she needed a magnifying glass to read it. Yet it was wonderfully clear. Was it the result of intense concentration? Before the War, Blitzen had had a loose, almost careless, handwriting. Now it was a fine, very small copper-plate. Certainly it allowed him to put much more on to paper than would otherwise have been possible.

On 22nd March arrived another long letter:

"I am told it was announced in the *St. Pancras Mercury*, or some such rag, that the 19th behaved well under fire. We certainly did, for we slept all through it. The bombardment was some miles away, and those in action were probably unaware of our existence, although we could see the flash of the shells as they passed through the air at dusk. We did not even know what place was being bombarded. To-day we saw a hostile aeroplane chased by an ally—or so we were given to understand. We could hear firing before the machines came into view, and fine little white clouds floated in the air in the direction from whence they came.

"The conditions of war are most curious at times. On our journey from the coast in the cattle train we were at first almost ignored by the inhabitants, mostly bourgeois—but as we got farther on and nearer the firing-line, they reminded us more of our journey in England, for they came running out of their houses and from their work to give us a silent wave of the hand. The pantomime was painful to see, for they were nearly all women who had borne some loss or sorrow—there was no smile upon their faces—they had seen so many many like us go! Further on we were welcomed by a grim gesture from the railway and field labourers. They drew their fingers sharply across their throats, stretched their capacious mouths, and pointed in the direction of the firing-line; suggesting, I suppose, we would get our throats cut there. At the feet of these crude men, primroses clustered, a cheerful yellow among empty jam jars and corned beef cans. We travelled thus for miles, through country similar to the Midlands of England . . . the people, the gestures, always the same. Also the plaintive voices of children crying for souvenir biscuits.

"There is a curious silence, too, among those I have met lately returned from the trenches—an almost brooding atmosphere. The first night I heard the thunder of guns in the distance and saw the flashes, I felt akin to the sensation of taking first Communion—best described by the contradictory term, a restless calm. Spiritually, it has a quieting influence, at the same time giving a physical restlessness. . . I am giving details in this letter that might be cut out by my Platoon Officer, of whom it is difficult to speak when he is censor. He is a decent youngster, apparently just down from Oxford. It is curious how old I feel now. I had my hair cut yesterday, and behold, as the shears traversed my thinning locks, shoals of white fell upon the waterproof sheeting which was about my neck.

"Thanks very much for the bit of gorse; one values such items in times like these. . . . Keep itself well, and be good for my sake. We are kept very busy and are very restricted in every way, which is just as well—All love,

"BLITZEN."

"*P.S.*—I want some fountain-pen ink in tablet form. I think Mabie, Todd & Lamb sell it. If I can, I will send you a few pencil notes of the place soon. Give my love to Mater."

In due course the pencil sketches arrived, and it seemed to Iris that they were even better than his work in the pre-war days. It was characteristic of Blitzen that he imbued everything which he touched with beauty, and the present sketches were no exception to the rule. "Our billet, rustic and unbeautiful," said the caption underneath. Iris disagreed—as portrayed by Blitzen, there was definite beauty. That he could have done such delicate work after months of trench-digging and worse, was little short of a miracle; so, too, was the length and frequency of his letters. They were mostly written in indelible pencil and in the same incredibly fine script, and she received on an average three or four a week.

"DEAR OLD SWEETHEART"—said the next letter—"Just a line to thank you for your letters and parcels, though I literally trembled at the thoughts of having more to carry. . . . We always have to carry our house upon our back now, and you know the weight of my pack when I left St. Albans! In addition to that we have had a 'woolly coat' served out—Teddy Bears, we call them—and I have that to carry in addition, hence every ounce of personal is of considerable consequence. It seems difficult to realise that I might not see you for another year, although, perhaps, we might be together in a few months.

"Truth to tell, I have been feeling rather blue of late—so blue, in fact, that I was tempted yesterday to attend a Battalion Concert—and you know how I hate those odoriferous functions. I was told the 'Hall' (an R.A.M.C. acquisition) was too full to allow even the entrance of a sergeant. However, I thought I would try, and, approaching, was greeted with these rather pathetic words, well sung, with much gusto:

> "She was so boss-eyed that when she cried
> The tears ran down her back.
> Ha-ha, ha-ha! ha-ha, ha-ha! ha-ha
> Ha, ha-ha-ha!

"Before me was a doorway crowded with laughing soldiers, silhouetted against the light within.

"The door was large with a shrine-like arch, and all I could see of the interior was an enormous *black crucifix*. The usual attenuated and modestly clad figure hanging upon it grinned down upon the motley crowd—I came away, stumbling in the dark, and the echo of the chorus followed me: Ha-ha, ha-ha, ha-ha, ha-ha—and whether it came from the figure on the cross or the soldier songster, it was impossible to say. I didn't sleep that night! THEY have been getting at me again, I suppose."

Iris shivered. She remembered a certain occasion at *The Hieroglyph* when both she and Blitzen had had a similar experience. It was after a somewhat lengthy spell of ceremonial magic in which neither of them had participated. It seemed to them both that the carved ivory figure was writhing in agonised torture, and the early light of morning streaming through the scarlet blinds caused the wounds to bleed afresh. They agreed that the excellent carving of the artist was responsible for the effect, and the light had done the rest—but neither of them had felt comfortable. There must be something definitely wrong somewhere, they had decided. Iris thought so now.

"Most dread of all"—continued the letter— "I am losing my sense of humour. So what with the weight of my pack, a heavy heart, the weight of years and orderly sergeant on top, I often he upon my straw at night and wish I had gone under at St. George's Hospital." (Then came the inevitable "Blitzen" touch.) "A laxative medicine, however, will probably put me right. The sex instinct is almost alarmingly missing. It might be that the square-hipped, flat-bottomed wenches are so unattractive. However, that is just as well, except that life is so uninteresting. I wish I had some paint or a little leisure time to adjust myself, but that, of course, is out of the question.

"To-day is Palm Sunday and I am enclosing a piece of green—I do not know what it is—they use it for sprinkling Holy Water, but most of the people here are carrying it about to-day instead of the usual Palm. It has been blessed, I suppose. . . . Please write as often as it can, for you are the only link I have with all my happy past. Good-bye, dear Heart.

"All my love and a good astral hug.—Always yours,

"BLITZEN."

By a curious coincidence she had sent him by the same post a "pantacle" in the form of a palm cross. On it was inscribed in Hebrew letters the name "JEHESHUAH," the letter "Shin" being in the centre of the cross and the "Yod He Van He" at the four cardinal points. Within the sacred name she had written her own baptismal name and the sobriquet of Bunco. She had written all the letters from left to right, and she had sealed the date in the correct manner.

Twice when endeavouring to "consecrate" it, the cross had been mysteriously struck from her hand, and it had seemed to her as an evil omen, but she had put that down to her own nervousness, and had forgotten the incident even before posting the talisman. Obviously their letters had crossed.

She and Mme. Strickland were now living at Hurlingham, close to the polo ground. It was a dismal spot, and Blitzen's letters were all that either of them had to look forward to. Fortunately, there was no shortage of them at this time.

On 1st April came the answer:

"Thanks for pantacle"—he wrote—"which, of course, I will keep in a safe place and place the proper value upon it. Letters are the only things one can look forward to, so, even if there is little or no news, write.

"Some of the officers have been up the trenches, also some of the sergeants, and I hope I shall have my share soon. Your letter with the pantacle was the first letter which sounded real genuine 'Thou' for a long long time, and it has made me feel tons happier." (Continued, 2nd April.)

"The weather has been glorious here this last few days. Heavy frost at night and brilliant spring sunshine by day. The fruit trees are just beginning to show bits of green which takes me back to last spring. How varied our life has been in a quiet kind of way! I wonder what is going to happen in the middle of this year?

"Dear old girl, never forget I regret nothing. Our life together has been very good on the whole. I was in hopes that experience would help me find myself, but so far nothing has happened. Perhaps it will come in the reaction. . . . I wonder what profession I will adopt on my return? At present I am in a Rembrandt mood, and feel I want an etching press and copper plates galore. One thing I cannot understand—the complete cessation of any imagination. The 'Energised Enthusiasm' idea is certainly proved in this case, but at present, of course, it is directed into a physical channel. . . .

"I have managed to get through my first week of C.O.S. without any charge being preferred against me, so I feel better. It is even worse than at St. Albans. Good-bye, dear old Sweetheart.—Always your same,

"B."

On 8th April they heard again.

"Thanks for Easter Sunday letter. A day may come when the picture you draw may be realised. We moved again yesterday, and I expect to receive my baptism to-night or to-morrow. I would let you know the result. I am more than glad. Unfortunately, we have got so immune to any kind of change and circumstances that it is likely to make less impression than it would three months ago.

"Everybody is in the highest spirits. Ten thousand songs are going at once, and the clatter of rifle bolts and trigger-pulling give the clue to the general trend of the minds of the men.

"I enclose sketch of our last billet, but I cannot draw for little apples. . . . Food has been very meagre lately, and everything here is terribly expensive . . . the word-pictures in the London papers of the luscious feeds Tommy gets are words, and words only. Still, life is very good, though rough. I went to a regimental lecture the other night given by a real live Bishop. It consisted mostly of pictures of churches the wicked Germans had destroyed, and we had cold boiled Jesus served up, and carved with a bayonet specially blessed by God Himself, and warm human blood for sauce! Easter Sunday we did two hours' bayonet exercise before 9 a.m., and then went to Divine Service in full pack, gun and 120 pounds of ball. Distant guns make a good substitute for an organ, and we sang, 'There is a green hill far away,' with real feeling. Truly, if Christ came again, they would crucify Him. We have a fine manly fellow for chaplain, and Christianity is a real live thing to him. . . .

"When we look out of the window here we can see the results upon the building of some of the German shelling.

"Good-bye, dear old Sweetheart. Keep up its spirits. The Bunco's all right and all is, so far, well."

"11th April.
"I am glad that you have settled on a little den for yourself and oh, Kiddie dear, I do hope you will be happy.

"Must close now, Sweetheart.—Your dirty, smelly, muddy old

"BUNCO."

"DEAR SWEETHEART,—Writing becomes more and more of an effort, and what seemed of interest yesterday is of no consequence to-day. A few weeks back the sight of a few wooden crosses at the foot of a wayside shrine conjured up untold possibilities; a week ago, to look over the breastworks into 'No Man's Land,' to see the German trenches 200 yards away and speculate upon the identity of the dead lying in the open, was an irresistible desire. Two days ago we willingly faced death to see the effects of our shells bursting in the enemy's lines, one poor fellow paying the extreme penalty. Twenty-four hours ago we were out and unprotected in that mysterious intervening space, putting up wire entanglements—not even taking the trouble to fall on our faces when the flares went up—it is such a trouble scraping mud off one's overcoat! In fact, it is difficult to understand all this work and trouble is WAR. From Egomania one drifts into Negomania! the only thing that really matters is to get through one's job. One soon gets used to the whistle, twang and crack of bullets and the deeper drone of shells. It is not easy when doing your work to remember that each of those bullets is stopped by something, and that something might be you or your pal. We still have to stand the test of a mad moment, when you fire like a machine gun at a rushing mass of men which nothing seems to stop. We still have to face cold steel and rush across the lead-swept track of a quick-firing gun. But I think one is much too busy to think or even dread till results. To me it is more trying to steadily carry a load over broken ground and no cover under the enemy's guns. It is useless to attempt to hurry, and the steady plod gives rein to the imagination. Fortunately, I have not suffered in that direction and I do not think I ever shall.

"The whole thing is most uninspiring, and dinner, rum or tea are always uppermost in one's mind—as at present, for I have an attack of heart-burn.

"The first twenty-four hours I spent actually in the trenches were the happiest and merriest I have yet spent. We were in a little fort all on our own with some of the Glasgow Highlanders. A biggerhearted, jollier lot one could not meet. All that they had was ours, together with many apologies for what they had not. One of their fellows got shot in that most valued portion of his anatomy which was likely to distress the lady to whom he was engaged, for bairns by him she could have none. Said his friend in deepest sympathy, 'And what will ye say to yer lass when she asks ye where ye are wounded, Jock?' 'Och, lad, I'll tell her if she were shot where the bullet struck me she wouldna be wounded!' Of lice they have a prodigious lot, and gambling is rife. Each man hunts for a large and leggy animal, these are lined up with as much accuracy as a Derby start, and wagers made according to fancy. When all is settled, each man lights a match and urges on his luckless steed to the winning post. . . . Horrible as this sounds, it is not really so bad as digging to fill sand-bags in the dark. A short while back, I could not get my spade through an obstacle. I felt about in the darkness with my hands and found that obstacle, 'hard and smooth and round!'—only it was soft and damp on the exterior and had hair upon it. To strike a match might mean death, so I just covered it up to deaden the stench and scratched an 'X' upon the spot with my spade to mark an unknown grave. After I had eaten my breakfast in the morning, I remembered I had not washed my hands. So you can understand that a 'Cooty' race makes a pleasant diversion. . . .

"As far as I can see the general method of fighting is by apparently friendly arrangement with the enemy, who are quite decent fellows who don't interfere with your work if you don't interfere with them. Of course, the snipers must keep their hand in, so just pot off a few of our fellows when a particularly pretty shot is obtainable. Ditto the artillery: they must find the ranges to a nicety and shell us until they've got it and then chuck up the job. Just before daybreak, both sides stand to and let off a round or two per man, and we chuck it for breakfast and kip down for sleep. About dinner-time we feel energetic so we fire a few more shots, then both knock off for food. At dusk we 'stand to' again, and take occasional pot-shots at our respective working parties. These parties clamber over the barricades, or rather breastworks, and advance say 50 to 100 yards and stick up hurdles or sandbags with barbed wire in front. These are covered by machine-guns. When the time comes we occupy them while the enemy shell us and try to capture them for their own use of course, we do the same with them. It is not always so. A time comes when an advance is made by one section of the line, and the other portions must re-arrange their positions accordingly. Both sides of the artillery then pound away; charges, counter-charges and attacks are made, and neat little mounds in very straight rows with a little wooden cross and an identity disc nailed upon it, very much in the centre, mark the place where heroes lie and rest, and can swear no longer at the length of the war and the Regimental Sergeant-Major. . . .

"I should not have been able to write this much, but I am on guard to-night and all are fast asleep. Tell the Kid to write to me, and also tell Audley to write. He must come over; he is missing all the fun."

Enclosed with the letter was a sketch with "*P.S.*" written upon it.

"You will notice from where I took this I can see the German trenches, which means that the Germans could also see me and potted accordingly!!"

"20th April.

"DEAR HEART,—I am very fit and am billeted in a farm barn where the snow comes in and the ducks quack just in my ear. The people, however, are awfully kind, and will do anything for me. Altogether we have little to complain of. . . . Keep your peeker up, old girl—All my love,

"B."

CHAPTER XVII

WITHIN a fortnight there had obviously been great changes, and Blitzen feared the worst. He must warn Iris lest she get the news first through the cold official medium of the War Office, or the yet colder medium of some London Daily.

"DEAR HEART"—he wrote—"It is ten to one on my day's work being finished out here, and, all things considered, it is well. If I go under, do not grieve, for I am pleased I shall be able to go first and clear a little way for you—if you really still love me. Good-bye, my dear one. Continue to live and live happily for my sake, so that when your time comes all will also be well with you. . . . On the other hand the gods may favour me and bring me back to you. *Somebody* will come back, and why not me? Always yours,

"B."

Enclosed with the letter were some cowslips and violets.

"These few flowers are all I can send you in proof of my thoughts of you. They were picked in a wood over which shells are whizzing. The weather is most glorious, all the fruit trees are in bloom, and both War and Peace seem very far away. The larks are singing, everything is worshipping Priapus, and even

Death seems to have discarded his rags and decked himself with blossoms."

The gods did favour him, for on 21st May Iris heard again. The letter described vividly his desolate surroundings, and one sentence seemed to stand out in letters of fire:

"The house is roofless, the window boarded up and stuffed with sandbags, the floor a mass of plaster fallen from the ceiling, the walls black with the smoke from our fire made from the staircase—*a picture and a framed certificate still hang upon the wall*, and at my feet lie these poor, tired devils over whom I am keeping guard through the night, so that I can write to you and think of all the happy days of studio twilight. I am dirty beyond description; the armpits of my tunic in rags and spotted with every kind of stain—save latter-day sins. If you asked me if I am happy, I couldn't tell you! . . . On the whole, the worst part of life here is the bad food and dirt. It is impossible to keep clean, and the monotonous diet makes eating a painful duty. People hear only the good things. In the papers are only recorded our successes, and, alas, only too few will return to tell the other story. Anyway, it is the wrong time to tell it now."

"Dear Heart"—he wrote a few days later—"You must not fret about me. The war is no different now than it ever was and my chances are as good as ever. We have just come out after a spell of some days—I do not know how many, and I am no worse off than when I went in. My cardigan was blown to bits and the glass and hands blown off my watch, and yet bar a bruise or two, I am as sound as a coco-nut. I looked like a slaughterman when I got away. . . One poor boy in my section had his leg almost blown off—about thirty wounds in him. I did my best to stop the bleeding and do him up, and I think he will pull through. His knee and foot were just pulp. It is torture getting them to the dressing-station. The trenches are too narrow to allow of getting round corners, so they have to be lifted above the surface, a most fatiguing task.

"For four days we were under shell fire day and night. Poor little M. got lost in a mine explosion. Captain P. is gone and—more" (the number evidently crossed out by censor). "W. is now Captain. Two of my boys caught it and stuck it awfully well. I don't like shell fire; it gets on one's nerves so. On the whole we took it pretty well. We are on the only part of the line where an advance has not been made . . . a little to our left we even lost ground. We are just in front of a famous brewery and orchard which the Guards captured about Christmas-time, and we have stuck there ever since."

"27th May.

". . . Imagine a clay dugout 10 feet long by 8 feet broad crowded with 23 tired men, all very hot and very tired and everyone of them scratching. The pineapple was worth pounds, and a loaf of real English bread a positive curiosity. We made our way to our present position through a famous distillery, which is a sight thousands of trippers would crowd to visit in the happy times of future peace.

"The roof of our dugout consists of an iron bedstead, a gateway, a door, and odd timber from God knows where. On the walls are drawings of the *Photo Fun* type. A shelf with a bunch of flowers in a broken bottle, the cover of a soup-tureen, a pitch-fork used as a grill, and a hundred miscellaneous articles.

"All are well and more than happy, *I* especially, after the two letters which came with the parcel.

"Must close now. In haste.—Love to all,

"B."

"SWEETHEART,—My letters, of necessity, have been short and scrappy of late—it has been a rather distracting time for us all, and coherent thought, thought at all, apart from the particular work in hand, is hard to acquire. Anyway, we have dragged through another ordeal, and are now preparing for a few days' rest away from the trenches. So far, my health and nerves have remained good, and if they (the nerves) can stand the shelling we have had the last fortnight, they will stand most things. The last week or two the Germans seem to have got in a new stock of ammunition, especially high explosive shells, which have played the devil with our trenches. . . . Thank God we are out of it for a bit. I think I have received all your letters and parcels, etc., but everything gets lost in the dugouts, as men come tumbling in out of shell-fire upsetting everything that stands in the way. The other day I wondered why my face and head felt so clammy, only to discover that I had been making a pillow of the men's breakfast bacon, the majority of which was fat.

"We managed to get into the canal and have a couple of swims last week, and it put new life into everybody; also a change of clothes, the first we have had in about two months. . . . I had my first experience of 'Gas' the other day. It is a most filthy concoction. If you get one mouthful of it, it makes you cough and splutter, and before you know where you are, your head is swimming and you run—straight to 'Kingdom Come.'

"We have only one Colonel in the Brigade now, and no Brigadier! The latter was shot yesterday. Perhaps it is as well to mention that the shot was not a punitive one. Sad to relate, I am rapidly losing my sense of humour. A great deal came away with my hair, which was shorn off under compulsion with a pair of horse shears. I had not seen a looking glass since the catastrophe until this morning when I discovered an interesting study of criminology gazing at me from a looking-glass.

'Long-headed N. German type,' I said to myself, not recognising the identity, but the reflection smiled upon the subject in pitying denial; 'a German would have made capital out of that'—nodding to the hair speckled cranium—'you're a fat-headed Englishman!' I thought it best to come away.

"It is difficult to think of anything worth recording. Things out here are so rough; not, however, the noble suggestions of Rodin, but a petty clipped effect overspreads everything. The country, of course, is flat, and that gives a diminutive appearance to everything. Existence is very confined, so is our range of vision, which leaves little else of note but bad language and phallic remarks. I think I shall have to resort to writing love letters, although they too would have but little in them, as they would be mere Catomitish (?) wastage. I see this lends itself to misinterpretation. I mean, I have no wish to use you as a mental Catomite. Passion of any kind is terribly lacking. If I were God or Kitchener, I would whip up the troops' sexual life to boiling heat, make rape an honourable game and loot a business. I guarantee the war would be over in half the time and the wastage of life much less. Honour is a thing without meaning here—or in England either, and men cannot put up a great show for the reward of 1s. per day.

"Anyway, I feel I have much more to return home for than I did when I started out. . . . A horrible but amusing pastime in the trenches has been to scrump for dead men's love letters and read them aloud. The amount of fair females who are sure of the return of those they love by every conceivable sign is prodigious. In reading these heterogeneous missives, one can easily imagine the quality, cut and material of their underclothes. Enough! I am, becoming too regimental—Love to you both,

"B."

"... I think if I return alive, you will find me terribly aged and lacking in interest. . . . Powdered, scented and rouged, I might pass muster as a broken hero with a bit of a past, but I am afraid it would be attractive to nothing above sixteen. In fact, the wicked uncle is the only part open to me to play, and I know that won't pass muster with you.

"What will become of the poor wee girl in the arms of a great heavy brute that I have become this last three months? I do not think, however, I shall ever trouble you again. My work, for the time being, is here, and that work is almost daily spinning pennies with Death. Why I have not died before, I do not know. There is a terrific fasciation in going out in front of the trenches, in seeing the Dread One come to one and then another, and leave you standing there. There is nothing I would love more than to come home to you all again; there is nothing I love more than to dream of that return and all that might be mine! And yet it seems so impossible. Sometimes I want to tell you not to wait for me, to go your way and be really happy, and yet the very thought of leaving you is too much for me. Often when I am 'standing to' in the trenches at daybreak, I see you sleeping there, wondering where your dreams are leading you. I seldom see myself figuring in your dreams except as something of the past . . . as the background behind the 'spot' lime-light to another scene. More than ever I see this life as an astral vision, with self-made emotions, self-made colouring and action. We make up the play with any materials we have handy, and call the material Fate. I want to end the play. I have made a farce in such a manner as would be approved by God Almighty as the judge—I suppose I really mean 'S.'

"To merely die in action not enough; it is not farcical. I must die a millionaire with not a penny in my pocket. I must die gallantly carrying a corpse into safety! I must die laughing at myself, and so far I have only learned to laugh at others. The love I bear to you . . . to all I have ever cared for, is only a form of self-adoration, self-gratification, the love of imagined possession."

And so the letter went on. Iris could scarcely bear to read it. She was well aware that she had acted foolishly at times, but surely Blitzen had understood. There had been no barrier between them at the last. But before many lines, the entire tone of the letter had altered. Complete rest was what he needed, she saw that plainly. . . . Yet how true was his diagnosis of her character.

"The world is fair, I know, and you have seen but little of that beauty, but because I know you have the knowledge that that beauty is but an illusion . . . an illusive state after which you crave, because I know you have that knowledge, I see you as I stand and look out into the night, a moth, a poor, beautiful little moth, battering its wings as it tries to rise and lose itself in the great moon overhead.

"I want to see you an Eagle, dear one, breaking its great wings, if necessary, in its flight towards the sun. For there is no life in the moon and mystery is never unravelled. Look to the Sun, the Giver of Life, for the hard facts of life are the only things that can really help. In fact, the analysing of these facts *is* the Great Work—as *I* understand it. You will say I have a morbid mood upon me. I have, but it is not only when I am moody that I think as I am now writing. . . . I have been practically living in an underground cellar for the last four days, and I suppose the one small ray of light coming down upon a small wooden table has put the mood of the cloisters extra strong upon me. Anyway, I cannot at the present get in touch with the others who, at the moment, are howling, 'I hear you calling me', and 'I'll make you love me'—emptying their bowels of sentiment, even as I, each in his own way.

"Your ring is nearly finished, although not yet to my satisfaction. I wanted the general shape to be that of a lotus, around which the universal snake, above which a circle of copper upon which you can have engraved the Key of Life. It is but a rude attempt, but it is made from the nose of a German shell (aluminium), and the copper circle a section of a bullet. Having no tools makes it a long job, and until these last few days I have had no time except for sleep. . . . I wish I could get my health back and feel purely animal once more . . . to dream of taking and crushing you in my arms, but it seems so far ahead, so absolutely improbable and yet, worst of all, I cannot forget you.

"B"

The weather was appallingly hot. Iris could neither eat, sleep nor think. What was it Blitzen had said in one of his earlier letters. "Get up before dawn, the air is beautiful then, and I, too, am always on duty at that hour! Try whenever you can to be in the open at sunrise, the stillness and peace will help you more than anything I can think of. It is good magic also!!"

If only she could. Usually she went to sleep at dawn. In the same letter he had told her of the terrible discomfort of the trenches and had also told her of his good job. "Very shortly I shall have a Trench Mortar Battery all of my own. At present, I am studying it up and getting experience, and that, too, is worrying work, as we make our own bombs, the detonators of which are composed of the highest explosive known, and very little is known of the substance. I hope in a few weeks to be attached to the Brigade Section, but at present I am only in reserve. . . . I am in the trenches again to-morrow for four or five days, and after that I hope we will have a bit of a rest. Since I first went into the firing-line, I have only been out of range of guns for four days. . . ."

On 8th July she had sent him a poem, a translation of a Persian hymn to Allah, *First Source of Light*. It had pleased him and he had written:

"Thanks for poem—it is more your old self again. In it you have largeness, the same passion that swells the breast of the sea, the jealous love that sends lowering clouds and the scorching passion of a desert sun. I think this is conveyed by the modesty of expression. It is of the gods you sing the best. . . . You complain of the heat. We have had such cold weather that they have issued overcoats!! Thanks for flowers (jasmine)—what do they signify?

"There was quite a lot I meant to write, but cannot put my mind (what is left) to it. All my love. —Always yours, Bunco."

In the same letter he had spoken of his intention of writing to S.

"But really there is nothing to write of save regimental stuff and that is censorable."

"Please note change of address and congratulate," said his next letter. "I got 'charm' safely—it is very jolly. It is, I think, the trade-mark of the T.S.

"I made a ring for you but it is too large and commonplace. It is not copper but aluminium. I cannot get on with the one I am making for you at present. I have made two attempts and failed. I wanted to give you a magical one, but all magic has gone for the moment. I am nearly dropping with fatigue. . . . I have only had my boots off four times in thirty days, and then I had to pick my socks off. I hear that the vicinity of C. Town was blazing with placards—'Heroic deeds of the gallant 19th,' or something like that. Please get half a dozen *Daily Expresses* of 16th July, and cut out the column in question and let me have them. . . . It is unbecoming to my modesty to write such things myself, but as others have done so I am quite willing to make the best of the affair. I am awfully glad I have got on to the brigade staff."

"2nd August.

"You will be pleased, I know, to hear we have at last turned our back on the trenches for a time and in a day or so will be out of the range of shells. We will be Army Corps in reserve for about three or four weeks. This will be the first time in four months.

"We have been billeted in many strange places. At the moment we are billeted in a *slaughterhouse* yard, with yelling pigs and 'booful' calves walking in to be killed." (Then followed the programme of the day. It ended up with an R.A.M.C. concert.) "Splendid band in the hospital grounds." Red-cross vans coming in and out with the wounded. The Gordons were there—and played their pipes—who should be the chief piper but the famous Findlater, V.C. . . . I gave a sprig of your heather to one of the Jocks and he nearly cried. All Scottish soldiers are called Jocks. You see our holiday has started at last, and with any luck we will go farther back still. I enclose a sketch I made the other day, but there is nothing in it beyond the fact that it is of historical interest. . . ."

"15th August.

"DEAR HEART,—I received your parcel and letter, the contents of both going a long way towards making me feel very happy. If you were with me now, with the certainty of death for us both—death, quick and sharp—I should die contented. I have slipped away to a slight prominence and lie in a bed of clover, and all around me are undulating fields, violent yellows and deep purple shadows, golden corn and verdant greens. Strips of shadow from the passing clouds creep here and there like saddened thoughts passing through a happy heart. Only the hum of an aeroplane speaks of war. Peasants are singing an evening song as they glean the fields, and a distant church bell speaks in its own language to all who wish to hear. The young lark is trying the strength of her wing, and the nodding clover bobs her approval of the song. Away back, healthy foul-mouthed men from London are singing their sentimental songs. Here and there a young mother listens to them, sometimes joining in the chorus as she rocks her 'Souvenir Baby,' wondering at the strangeness of these noisy English; wondering if the masterful English father will return to claim his child and her. They are very proud of their souvenir English babies. . . . A little child, months ago, tied a piece of red string on to my tunic button, the only thing she had to give me as a parting gift. I kept it as a mascot and twined your piece of green around it. I managed to keep it tied to my button until ten days ago. The day before I left the trenches a shell came after me. It failed to do me any harm, but when I got free of dirt and sandbags I found my two mascots missing! I expect you will find me changed also, dear Heart. I have had to scheme hard to hold my own against old hands at the game. A lot of jealousy is caused because I can laugh and talk to an officer and have tea and play cards with them, while those who have been in the regiment for years and are my seniors are left to walk the trenches and are not allowed in their dugouts. Consequently, if they can let me down, they will. This has made me creep even more into myself.

"Well, dear Heart, the great cave of the sky as assumed a purple hue, and through the entrance a few golden shafts are tipping the distant clouds, with a tinge of red. Far in the distance an occasional spark will flash in the sky—they are shells bursting. A pale crescent moon is struggling into life, and before she has half uncovered her face I shall where those sparks are great flashes of flame. Perhaps the gods will spare me for yet another spell. Perhaps I may still come back to those sticky little arms and feel a foolish little head rest comfy on a hard chest. Poor little Kiddie-wee. I feel such lots older; I want to make you happy and contented, but God knows if it rests in my power to do so.

"The Angelus is tolling. Not a soul is in sight. A wonderful hush is in the air and the world seems suddenly empty. Only vague thoughts are left me, some memories of little joys and their balance of pain. In a few minutes I must be back amongst the clatter and noise, ribald laughter and coarse oaths, and I know I shall feel very, very lonely. But somewhere from my corner in the straw I shall be able to look into the shadows, and perchance a beautiful white face with an absurd little drooping mouth will come and beckon me with her eyes, and take me over the path of years to the shadow of a slanting roof where a little black kitten darts in and out, a dying fire flickers and a pair of arms stretch themselves out for me, and perhaps in their embrace I shall forget the path that I have trodden, until the bugle calls me to tread that weary road again.—All my love,

"B."

"*P.S.*—I've nearly finished your ring, but it is very fragile and the shape of the lotus is almost lost. It has taken the spare time of three days to get the little piece of copper metal fitted in. Write me a 'booful' long letter soon, as I am very bored just now. In the words of the song:

"I, I, don't want to die,
I want to 'ome."

I have no news, and unless you write to me I can find nothing to write about except shop, and that I want to forget."

"Dear Old Sweetheart—I am now in charge of the whole Brigade Battery, 4 guns and 40 men. We are trying to get our leave as a Brigade unit, but I don't know if we can pull it off.

"I am now having a complete change in camping-out. We have each made a little shelter out of branches, leaves and waterproof sheets and the country around is most charming. The harvest is being gathered in; our regular officer has gone home on leave and his substitute does just what is told, like a good boy. He is an old Fleet Street hand and knew Mueller of The *Tribune.* . . . His outlook is typically journalese, and every that does not coincide with his point of view is bad, bad art. I seem to know him. Probably I have met him at G.O.'s.

"I struck a weird house, of which I meant to tell you; quite a magic place where people take off the mask they wear and are their own selves. In point of fact it was like watching a cinema film and I enjoyed it immensely. I would have written of it last night, but I had no candle and out here all lights of it are *supposed* to be out by 9:30.

"Have had no time to put in any more work on your ring. . . . Re my short hair in the photo, it looks short because it is almost quite white. . . I am sorry I am so dry to-night. Somewhere at the back of my head a long-faced little Pierrette is spinning on a spindle toe and a wan and chill Pierret putting grass in his shoes to stop the holes. His tears have rusted the strings of his instrument and he can twang it no more. Pierret and Pierrette are very much in my mind of late. I wonder why? Clown, too, is often there. I think it must be the gossamer tints of the evening that suggest them to me, and at night I spend many hours walking up and down amongst the 'shelters' wondering what dreams are hovering there; wondering what will become of all these peaceful slumbers *après la guerre.* I cannot help wondering also of my own welfare if I should ever see the end of this war and return sound and fit. Try as I may I cannot raise the veil, and that is why I feel I shall stop here till the end.

"It seems almost in the period of my childhood when I look back to the time you were staying at Hatfield with me. I must have passed through many phases since then, and they have doubtless left their mark. You too, I expect, are altered more than you realise. How strange it would feel if we met again!

"I must close now. The dew is damping the paper and I have not my tunic on. It is most bitterly cold here at night, and it is difficult to sleep even with an overcoat on.

"Still, it will harden us for the winter. Good-bye, dear Old Girl.

"B."

"3rd September.

"SWEETHEART,—Your letter sounded very blue and I fain would cheer you up, but I haven't a single idea in my head and there is nothing worth recording. I have had the old black cloud over me for some time; I would drink it off if that were possible, but only very light wines and French beer are allowed to be sold, and they are even more horrible than the Horror itself.

"Make it straight with K. for me if you can. If am afraid my letter rather upset her. In point of fact I had buried a pal, and felt very bitter that he should be lying peacefully there, with a clean sheet to start upon, while I only had my dirty, smudged and overscored record ever before me. Thank God! I had written your letter first, for I fear I should have struck out just as wildly if writing to you. . . .

"Will write as soon as I feel myself again.

"Poor old Captain 'H.' copped out the other day. I am sorry he is gone. Shot through the head.—All my love.

"B."

"8th September.

"DEAR OLD SWEETHEART,—I was sent away, back for ten days, so I received yours of the 30th, 6th and 3rd all together. I have been awfully busy as I have the whole battery still on my hands officer and no junior sergeant to help. I will answer your letters in their order.

"Pierrot's shoes are only metaphorically in holes; one cannot imagine the picturesque wanderer in new boots or free from dust and mud! Yes, I am often very mizzy; there is so much I should be able to do and yet it seems so impossible. There is nobody to whom I can 'talk'; the war itself is so absurd (from the philosophical standpoint), the sufferings so great and the pleasures so trifling. It is all so cold, so calculated; the monotony stagnates one's blood. Even the Germans who tried to fashion the war as war has been understood through the decades of Time, even they are getting nauseated and flat.

"I am sorry to hear of Laura, and I am glad you are doing everything in your power to help. She and I have never been good friends, but I think she would value a little genuine attention from you. Here I have to stop-more orders just come in, so will continue to-morrow."

CHAPTER XVIII

"9th September.

"TO continue. Regarding your inclination to follow the Flapper if I don't come back, although our nickname is 'The Suicide Club' (or the 'Gas Pipe Brigade ') I have no intention of throwing my life away for or nothing. Something is bound to happen soon (naturally, I cannot go into details) and then I shall do my part with the rest. I only hope to God we get an officer before then—I don't like the idea of going into any big action on my own, and have thirty odd men's lives hanging on my hands!"

(Followed two sentences crossed out.)

"Regarding your intention to remove, I don't somehow think it really wise. . . . If I do come home I should dearly love to come to some little garret-room just big enough for you and I. Of course I do not want to tie you down, but I think of the two you are better where you are. . . .

"I must close now. Keep on loving me, dear Heart, if you can. It won't be thrown away. Love is not a finite thing, so it won't matter much if Love is really there whether I come back or not. If you and I are infinite, must not our love be infinite too? Good-bye. All your own,

"B."

"11th September.

"*P.S.*—The Brigadier came down and questioned me about a thousand and one things—about ammunition supply, etc. etc. He is a wonderful man. I got through all right, for he sent down his Brigadier Major in the afternoon to go further into the matters I had put to him. Everything I asked for was granted, including *arrangements for leave*, so I might have a few days in England yet! Altogether I feel very satisfied with my day's work.

"B."

"Thank God!" said Iris devoutly. She spent some time looking round, and found a really charming top room that in many ways suggested their old Adelphi studios. It was empty, and in imagination she saw how they would arrange it. There was everything that Blitzen would like, even to the skylight, the wide window-ledges and the surrounding short balcony. All her bad presentiments had vanished into thin air. She wrote enthusiastically.

"SWEETHEART"—came back the answer, posted 22nd September—"Thanks for dear letter; I have no time to write in detail. I am well, I am happy, I am busy. I am sleepy. I am *not* hungry. I am dirty, and I love you. Good-night,

"B."

Then followed a week of sickening suspense.

On 30th September Iris received an official postcard, dated the day before:

"I have been admitted into hospital, wounded, and am going on well. I am being sent down to the Base. Letter follows at first opportunity.

"B."

She had not the faintest notion where the Base could be, and there seemed no possible means of finding out. In desperation she stopped a soldier in the street and, "1st or 2nd Canadian General Hospital," he told her, "but I don't know which; they are some way apart. I should write to them both." Write! She must telegraph, and she hadn't sufficient money for prepaid telegrams to both places.

Yet she dared not wait. "They'll never allow a telegram to pass," some ignorant and well-meaning fool had told her, "but if he is very bad they may send him home." Yes, perhaps *now* they would send him.

What should she do? She telegraphed, reply paid, to the 1st and 2nd Canadian General Hospital: "Any progress? Anxious. Iris." They couldn't, she thought, prevent *that* from reaching him. Yet in all probability its very vagueness was an error. Five more days of mental torture, and a card from Blitzen himself. It was from E. M. Ward, Canadian General Hospital, but a heavy censor stamp had obliterated the number of the Hospital—4th October it was dated.

"I am wounded badly in thigh, bone is broken. I do not quite know what they are going to do with it yet. Pray that I can stand the pain." (Then to the side of the card in a smaller script) "All my love.

"B."

At the same time came a letter from Blitzen's sister, saying, "He would be sent over to England," and also speaking of the splendid account that had been given by the Brigade-Major of his gallant conduct in the field. He had won his sword, as he had promised her. How proud Iris felt of him! It was dreadful that he should be so badly wounded. But once in England he would be well looked after. He was returning home, that was the all-important thing. They would wire her and it was bound to be soon—so various friends had assured her.

6th October, and a telegram from Le Treport. The boy waited, there might be an answer.

Iris was almost too excited to open the envelope. Blitzen was coming home. Perhaps it would be next week, perhaps it would be to-morrow. She stared at the paper, and for the fraction of a second could see nothing, then she looked at the boy.

"There is no answer," she said tonelessly. With a scared expression the boy hurried down the steps.

It was the answer to her prepaid wire, and was from the Matron, 2nd C.G.H.:

"Death occurred 4 p.m. Oct. 5th. Funeral takes place 1 p.m. to-day. Writing."

Alone in her room Iris realised for the first time the true meaning of the word "Hell." Mechanically she had written a number of telegrams, and had sent the landlady out with them. The woman's ill-timed chatter would surely drive her mad if she did not go away. The post office was some distance down the road, and it would ensure her absence for a little while. At first she felt completely dazed, and it was several minutes before the full significance of the dreadful truth came home to her.

Blitzen had gone—gone, and now she would never be able to tell him of the thing that had been worrying her for so many months. How in a certain important matter she had disregarded his wishes, and how sorry she was. She had in-tended to do so when they met; writing so often was the cause of hopeless misunderstandings.

That is why she had not told him in writing. And now nothing remained to her but unavailing remorse.

For her own torment she cared but little; it was the thought of what Blitzen must be suffering now he knew that she had failed him. In the exaggeration of her grief she saw everything in the blackest colours. She was responsible for his death; she was responsible for all he had suffered in the trenches. "O God, let me suffer anything, *anything*, but don't let him suffer more." So she prayed in all sincerity, little realising that in the vehemence of her grief the prayer was already answering itself.

Blank horror seized her.

She was not. She was nothingness. She was. . . conscious blackness. Yet that same nothingness, that blackness, was surrounded on all sides by an iron wall that reached from heaven to hell.

So it would be for all eternity—relentless nothingness, inexecrable blackness.

Somewhere in the darkness behind that iron wall was Blitzen. He was suffering; he was alone. He also was in the grip of that inexorable conscious nothingness—that blackness. Her cries would never reach him. She would never be able to help him. By her own foolishness she had shut the door. He would never know that she had cried. Her own voice as the sound of another's came to her from an infinite distance. It was the first sign of returning consciousness. She was as a tired swimmer raising her head from beneath the waters of a black flood.

Days and weeks passed.

Little by little Iris learned the details of Blitzen's death. He had been Acting Sergeant-Major of the Trench Mortar Battery, 141st Infantry Brigade, and had been badly wounded at Loos, 25th September.

With a broken thigh, and suffering agonies as he must have done, he had yet managed to take many notes and get much valuable information for the General. Days after, the stretcher-bearers had found him. Ten days later he had died of tetanus. Why they had not found him before, no one seemed able to tell her.

The Brigade-Major paid a glowing tribute to his gallantry, the matron of the hospital spoke of his courage and patience—and she heard on all sides from both officers and men of the many fine things he had done, but it was a long time before she could piece together the various bits of information. Why, she reflected, if he had behaved so magnificently at Givenchy (and she had the testimonial in his platoon officer's own hand-writing), why had he not been recommended for the honours so obviously due?

"I didn't think of it at the time—our nerves were in such a state, but I'll do anything I can now," so Lieutenant S. had told her.

Thereupon she remembered a letter Blitzen had written in the latter part of August, describing his company officers: "Lieutenant G., a rotten little snip; S. worse. Lieutenant H. is the only gentleman in the crowd, an Oxonian."

What might not that brief description cover?

One thing was plain. Had he lived he would undoubtedly have won his commission. He had indentured weeks before, but the Colonel in whose hands the matter lay fell with him at Loos, and the papers could not be traced.

So, too, with regard to honours. "Had he lived he would undoubtedly have been singled out for distinction, but except in the case of the V.C., posthumous honours were not given." So they had told her at the War Office. After six months' hopeless striving, Iris gave it up.

After six months' waiting she received his effects. Of the latter nothing remained but a recent diary, a few letters and photographs a crucifix and the "pantacle."

She read the various entries:

25th September.—Wounded.

29th September.—Had leg dressed second time since Saturday! Still no splint.

30th September.—Settled down a bit. They made a splint for me but it wouldn't fit. Awful pains. Moving these broken bones is like being in the lowest depths of Hades.

1st October—(the last entry).—Pheasant shooting begins to-day, as if I didn't know.

✳

Iris looked forward to the air-raids. They were the only occasions on which she slept. She had promised Blitzen that she would never take her life, but there was always the chance that it might be taken for her.

She liked the sound of the guns. It reminded her of a thunderstorm, and since she was a child she had always loved the sound of thunder. There was something so grand and elemental about it. As she always slept through a thunderstorm so she slept through the raids. When an air-raid took place in the daytime and she was out of doors, she always refused to "take cover," saying that she preferred to be killed in the open, and those who shouted at her were always too much afraid to forcibly insist. How queer it was, she thought, this clinging to life!

What did most of the people around her get out of it? Yet most of them seemed terribly afraid of dying.

She was not and never had been afraid of death; now she would gladly have welcomed it. She ran every imaginable risk, and all to no purpose.

Seemingly it was not to be.

What was it Blitzen had once told her?

"They are not going to let you off so easily, you have lots more to go through yet."

✳

Iris had not written to Svaroff. Why, she did not know, but she dreaded his learning of Blitzen's death. If there were anything queer about the man (and she had often felt that there was), might he not start experimenting with Blitzen, now that conditions were favourable? It was a dim fear that she could not analyse, but she felt she was right in not telling him.

Their few mutual acquaintances, she hoped, would not tell him either. . .

The shock consequent on Blitzen's death had had one curious effect upon her. She conceived for literature, and for poetry in particular, a complete loathing! She felt that she would never write again, and most certainly she would never read.

What a ghastly mockery it all was, and what incredibly callous persons poets were! They put all their sentiment on paper, for the simple reason that they felt nothing.

The thought of poetry filled her with something very akin to nausea.

From necessity she worked at the War Office.

She lived alone. She had no time for dreaming.

Occasionally strange rumours reached her concerning Svaroff:

"He was a spy in the pay of the Germans"—"He was editing a newspaper which was violently anti-British"—"He had helped German prisoners to escape"—"He had become a naturalised American."

Iris attached as much importance to these rumours as she did to the pre-war paper accounts. Quite apart from what he might or might not be feeling, Svaroff was not such a fool. Of this she felt certain.

✳

It was some five years later that she first had a letter from him. He wrote very sympathetically about Blitzen, though the letter was strangely worded.

"Subconsciously," he said, "I was very fond of him—he was snowed under by your personality—you must not cry out against Fate; you must face it squarely—that is what we are here for."

Iris left the letter unanswered. She had started to write again, and to her great relief found that she could still do good work, though the style had altered very considerably. There was less superficial beauty and much greater depth. In a word, she had found herself, and in so doing was helping others to find themselves. The realisation of this brought with it a definite comfort. It also, strange to say, brought her definite recognition and recognition in quarters that counted.

Would Svaroff care for this new style? She sometimes wondered. But she would not write to him.

Once again he wrote to her: "I shall shortly be in England for a few days, the exact date I will let you know later. I hope to see you before I leave." Then came the promised letter. Later came a wire: "Meet me at Victoria Station 2 pm. Continental Express."

Iris got there two minutes early, and then wondered what she ought should do.

Ought she to wait on the platform? And in any case, which platform would it be? She had always been hopelessly lacking in a sense of time or place.

What a pity if she were to miss him. She no longer felt the vague fear that had obsessed her at the time of her great loss. She wondered what he would look like after six years.

A dark-bearded man who had been watching her for several minutes came up slightly smiling. "I think there is some mistake," she was just about to say, when the stranger's smile deepened.

There was no mistaking those eyes nor the hands which still carried the ivory cane.

On the little finger of the left hand was a serpent ring which reached to the base of the finger-nail. "Love is the Law, Love under Will" he said, and held out his hand. Iris took it, then:

"Why the disguise?" she said. "I should never have known you."

"Of course you wouldn't," he answered. Then, "If you really wish to know, blunt razors," he added laconically.

"It is quite a chance you found me," she said.

"I had no idea where to look for you."

"There is no such thing as chance," he reminded her, "and where does all the world meet but under the clock? Let us have some lunch. I don't like Stewart's and neither will you, but it's most conveniently near."

How little he had altered, she thought.

"Well, what are you doing?" he asked, as they left the restaurant together.

"Writing a bit," she said, "but life is pretty dull."

"Life is precisely what we make it, so rid yourself once and for all, young lady, of any such foolish notion."

"It may be for you," she answered. "You go just where you like, when you like, and do just what you will. So why not? You speak from experience."

"Well, and why don't you? There's nothing to prevent it, I suppose? In the paraphrased words of Issa Ben Miriam, 'Come thou and do likewise.'"

"I can't possibly," she said, and she gave him several reasons.

"Just the same as ever," he remarked. "Whenever persons try to help, you won't let them. Now if you were to come to Corsica, as I wish, you would soon be doing the most magnificent work. It's a lovely place. Why not come?"

"I'm sorry," she said, "but it's impossible."

"So it seems," he remarked.

"Well, I'm only over here for a couple of days and I've quite a lot to do, so once more we part. But I'll do what I can for you before I leave. Can I give you a lift?" he added, as he hailed a taxi.

"No thanks," Iris said. "It was nice seeing you again," and she moved away in the opposite direction.

"Good-bye," he called after her. "Don't forget. Do what thou wilt shall be the whole of the Law. When you have realised that, half the battle IS won. Good-bye."

"Good-bye," she answered.

CHAPTER XIX

A T three o'clock in the afternoon, in the latter half of July, there are, if the summer has been a warm one, few places hotter and stuffier than London. As he crossed over from Villiers Street into the Strand, Vladimir Svaroff felt decidedly depressed, but it was not the heat of the day which alone depressed him. Since the time that he had talked with Iris at Victoria Station, ten years had come and gone and outwardly they had left their mark.

He was much stouter, some persons called him fat, and his hair though still dark had receded considerably from the temples. Loth as he was to admit the fact to himself he was getting old, soon he would be numbered in the category of those, who according to the dictum of the younger generation had no right to exist—whose proper place should long ago have been the lethal chamber. How incredibly callous they were this younger generation!

Yet only yesterday, it seemed, he had been their foremost spokesman; they had looked up to him, many of them, as to a monument of wisdom. Now, it seemed, a new set of youthful pioneers had arisen, who knew not Joseph. No, nor what is worse, did they show the slightest wish to know him. Decidedly it was depressing. What did that poem of Charles Lamb say? "Gone, gone are the old familiar faces." Did Lamb once feel as he was feeling now? Presumably he did, presumably many men had felt the same. There was not much consolation in the fact—truth to tell, it but added to the depression to know that history but repeats itself *ad nauseam.*

In swift retrospect Vladimir went over the events of the last twenty years, events in which he had played so big a part. The launching of *The Hieroglyph*, the Republic of Genius, the suicide of the Flapper. He at all events had not been responsible for *that* catastrophe, though inevitably he had been blamed. He had not even troubled to refute the charge; if people cared to be fools let them.

Then had come the War and the death of Blitzen! He had always been sorry about that—still, who knows, perhaps of the two of them Blitzen was the better off.

The train of thought continued itself. Vincent who had died in Burma; Laura who had followed five months after Blitzen; Audley, that youthful Adonis, who had but recently joined the great majority! Ivanoff, killed in the war; Selden, died of enteric; Harrington Hobbs, definitely insane; Newton a hopeless neurasthenic—a host of others who had gone under. Had any of the old set come through? Ah, yes. Somewhere or other there was Iris Hamilton; he had not yet heard of her death, so he supposed she must be still living. Queer girl that. Never let herself go, never knew her own mind—but had definite genius all the same. Suppose she'd be a woman now, or would she ever be that? Vladimir smiled to himself, and a passing stranger, glancing suspiciously at the interesting looking foreigner, edged away. "Queer cove that" was his mental comment. To smile at a joke that is not shared by others is a sure mark of madness, especially in England. Vladimir read the thought even whilst noting the action, and he smiled again.

What had he done with his life these last ten years?

He had stayed at most of the capitals of Europe, and at a good many capitals farther East. He had been accused of ritual murder in Westphalia concerning which he had had at the time no knowledge whatsoever. A silly young ass experimenting with drugs had taken an overdose and he had been blamed for that also. Young women, with more money than brains and less morals than morons, had flung themselves at his head and he had been accused of alienating their affections from their rightful owners. How asinine it all was! If the young women had not been good-looking would anyone have troubled where they deposited their worthless loves? Jealousy—that was at the bottom of it all. Svaroff felt profoundly bored.

For some months past he had been experimenting again with drugs, and there had been some interesting results, but he wished there were someone with whom he could discuss the matter. He had of late hit upon quite a good mixture, a concoction of three, in which opium played a fairish part, but he had run out of the latter. Well, he would get some, and he would make a goodly brew.

Thank heavens his imagination remained. He would write a damned good story. He would show a few of these moderns who thought they knew everything just what they didn't know. That would mean going to Limehouse. Well, why not? A man carrying a large basket of flowers on his back came quickly down a side street by Aldwych and all but collided with him. This was the last straw. Svaroff, jumped on to a passing vehicle.

"Aldgate," he asked.

"Yes, sir" the man answered, punching a ticket, "very hot isn't it?"

"Very," Svaroff answered for the hundredth time that day!

Where Aldgate branches off into Commercial Road he took a tram.

"Burdett Road," he said. If one were being watched, and one never knew these days, it might be as well to put the watcher off, to suggest that one were going in the opposite direction.

From the top of the tram-car Svaroff looked out, noting with amusement the foreign termination of the names on the small crowded shops—the "ovskys" the "skis" and "steins"— the "offs" "bergs" and "manns," with many another and stranger name that suggested the Far East.

Seemingly there was not an English face or name among them. The women seemed mostly Jewish; the children playing on the pavements had magnificent heads of hair, many of them a wonderful auburn colour—they were animated, and all of them looked intelligent and happy.

"A curious childlike race," he mused, "emotional as are all children—amazingly responsive to kindness. Yet on occasion profounder than hell itself. Do any but their own countrymen ever really know them?"

"Christian Street! And not one Christian in it—Jamaica Street, and every resident a criminal (or said to be); Sidney Street, of 1911 fame, Arbour Square, Albert Square, Old Church Street—Grosvenor Street—My God! What hovels, and to think that whole families live in each!

"Yet in some curious way there's a spaciousness that one does not experience in the West End? What is it? Is it purely psychological? Is it the mass-mind of the people? Ah! The houses are so tiny they do not shut out the sunlight—after the corridor-like mazes of the West End, after the sky-scrapers of Oxford Street and the Strand, it is like being on the crest of a hill." So Svaroff's thoughts ran on. Burdett Road at last; and quickly alighting, he crossed over to West India Dock Road. He walked on the right-hand side of the road past Jack's Palace on the right and the Asiatic Home for Seamen on the left until he reached Limehouse Causeway passing on the way doss-houses, lodging-houses and small Chinese restaurants, in the doorways of which stood clean-shirted men with white collars and mask-like, old-ivory coloured faces. Their high cheek bones and strange slitty-looking eyes reminded him of the figures on a screen. (How true to type were the old artists and craftsmen!) Passing, too, the sailors homes and the Jewish outfitters for seamen, with their blue linen slacks and high seamen's boots.

He turned down the narrow street known locally as Chinese Causeway, looking with interest to right and left. He was beginning to feel like a character in a Jacobs novel. Ah Sing's little shop was halfway down and on the left-hand side. Would Ah Sing still be there? No matter if he were not—not for nothing had Svaroff lived in Shanghai, Pekin and other places. They were, on the whole, a cultured race. An apt quotation from one of their favourite philosophers plus, of course the necessary gold, and one could usually procure what one wanted; at least he, Svaroff, had always done so.

A lightly-clad child, looking like a toy from a Chinese cracker, ran just in front of him, and a black-and-white cat washed its face in a neighbouring doorway—a wrinkled old face smiled at him in a welcoming fashion from the dark paper-hung doorway.

Could it be Ah Sing? It was. This was luck indeed.

"It has been bright all day, but now indeed does the sun shine," said the old man.

"The sun kisses the lotus-petals that the dew has washed," murmured Svaroff. "Are you alone?"

"Entirely."

"That is good; then we can proceed to business," and Svaroff took from his pocket a large, square envelope made of rice paper, on the top left-hand corner of which was a red glyph in Chinese letters.

Ah Sing bowed, then led the way to an inner room. He lighted a joss-stick, murmuring a few prayers before the God of Luck, then turned to a small ivory cabinet which contained innumerable small drawers. He opened one which was empty, but carved in the inside with a floral pattern of lotus flowers;

on the outside was a rayed sun above a pool. Ah Sing pressed the centre of the sun and an inner drawer opened behind the lotus flowers. In the inner drawer were several small packages. Ah Sing took out two and handed them to his visitor. More compliments passed between them, and promising to return, maybe at no distant date, Svaroff took his departure.

Outside in the hot street he hesitated for a few seconds, then seemingly made up his mind. He would not return the way he had come. For one thing, it would mean passing the Police Station; and (like the Artful Dodger) in these days he was too well known.

It was now nearing four o'clock and the day was Saturday. Everywhere it would be crowded, but on Limehouse Pier there would be quiet, fresh air and room to breathe. He walked to the end of the Causeway, crossed Three Colt Street and entered Thames Place.

How narrow the street was! Paved with cobbles, and the tall buildings seemed to lean one to the other in friendly fashion, even as old cronies in the act of exchanging secrets. On his right hand was the back of a large granary warehouse, chiefly windowless, but had there been windows, from the upper storey residents could with ease have shaken hands with their neighbours across the way. The scent of the warm grain was in pleasing contrast to the malted aromas he had just left behind him, and a cool wind from the river—the first he had felt that day—played refreshingly upon his temples.

Svaroff took off his sombrero (a fashion in hats he had always affected) and with an audible sigh of relief, walked on to the floating gangway.

A few loafers, idly smoking or sleeping, and one or two children playing by the mud flats, were the only signs of humanity to greet his eye, but on the pier itself was considerable activity—slackening and hauling in of ropes, moving of large bales, and, in one corner, the making and drinking of tea in large cans.

The river swept round in a grand, almost circular curve, dark glassy-grey in colour, save where here and there a dancing ripple caught the light. A few gulls, with indescribably graceful motion, swooped down upon the barges; then, without a break, continued their flight in search of fish. No sound broke the stillness but the plash and lap of the water.

How soothing it was, yet how full of pulsing life! Out of the hazy mist the vague shapes of the warehouses and the giant wharves rose with the indescribable fascination of a dream city. The beauty of it gave one almost a pang. It was intangible, wonderful, a dream city of the gods, a place of infinite mystery—a city to appear and disappear in a night. No wonder Whistler had loved it, and Turner and a host of others!

For a while Svaroff recaptured the happy enthusiasm of his boyhood—if only he were forty years younger he would go to sea. The freshness, the freedom—what had the land to offer in comparison?

A smart-looking tug was coming up on the left, and as it reached the jetty it moved slowly round in order to take in tow a large, clumsy-looking barge. Vladimir watched with interest the throwing out and hauling in of the ropes—the final lashing, stern end on, of the bulky-looking craft. As the two passed him he noticed the name of the barge—*The Anna*.

How many years was it since he had thought of his mother, and how many years since she had died? Ten, at least. And how far had he been responsible for her comparatively early death? He preferred not to think. After all, her complaint had been a common one and she might have died in any case.

For a while Vladimir brooded over the mystery of mother-love—the amazing courage, the self-sacrifice, the humility, yes, and the pride—the pride that would never give up hope, so long as life lasted, in the child of her love. He had, in imagination, often likened himself to St. Augustine and his mother to St. Monica, though the latter had been of far sterner and less compromising stuff than had Anna.

The gangway rocked with the moving of the water caused by the passing vessel, and as it passed to the right of him, his attention was attracted by the huge, moving crane, from which a large, square package was being lowered to the boat below. The package was safely deposited, the rope drawn up, and yet another and yet another package deposited. Could it be tea?

But the place was surely a granary wharf? It might be several things. How rhythmically the whole thing worked. How in unison were the men. Their movements had, somehow, almost the leisurely activity of an ordered dance; there was cheerfulness mingled with their toil; there was grace in their movements. The name of the boat was *The Perth.*

Vladimir watched them for quite a long time. There is always a tremendous fascination in watching others work, especially when their movements are rhythmical and please the eye. Hence, perhaps, the crowds, which, no matter how hot or how cold the weather, one can always see looking on at the repairing of a road. Again the gangway rocked, the water began to move more swiftly, and he realised that the tide was coming in. He must have stood there nearly an hour! Well what matter? He felt better—and in some subtle way he felt cleaner. But if he stayed there much longer he would be courting attention, the one thing at the moment he wished to avoid.

He retraced his steps up Thames Place, turning to his left up Three Colt Street and from thence into the gardens of St. Anne's Church.

Again he was struck by the peacefulness of it all. A few old men, shabbily dressed, were resting on the garden seats; they were smoking clay pipes, and they looked quite contented. To the left of him, as he faced the entrance to the church, was a memorial of some kind: the figure of Christ, considerably above life-size, held up the right hand in blessing. Almost it seemed to Vladimir for a moment that the figure saluted him in Eastern fashion. The thought of returning to his Bloomsbury lodgings became suddenly distasteful to him. Why not have a look round the church—there was sure to be some good carving, and it would help to kill time? Vladimir entered almost with the feelings of a trespasser. It was so many years since he had entered a church. Two or three little girls, children, were kneeling before a side altar. That is unusual, he thought. Are they asking for some special toy? After a very little while they got up, and taking some picture-books from an adjoining set of shelves, began to read. They looked a happy little group.

He wandered round, looking in leisurely fashion at the wonderful carvings. The pulpit was especially fine. There were roses, lilies, thistles and wheat.

In the centre of one of the roses the old craftsman had actually carved a bee. Here was realism with a vengeance; but how different to the modern travesty which goes by that name! The artist (whose name has not come down to us) had even carved on the insect the two sets of wings, one superimposed on the other, and by making one set a little longer, had cleverly suggested their transparency.

The left top wing of the insect was missing: perhaps it had been too often handled, perhaps it was due to the delicacy of the work! Vladimir wondered how many besides himself had noticed that touch of conscientious realism and exquisite artistry. He wandered round the church and he wandered out.

What should he do now? Perhaps, after all, he had best return.

Once again in Commercial Road, a familiar sign caught his eye—two large interlaced triangles. What was the hexagram doing there? But in an instant the writing below stood out boldly: "The Synagogue of the Congregation of the Sons of Jacob." "How queer," thought Svaroff, "of all the many odd places I have been into I have never yet been to a synagogue."

226

He pulled his hat yet lower over his eyes, slightly raised and stiffened his shoulders in Oriental fashion, and crossing the road, quietly entered the building. Inside, profound disappointment seized him. The place was dull and gloomy—it differed scarcely at all from the meeting-houses of his boyhood. Save for the talliths of the men and the brighter dresses of the women (stout specimens of which looked down upon him from the gallery), there was little to distinguish it from a Nonconformist chapel. There was no chancel, altar or steps, but at one end of the room was a raised dais and a squarish box, representing presumably the Ark of the Scroll of the Law.

He had not time to notice further, for the old beadle had seen him and, noticing he was a stranger and well dressed, had courteously come up and asked if he would not "go up" and "read the praises of our Father?"

Svaroff recoiled as though he had been stung; for a moment he was once again a boy of twelve, listening to the talk of his father with the Rabbi Elhanan. What had he not been guilty of since then! The old man noticed the movement, but misread the cause.

"Goy?" he asked. There was a slight touch of hauteur in his voice. "I understand, but it is not usual——"

Vladimir did not wait for the finish of the sentence; once again he was out in the street. Almost as a man pursued by demons he crossed the road.

"Strange," murmured the Jew. "The man was as ill at ease in the House of God as the Bee in the honey-pot: attracted by the sweetness in spite of the danger, yet, once inside, anxious, above all things, to get out. Very strange!" And he thought on the matter more than once that evening.

✳

Meanwhile, in search of distraction, Vladimir wandered through Watney Street and Watney Market.

He was restless and *distrait*, dissatisfied with life and with himself. He watched the crowd buying and selling, caught here and there a joke with accompanying burst of good tempered laughter, heard the excited shouts of children at play—all the world appeared to be happy save himself.

Up and down the street he wandered in and out among the stalls. Returning up the street for the second time, the church of St. Margaret, set a little way back and midway amongst the market stalls, caught his eye. He noticed the ultra-modern lettering on the notice-board, and also that the door was open. He wandered in. It was a cheerful place; judging by the number of candles and side pictures, decidedly ritualistic. The ceiling was blue and white plaster, after the style of St. Anne's though less magnificent than the latter.

Again he noticed three little girls playing in a corner.

Perhaps they were there to prevent stealing, perhaps to prevent other wrong uses of the empty church.

Anyway it was a good idea, who ever had thought of it, and seemingly it was peculiar to East End.

As a firm believer in the influence of Place through the means of auras and vibrations, it was likely, he thought, to have quite a good effect on their infant minds. Decidedly a good idea.

One other thing he noticed—the amazing cleanness of the scrubbed boards. In the midst of so rough a neighbourhood, such cleanness bordered on the occult.

The occult! Ah, therein perhaps lay the solution to the riddle. Perhaps the vicar of the place was that very rare thing amongst Anglican clergy—a mystic?

Vladimir came out of the church and walked quickly towards Commercial Road. As he was nearing the end of the street he became aware of hurried footsteps behind him.

Automatically he turned round, to be greeted by a young man dressed in grey, and wearing a strange-coloured orange tie. From the pale, subtly remote face of the young man looked out the eyes of Strickland. "Mystic and psychic if ever there was one, even as he was," thought Svaroff; "also, unless I am much mistaken, an artist and 'modern.'"

"Did you wish to speak to anyone?" said the youth. "I'm from the Vicarage; I thought perhaps that——"

"No," answered Svaroff, "I was only in search of local colour." ("A curious boy," he thought; "lonely as I myself—that, perhaps, is why he followed me.") "Oh," said the youth, "I'm sorry," and he seemed literally to melt away, for he was there one minute and gone the next. Most probably he disappeared amongst the crowd, but to Vladimir the little incident had the unreality, the peculiar quality and strange flavour, of a dream.

He turned back again into Watney Street, walked to the other end and this time entered the Polish Church.

The usual odour of stale incense, mildew and old calf, assailed his nostrils. The place was dimly lit and he noticed a profusion of the usual tawdry statues, only here they seemed more tawdry than usual. There was, however, a definite power in the place. Vladimir felt, as he had always felt in Catholic churches, as though unseen eyes were watching him; he also felt faintly unwell.

"Why on earth don't they ventilate the place?" he thought irritably—he did not like the vague feeling of fear following on a sense of the supernatural that was slowly creeping over him.

It was nearing six o'clock, the time for Saturday confessions. He noticed on the left of him, some little way below the altar of the Sacred Heart, a confessional box. A light was burning inside—obviously the good Father was waiting.

For the first time that day an impish feeling took possession of Svaroff. He thought of the story of the Sailor and the Nun.

Why shouldn't he give the father-confessor a confession that was a confession—something to make the good man sit up.

He would; it could do no harm, and it might (who knows if there were not some truth in these things) even do good.

Without a moment's hesitation Vladimir entered the confessional.

Instantly the light went out and he found himself in complete darkness. Then, only, did he realise the hardihood of his action. He had taken the plunge; he would have to see it through. Not to do so would savour too much of cowardice.

Before he was aware of it, perhaps through force of old habit, he was on his knees, his head level with the grill. As yet he could see nothing; then he was conscious that the priest was pronouncing the blessing. The whispered words falling eerily on his ears seemed to have in the darkness some strange mantric quality. Instinctively he bowed his head. It was as though some unseen Power were bending over him, wrapping him in, protecting him—but it was a power from which he shrank. The sound ceased and Svaroff looked up.

Then it all came back to him, the familiar surroundings of a confessional. The crucifix near his head, the grating of perforated zinc, and beyond it, dimly outlined, the white coat of the priest with its two dark strips down the middle—the purple stole, of course. The face was hidden by a hand on which the head rested, but the ear was near the grating. It was several seconds before Svaroff had taken all this in, and it was not surprising, therefore, to find that the head on the other side of the grill turned a little, and he was brought back to a remembrance of where he was and what he was there for, by a whispered question:

"And how long is it since your last confession?"

It was distinctly a young voice. This, because of his own years, made Svaroff very uncomfortable, but in a way it helped to strengthen his perversity. He would give this fledgling something to think about.

"Thirty-three years," he answered casually. He paused. Again there came a whispered question: "And since then?"

My God, what hadn't he done since then?

Svaroff felt himself grow suddenly hot as a ghostly memory protruded itself. He was glad his face could not be seen. He spoke in a very low voice:

"Years ago—I was practicing magic—I killed an animal in a particularly cruel and horrible fashion. I do not know what devil obsessed me at the time—actually I am very fond of animals."

"How often has this happened?"

"Only once, thank Heaven."

From the other side of the grill came a slight sigh of relief.

He is probably fond of animals, thought Svaroff; perhaps he has a cat of his own. Again a hot wave of shame swept over him.

"Yes? And then?"

"It was in India. I was leading a mountaineering expedition. I sent two natives to what I knew would be their death. They were fine men, but not sufficiently amenable to discipline. I sent them ahead with some baggage; it was 19,000 feet above sea-level—they perished in the snow. I gave it out they had deserted. No questions were asked."

Again Svaroff was silent. Confessing was a difficult business, he reflected. If only the priest would make some comment. His very passivity was throwing Svaroff back upon himself. For the first time he was facing squarely the mirror he had so often held up to others, and the image he was seeing was not a pleasant one.

"And what else can you remember?" came the gentle reminder.

"Oh, well, I've had lots of relations with women, both married and single," he said, with affected carelessness.

"I can't remember how many, but I'm not quite the Don Juan some persons would make me. If the women were but an episode in my life, I equally was but an episode in theirs." He paused, then hurriedly continued, "There was one, however, who was different. She was the cause of my divorce."

"Yes?" said the priest encouragingly.

"She was a Polish Jewess—very beautiful. She had hair like the tawny mane of a lion and the shy, wild eyes of a nymph. Her——"

"Do not tell me her name—and there is no need for description."

"She was sixteen years of age when I met her," continued Svaroff, "and had been most carefully brought up. I made love to her. I was the first man she had ever known. One day I took her out and gave her too much wine. The poor child was not used to it. The usual thing happened."

"Did you promise her marriage?"

"I suppose so; one usually does in such cases."

The priest slightly shifted his position.

"And then?"

"There was a child, a boy—I had it registered in my name—I wished to adopt it. I offered to care for it and for the girl if she would leave her people and live with me. She refused to do so, so I abandoned them both. She and her people were proud; they did not sue me."

"Did you offer to marry her?"

"I was already married. But to be honest, I had not thought about it. I wanted the boy. My wife got to hear of it and she brought a divorce."

"Did you subsequently inquire after the girl's welfare?"

"I did not. She had refused my offer. I was not interested further. Later I heard that she had married. After the way I had treated her she never could have loved me."

Svaroff had entered the confessional in a spirit of jest; by tensely slow degrees he had become increasingly serious. "What troubles me most," he said, "is the thought of the boy.

If he chanced to resemble his father, life must indeed have presented many difficulties."

"I should not worry too much about that," said the priest soothingly. "Is there anything else?"

Svaroff paused for a moment.

"For years," he said, "under the guise of spiritual instruction I exploited the weaknesses of young men and women, I placed temptation in their way, and I despised them when they fell."

A great weariness had suddenly come over him. For twenty-four hours he had not eaten and for days he had not slept. "I can't of think of anything more," he said. "Of course I've told the usual lies and have been dishonest like the rest of the world—on occasion I've given way to great anger—but those are the memories which stand out. I'm an outcast from God and man—it is not necessary to tell me."

He spoke with great bitterness.

To his surprise the young priest talked very sensibly.

He reminded him it was the end of a man's life that counted, not the beginning or the middle.

"The great thing," he said, "is always to rise up, no matter how often one may have fallen. To look forward always, never to dwell among the shadows of the past. To make a more frequent use of the channels of grace that are ever open, to come more often to confession. Remember that the orphan is God's special care. The son need not have been taught to despise the memory of his father." He spoke cheeringly and hopefully. "Say for your penance three Our Father's and one Hail Mary once a day for the next week, and renew your act of contrition."

Svaroff endeavoured to collect his thoughts, but found instead that he was listening to the absolution.

The priest's voice had a note of triumph in it as it rose in the middle. . . . "*Deinde absolvo te a peccatis tuis in nomine*

Patris et Filii et Spiritus Sancti. Amen. Go in peace, and pray for me."

So, it was over. It had not really been so very bad. If only he could believe. He felt none of the exaltation that is said to follow on a good confession, but, on the whole, he felt better.

Why not give the thing a trial—at least as good a trial as he would give to a magical experiment?

He came out of the confessional and knelt down.

He repeated the three "Our Fathers," and had reached the "Hail Mary" when a sound broke the stillness.

A small boy in a cassock, and wearing large hob-nailed boots which rattled noisily on the marble of the chancel floor, had entered from the left and was beginning to light the six large candles in preparation for Benediction. At the same time the priest was coming out of the confessional; as he did so he switched on the light.

For a moment Svaroff felt his heart beat widely, then stand strangely still. Over the door of the confessional he saw his own name in capital letters: FR. VLADIMIR SVAROFF. The young man leaving was as the early, unspoiled image of himself.

As a man in a dream he rose unsteadily to his feet. Drawn by a force he felt powerless to resist, and with the wooden steps of a sleep-walker, he followed the young priest up the aisle.

CHAPTER XX

IRIS was working on her third book of poems. She looked out of the window at the typical English sky and sighed wearily. Really, she thought, it's about time I had a holiday; Heaven knows I need one. Since the end of the War she had devoted herself entirely to literature. Five years of deadly reviewing, the translation of a philosophical work by an eminent French author, the writing of a number of articles on out-of-the-way subjects, plus the writing of an equal number of short stories, had left her very little time for outdoor amusement, and practically none for outdoor exercise. Her small army pension did not permit of the luxury of a maid, and, in American parlance, she did all her own "chores."

"Something will have to be done very soon," she reflected, "or I shall go all to pieces."

It was over twelve years since the day she had last seen Svaroff, and she had seldom thought of him since. A couple of years ago she had heard that he was in London, and had also heard that he had altered considerably both in appearance and in other ways, but he had not troubled to look her up and she made no further inquiries concerning him. Perhaps if she continued to "peg away" just a little bit longer she would receive sufficient recognition to make that that long-desired holiday an accomplished fact.

She had been saying this to herself for some considerable time past; and it seemed just as far away as ever.

She sighed again; then, opening a strange-looking Chinese box, lighted a cigarette.

She thought of the reviews of her last book of poems. They had been excellent, and there had been no log-rolling, no reviewing by friends or acquaintances, celebrated or otherwise, to whom she might have kow-towed or "toaded." That perhaps, was really the trouble. She never could or would kow-tow or "toady"; neither could she pretend to admire what she did not. Hence, to the public at large, she was still unknown—yet, despite this, she had much for which to feel thankful, she reflected.

She had been acclaimed by the foremost London Monthly as being "in a front place among her contemporaries." Another eminent Monthly had said of her work, "Gold, from a true mint, reacting rightly to all the tests—she has yet to come into her own."

Another had stated that her work was "comparable in excellence to that of Tennyson or Shelley."

"Without writing an essay," the reviewer had said, "it was difficult to appraise this book aright. It is work of enduring worth that anyone who reads will never forget."

That review, she had been told, was by a young Cambridge graduate, but she had never asked his name.

What had *The Imperial* Review said? "She is a mystic, as true poets should be. . . The book shows an unusual range of thought, and is free from the jolting obscurities which seem to make some modern reputations."

"Modern reputations, aye, there's the rub," as Shakespeare would have said. Therein, perhaps, lay the solution to the whole riddle. She loathed modernity with her whole heart and soul. Why, she had not even cut her hair!

She got up and walked across to the mirror. Was she so very different to the young men and women around her? She supposed she must be! That, perhaps, was why they showed so little sympathy and even less understanding. How awful if she were really getting old and were beginning to look it!

Like all persons who have an intense love of the beautiful, the thought of old age and all that it conjured up was almost terrifying to her. She looked at her reflection in the mirror, then suddenly smiled. No, she had nothing to worry about at present. She was certainly rounder than she had been twelve years ago; her features had lost the absolute childishness that they possessed, and, the whole face had gained considerably in strength but she still looked young. "I've never been to a beauty parlour in my life! I don't make up! I've never tinted, hennaed, or touched up my hair, and I hope that I never shall. When the time comes that I am really old, I hope I shall have I sufficient stoicism to accept the fact bravely. But I mustn't get fatter—it simply won't do!".

She wandered round the studio. On all sides of it she saw portraits of herself—delightful studies by Blitzen, done just before the War.

What a serious, dreamy-looking little thing she looked in most of them. What frail wistfulness was there—what intangible mystery! Had she really been as beautiful as that, or was it just Blitzen's idolatry; had he always seen her through rose-coloured glasses? She wondered.

In one of the portraits she was like a Florentine youth— most persons took her for a Rossetti. In another, the only portrait in which she was smiling, a roguish little face with dancing, half-closed eyes, looked out from beneath a cockaded tricorner hat.

What an artist the world had lost in Blitzen!

But she had no thought that he had ceased to be.

Somewhere, in some other world, he was still painting— she felt sure of it—but it was on a larger canvas and with goodlier colours.

She returned to the divan, curled herself up and continued writing.

"How on earth you can write lying down passes my understanding," Blitzen had once said to her.

"I have to do all my thinking walking up and down the room or else tearing along the street."

"I know," she had laughingly replied; "but you forget that I'm a quarter Oriental; I suppose that blood always tells. Not only do I prefer to write lying down, but I prefer to eat lying down. I like my meals reclining on a couch, Eastern and Roman fashion." "Little sybarite," he had answered.

She smiled to herself at the recollection; still the same old habits, she thought.

A ring at her bell, and a letter by the four o'clock post. It was from Newton, of all people—Newton whom she had not heard of since 1914. She wondered what he could want?

The letter was from a place in Sussex, and was dated 4th August.

"Dear I. H."—it ran (in the same spidery scrawl as of yore)—"Salutation and all good wishes to you. Can you come down for the week-end, or longer if possible? Quite a lot of famous persons are anxious to meet you. We also would greet thee.

"Congratulations on the 'pomes'—you know you really are a poet—'et ill Arcadia ego—so we can say it with confidence. By the way, I am married I forgot that—you'll have to meet L.; she's heard all about you and wants to. Meet you, I mean, of course.—Thine ever,

"Benjamin."

"And some persons say there's nothing in telepathy," Iris remarked as she laid down the missive.

"It's true I wasn't thinking of Newton, but here am I, badly wanting a holiday, and here comes an invite. Well, I'm for accepting." And without further ado she answered the letter.

She decided to travel down by motor-coach from Victoria Station in order to see more of the country, and on the following Friday morning found herself comfortably ensconced on a front seat of one of the Southdown Coaches.

They went down Sloane Street and King Road, Chelsea, first, then through a number of mean looking little streets in Fulham and Hurlingham. It seemed some considerable time before they reached Putney Bridge, and Iris gave a sigh of relief as she saw the stretch of familiar water, with its beached boats and wide sweep of trees on the right, and on the left the little old church with its sundial and well-known motto, "Time and tide wait for no man." A few more minutes and they had passed Putney Common and Putney Heath, then Richmond Common, and so through the town of Richmond.

Once out of Richmond, past the Star and Garter Hotel, and one had the first intimations of the country. The trees met over the road, and soon there were woods on either side. The landscape in the distance reminded Iris of the panoramic views seen through ivory pen-holders and such-like—the occasional finds of her childhood. They passed Kingston Canal, dark green and sleepy-looking, with overhanging trees and clusters of daisies on the banks then past the Thames on the right, like another broad canal, and they were definitely in Surrey.

She noted the beautifully kept gardens on the Upper Brighton Road and the scarlet poppies by the roadside. There had been at intervals through the day sharp showers of rain, and it gave a vividness of colour to the massed flowers and heavily foliaged trees.

Leatherhead at last! and then, what wooded slopes and glorious trees and hedges! Great clumps of giant pines, and mighty beech trees on either side; then Boxhill on the left, clean and sparkling after the rain; more wooded banks, and at last her first real sigh of the Downs, with Chanctonbury Ring like a dark-green *beret* perched on top. She got out not far from Washington—surely the loveliest spot in the whole of lovely Sussex—and, following a signpost, walked across the Downs in a southerly direction.

How fresh and beautiful everything looked, and what a clean salt tang was in the air! And to add the last touch to perfection a wonderful rainbow appeared, spanning in a great curved arch from hill to hill like a jewelled bridge of the immortals, the delicate sevenfold colours made softer and clearer by contrast with the dark grey of the clouds and the darker green of the trees, belts of which ringed the slopes or clustered in the hollows. . . .

For the first time in many months Iris felt radiantly happy. She walked with an elastic step over the springy turf, stopping now and then to admire a blue-mauve scabious or to smell the small wild thyme.

By the time she reached Ivy Cottage, the place of her destination, she had quite a collection of gay wild flowers tucked in her blouse and tickling her chin. She had also for companion a delightful black-and-white sheep-dog, which, as though reading her thoughts, had run on in front of her, every now and then returning to show her the way.

Altogether the day had started admirably.

A straggling, unkept garden, such as she loved, in which roses, tiger-lilies and gladioli struggled for the mastery with mauve daisies, sweet-briar, jasmine and honeysuckle, surrounded a charming old-world cottage on the walls of which the ivy struggled with the vine.

What a wonderful place, she thought, as she walked up the path preceded by the friendly tail-wagging dog. "Hello I. H.!" called a voice. "So *that's* where Nell had got to, was it? Bad dog to go without its collar! In you go, you old reprobate," and a wild-haired figure, half smothered in downland clay, with a three days' growth of beard on his chin, and much grass and bracken sticking to the rumpled clothes and still more rumpled head, raced down the steps to meet her, kissing her effusively on both cheeks. "It's good that you were able to come," said the trampish-looking person with much friendliness.

So this was Newton?

"You've hardly altered one bit!" she said, with well-feigned candour.

"Neither have you," he answered, stopping to view her admiringly. "Still as beautiful as ever, I. H.! You've *expanded* in some ways, shall we say, but it's definitely an improvement. In the old days you were just too aetherially thin. The old Guru and I used to vow we could blow you round the studio."

"I guess you couldn't do that now," said Iris, laughing.

"No," said Newton, and he smiled rapturously.

"Ah! Here comes Laetitia," he said; "nice old-world name, isn't it? just fits in with the cottage and garden—what?" And Iris was introduced to Mrs. Newton.

He talks of her just as though she were part of the furniture, she thought; how funny men are! But she liked Laetitia, and seemingly Laetitia liked her, at least she said so.

They went indoors and Iris was taken up to her room, where further pleasant surprises awaited her. Three lovely looking cats and two adorable Persian kittens walked purringly to meet her, and the room itself was all that could be desired.

There were casement windows along two sides of it, through which one had a glorious view of the Downs, and the room was charming. Soft grey in colour, with lovely old-world prints upon the walls.

The modern furniture was simple and harmonious and there was an electric switch above her bed and plenty of electric lights; but the cottage itself was Early Jacobean and genuine at that.

"I don't like old places," Mrs. Netwon confided, "so I insisted on having every modern convenience. I've electric lighting everywhere, Hoovers to do the cleaning and, of course, a telephone. Only one thing that I've been barred and that's a wireless and gramophone." She spoke rather regretfully, as though the latter were a definite loss.

"Personally," said Iris, "I adore old places, and I shouldn't have a telephone though I know they are convenient. As to gramophones and wireless, if you lived in Chelsea you would soon realise that they are an invention of the devil."

The two of them laughed. Then, "I expect you'll want to be left for a little," said Laetitia; "tea will be ready in a quarter of an hour. I'm sure you must be dying for some. I hope you have everything you want. Doris is a good girl, but young, barely sixteen—I'm training her; occasionally she forgets things."

"Everything is perfect," said Iris, "and it was most awfully sweet of you to have asked me down."

"Now I've seen you, I'm sure we shall get on," was the answer, "but it's more than can be said for some of Taddy's friends. Before I'd seen you I'll admit I was distinctly nervous, but I liked you at first sight, and I always go by first impressions."

"How strange! So do I," said Iris, and she smiled again. "By the way, who is Taddy?" she asked.

"Taddy? Oh! That's Benjamin. Newt is the short for Newton. Taddy's a sort of newt. I called him it for fun once, and the name has stuck ever since, but I seemed to know you so well that I took it for granted you'd know—one feels that way with some people. Curious, isn't it?"

"Very," said Iris, as she turned to open her suitcase, and turning to speak again, found herself alone.

"She's not pretty," she said to herself as she brushed her hair before the mirror; "far too much like a Creole; but she has a very dainty little figure, not too thin, and most definitely she has charm. I like her, and I'm sure I'm going to enjoy my stay here." She washed her hands and face, changed from her travelling-dress and went downstairs.

They had tea in the oak-raftered room that looked on to the front garden, seated on Jacobean chairs at a gate-legged table, with a fine old spinet in the corner and pewter jugs gleaming above the settle. Laetitia had not had her way altogether in the matter of furnishing, it would seem. They were joined early in the meal by the three cats, who had the most excellent table manners, each keeping to his or her chair, and awaiting their milk and cake with the feline resignation born of true cat-aristocracy and blue-blooded Persian ancestry, but the kittens rolled and tumbled on the hearth-rug, as is the way with kittens all the world over.

After tea Laetitia excused herself, as she had some accounts to settle, and Newton took Iris for a short walk.

"We'll go over, to-morrow," he told her. "I'm half expecting some people to-morrow or we'd go then, and its possible my cousins may be coming. Claude plays, and Desmond is quite clever in his way. He had a rotten time in the War and has not got over it yet. I was lucky—got invalided out very early—blood poisoning," he explained; "that's why I shave so seldom." They talked of books, then of *The Hieroglyph* and Iris reminded him of the funny sayings and doings of that time.

"By Jove, how you bring it all back; marvellous times they were weren't they? What a memory you must have!" And for a moment it seemed to Iris as though she were listening to the ghostly voice of Svaroff speaking at her first visit.

"Yes. I sometimes wish I hadn't," she said.

"But all this is history; we're making it," pursued Newton with cheerful egotism. "You ought to write it up."

"Do you really think so?"

"I do," he answered seriously.

"Well, perhaps I will some day," she answered. "I've certainly met some rather strange persons."

"The things that have happened," said Newton, "nobody knows, nobody ever will know! They're unbelievable, some of them; why, I've lived at least six separate lives since this, my last incarnation, and I dare say you'd have quite a lot to tell if you chose to."

He looked out into the distance, and for a while they walked on in silence, each busy with their separate thoughts.

Would she have much to tell? thought Iris; not so very much. There had been for a time a very pleasant friendship with Hildebrand, the publisher. Nearly three years it had lasted, and then one evening he had proposed to her. After that she had never seen him again, and a year later he had died, and on precisely the same day as Blitzen. She realised, too late, that she need not have kept away—she had suffered from ultra-sensitiveness. But she could never have married Hildebrand. Friendship was one thing, but marriage was far too intimate a relationship. He had said he would be happy simply with her companionship, and she had always liked to talk to him, but would any man, least of all a Jew, have really been satisfied with just that? Yet! perhaps, after all, she had misjudged him. She hoped that now, at least, he would be able to understand the reason of her silence.

Then she had met Hanbury Haines, a man twenty-five years her senior, and for a while had placed him on the highest of high pedestals. Hanbury was a barrister, a clever writer, and, as she subsequently found to her cost, a finished rogue and scoundrel. He was also a very fine actor—that, probably, should have been his vocation—and for the best part of a year he had completely taken her in. But she had soon found out that he was both a liar and a coward and, having done so, had ceased to care. She could never love where she despised. In this respect she was assuredly more fortunate than the average woman, who seemed quite able to love what she knew and admitted to be contemptible.

Women were queer creatures, she reflected.

But the disillusionment with Hanbury had marked a turning-point in her life. Up to that time she had trusted implicitly the persons of her own class; she had imagined that no gentleman ever told a lie and as to his being a coward, why, the very thought would have been ludicrous to her (only louts and cads told lies and were cowardly); now, well nothing would ever really surprise her. The child ready to worship where she loved, and to trust where she worshipped, had been cruelly slain. She could never rise to life again.

Yet there had been no common physical union with Hanbury; her natural fastidiousness had once again proved her safeguard in that direction as it had in the others. How a thousand times that had been fortunate.

After that she had taken to writing again.

"No," she said, in answer to Newton's last remark, "I might have had quite a lot to tell had I acted differently in some respects, but my life for the last ten years has been singularly uneventful. I've felt a tremendous lot, far too much perhaps, but that hardly makes history except for myself. If supper is at seven and L. is so punctual, and we are returning by the longer way, oughtn't we to be going back?"

"I suppose we ought," said Newton.

CHAPTER XXI

IRIS went to bed early that night, and she spent the greater part of next morning lazing in the garden, playing with the cats and alternately reading Newton's poems. He was too fond of affected words, she decided, and that spoilt much that was otherwise excellent! What sane English person in the twentieth century ever talked of "coolth" and "spilth"? And Newton, being entirely foreign, prided himself on his knowledge of English; evidently (like certain savages in the matter of medicine) he fixed on a word for its rarity and unusual flavour!

In the afternoon the cousins came to tea. Claude was the exact antithesis of Benjamin, neat and dapper in his person almost to a fault, but essentially suave and cosmopolitan in his talk and manner; and he played the violin remarkably well. Desmond was sensitive and retiring. Iris had the feeling that he ought to be petted, like a rather pathetic child whom the world has used ill, and this, as she subsequently learned, had actually been the case. The five of them spent a very pleasant evening together, but in spite of much pressing the cousins refused to stay.

"We may see you later at the Haven," Claude explained. "We're going there very shortly for some sun-bathing."

"Good," said Newton, and they made their farewells

"Well, how do you like them?" he asked, after they had gone.

"Very much," Iris replied. "I don't know why, but I felt intensely sorry for Desmond—he's been hurt quite a lot, hasn't he?"

"Quite a lot, and in more ways than one. He quite took to you, by the way."

"Did he? I'm glad of that. But tell me about the Haven. Where and what is it? Everyone seems to be talking about it, and I feel rather out of things."

"Well," said Newton, "it's a sort of informal colony where everyone does as they like, and where, so far, the law hasn't interfered. They're mostly artists and writers who go there, but occasionally one finds a Philistine; however, they seldom stay long, so it's quite all right—the Philistines, I mean."

"Oh! A sort of garden city place? *à la* Letchworth?"

"Heaven forbid! The Haven's the *Haven!* You'll understand when you've once been there," said Newton proudly.

Evidently the Haven was much to his liking. Iris looked across at Laetitia for confirmation.

"It's a rotten place," said the latter simply, "but if it pleases you to go, Mr. Benjamin, go by all means. I'm going to a dance at Hove; much more fun."

"*Chacun à son goût. De gustibus non disputandum.*" was the mixed and somewhat sententious answer.

"We're the exact opposites," he explained to Iris, "that's why we get on so well. She"—referring to his wife—"hates poetry, and I detest dancing, so there's no competition."

"One poet in a household is quite enough," said Laetitia; "*someone* must do the cooking and keep the place clean, how otherwise should we exist? I often wonder how I do it, but I do!"

"I think you are marvellous," Iris said, and she meant it.

✳

On Sunday morning, as arranged, she set out with Newton across the Downs. She was returning to town in the evening, and had determined to get as much walking as she could while the fine weather lasted.

It was a lovely day, with a fresh wind blowing from the sea—some five miles off, feathery clouds sailing overhead in a sky of deepest blue, and great masses of gorse and purple heather dotting both hill and hollow.

Iris told Newton of some of her early experiences when she had seemed to leave her body at times and had sensed the spirit of Nature as some great beneficent being. One feels it here very much, she said "the brooding calm of the Vast Countenance filling the heavens—vast forms upon the horizon, majestic, godlike. Don't you think so?"

"I do," he answered. "I know exactly what you mean. It is the spirit of the old gods. They are very powerful here, yet. It will be some time before civilisation drives them out; but it is doing its best. Look at that!" and he pointed to a hideous steel construction which broke the beautiful line of the hills.

"Why, they're everywhere!" said Iris. "What is it?"

"Something to do with the electric cables," he answered. "We protested, those of us who cared. But what can we do? We were out-voted and here the abominations are, and there they'll stay, I suppose!"

Iris sighed with genuine depression. "How they must hate it," she said, "the grand old pagan gods, the true lords of the hills."

A light wind lifted the hair from her forehead and with an almost unconscious movement she opened her arms wide as though to embrace the unseen presences that filled the place. Upon her face and in her eyes was the rapt look of the mystic. She had forgotten that Newton was there.

"You ought to live in the country, I. H.," he said, and with a rush she came back to earth.

"I know; I was born in Sussex, and not so very far from here. That, I suppose, is why it tugs at me so. It almost hurts at times."

Newton looked grave.

"Why don't you try to find a cottage and do as I do?" he said.

"If my next book is a success, I shall," she said.

For a few minutes they walked on in silence, then Newton again spoke.

"The Haven is over the crest of the next hill, down in the hollow," he told her. "It's quite an interesting crowd that we'll be meeting. There'll be Reginald Mayflower and Gerald Carteret and the great Clarissa—Clarissa Montague Jones."

"What names to conjure with!" said Iris laughing. "What do they do, all these people?"

"Bower writes, Gerald's a journalist, and Clarissa paints— futurist wallpapers and house decorating, I believe."

"I see," said Iris.

And now they had reached the crest of the hill and were looking down on the Haven, the outskirts of which they had reached.

A profound disappointment seized Iris.

Why, it's just like a gipsy encampment, she thought, but without the occasional picturesqueness of the latter.

Mean-looking huts were scattered about haphazard; the gardens, in many cases, were mere refuse heaps, and there was no attempt at any sort of order.

"Hullo, Benjamin!" called a girl's voice, and a hefty-looking wench, wearing shorts, no stockings, and a blouse very much open at the neck, passed a little way below them on the hillside. She was carrying a collapsible bucket full of peeled potatoes; beside her walked another wench, similarly dressed, but with flaming red hair. The latter looked at Iris with open curiosity. Iris felt slightly annoyed.

"These people," she said to Newton, as soon as they were out of earshot, "make one feel as though one had gone to some morning performance in evening dress. Am I so very peculiar?"

"You look jolly nice," he said, viewing her white linen semi-nautical dress with evident approval, "but of course shorts and that sort of thing are the latest fad at present; they save laundry—and besides, being natives of the place, you're a sort of a foreigner to them.

"Why, there's Reggie!" he exclaimed, and from a distant hut a tall youth waved to them.

Newton hastened his pace, and soon he had reached the bottom of the hill.

"This," he said, turning to the youth, "is Reginald Mayflower, otherwise known as Evangeline—Eva for short."

Iris saw a loose-limbed, rather lanky-looking boy wearing a blazer of many colours. His face was girlish, he had a weak mouth, a weaker chin (and I'll swear his hair is permanently waved, she thought) but he had quite a good forehead.

"How do you do?" he said, holding out to Iris a limp, rather clammy hand. "I've been wanting to meet you for some time; I liked your last book of poems." He had a lazy, affected voice, and spoke with the soft, lispy drawl that she was beginning to associate with the would-be intellectuals of twenty or thereabouts.

"I'm glad you like it," she said, and thereupon lapsed into silence.

"Has Gerald come?" Newton said.

"Yes. He's just getting rid of his kit; I'll take you round by the other side," and Reginald piloted them skilfully round the hut and so in by another entrance.

"Do take your things off, as much as you like," he said; "if you've walked from the cottage, you'll want to, I expect; you'll be tired, I mean." Then, turning to Newton, "You know the geography of the place, so I'll leave you to make all the introductions," and he dashed out.

What an extraordinary young man, thought Iris, and turning she picked up a book from the window sill.

A tall figure darkened the doorway, and again Newton introduced her.

"Gerald Carteret," he said, "I believe there's really a 'de', but for some reason he's dropped it."

Iris looked up and for a minute was genuinely astonished, for she found herself facing the handsomest youth she had ever seen in her life.

He was tall, excessively slender, and graceful both in carriage and in build, and had features of a slightly Jewish cast. His tawny-hazel eyes were long, well set and heavily fringed; his ears small, well shaped and set high up on his small, well-shaped head, and his forehead was wide. His mouth was a vivid red, narrow, curved and slightly smiling; his teeth, white and even; but the strangest feature of all (that which gave character to the whole face) was the eye brows.

They were excessively dark and heavy, and came down in a great sweep, meeting at an angle of forty-five degrees above the bridge of the nose. There was about the face a faint look of unconscious arrogance and a definite power. He looked at Iris and she looked at him. There were few persons who looked at her squarely, like that; for a moment she felt that she was his sister.

Of whom did he remind her? Hadn't she cousins on her mother's side named Carteret? She remembered the family album and saw the strong family likeness. She told him about it.

"Then we must be third cousins," he said. For a moment his face lit up and he looked pleased, but almost at once it relapsed into its usual youthful unhappiness.

Lucifer, thought Iris, or is it Mephistopheles? It ought to be the former. His voice, when he spoke, had a slight lisp that was evidently the latest London fashion, but it was not so much affected as inexpressibly tired and very soft. She had the greatest difficulty in hearing what he said—altogether he intrigued her vastly.

Newton had temporarily vanished, so they talked together for quite a time. The boy was quietly dressed, she noted. He had ideas of his own, and seemed to have read a tremendous amount.

What could he be doing down at the Haven? Then she remembered his profession. He's in search of copy as well as amusement, she thought, but even Newton hasn't guessed. How funny!

And suddenly she laughed.

"What is it?" he asked.

"Why, none of them know why you're down here, but *I* do," and once again he smiled. She wished he would smile oftener; he looked so very much nicer when he did.

"You won't tell them?" he said, with boyish eagerness.

"Of course not," Iris answered; "besides, it would spoil everything if I did," and at this juncture Newton joined them with Reggie.

"Claude and Clarissa are coming down the hill," he said, "they'll be here in five minutes; sure you've got enough grub, Reggie?"

"Tons," was the answer.

"Very well, I'll help you to get things ready," and he wandered into the small kitchen.

"Can I help, too?" said Iris.

"Rather; I'd ask Gerald, but he never does anything."

"No. He supplies the necessary ornament," Iris said.

"Yes, he is rather wonderful; but, I say, won't you spoil your dress? You ought to have taken it off!"

"No, I oughtn't. I'm used to pottering," Iris answered.

"How frightfully keen they are on undressing," she thought amusedly. And then, it seemed, she was being introduced to Clarissa.

Clarissa was a tall, thin girl with platinum-blonde hair; round shouldered, and with long arms which hung loosely from her shoulders in ape fashion, and her dress was very short.

She had a round babyish face, a calculating mouth and good mathematical forehead. Her eyes were large and blue, and she made the most of them; now opening them wide in baby innocence, now looking intensely grave, but taking care always to keep them well in the view of the person to whom she was talking. Her voice was high pitched and very affected; her persistent habit of staring was almost hypnotic in its effect.

It was Clarissa who suggested they should lunch on the grass outside, and in a few minutes she was ordering Claude and Reggie about as though the place belonged to her; but Gerald, Iris noticed, kept carefully aloof, though more than once Clarissa tried to rope him in. Later she made every possible excuse to touch one or other of the men of the party, and was always, on the pretext of showing them a book or flower, getting them to look over her shoulder, or else leaning over theirs.

After a while Reggie broke away and Clarissa fastened on to someone else, and Iris, who had gone indoors from the heat, overheard the following conversation:

"I wish that wench would wear more underclothing; every time she leaned forward I could see right down to her waistline and it wasn't as if she's got a decent figure either," the speaker pursued in aggrieved tones. "Horrid little pointed things and nobs like great unripe raspberries; all out of proportion. Gerald detests girls—and I'm not surprised."

"Every sensible man hates women," said Gerald calmly, "they're such hypocrites for one thing—always pretending they want your friendship and yet angling for something else! Always trying to lead you on and yet always pretending they are not! They are never satisfied unless you make love to them, and even when you do they sometimes pretend to be shocked. I've *no* time for them—older women are much better, one *can* have a friendship with them."

"Don't you be so sure, my son!" was the answer. "I'm not an Adonis like yourself and I am not frightfully clever, but even I get pestered at times. What must you have put up with?"

"Nothing," was the answer. "I don't allow myself to be pestered. If I think they are getting troublesome I tell them I am married—that always works."

"By Jove, that's a great idea; I never thought of it."

Gerald smiled with an amused, languid grace. "Yes, but you don't blurt it out, not unless you *wish* to be rude. You just make some casual reference to it. 'When my wife and I were down at Mentone,' or whatever place is most likely to arouse her envy. It's quite simple. Try it and see."

"You must have had a lot of experience," said his friend admiringly. "What *haven't* you done, Gerald?"

"I've done *everything*," replied that youth, with the air of a conqueror.

"Nice boy," thought Iris. "He's not 'sexy' so I like him," but she had the greatest difficulty from laughing, and she dreaded lest they should enter the hut; for if they did, they were sure to know that she had overheard. Fortunately, they walked away, and a few minutes later Newton came in to know if she were all right.

"Yes, I'm cooler now," she replied. "What's happening next?"

"I am going to read *Attis*, my latest masterpiece," he replied, "and after that there'll be some nature dances. We shall all wear loincloths; it's the curse of custom to which we all bow, but it doesn't really interfere with one's movements. I can dance quite well in one," he said.

Iris stole a glance at Newton and saw that his face was perfectly grave. Did these people really take themselves seriously?

"Yes," she said, "but with loincloths there'd probably be more uniformity, and even the most pagan dance needs a little restriction, otherwise, of course, it's not a dance; and if the loincloths are all the same colour," she added quickly, "the general effect might be better."

Newton looked at her suspiciously, then seeing that she did not smile, "Well, we *had* thought of having different colours to represent the planets," he said, "but we couldn't get the stuff in time, so we've to be contented with white."

As he spoke, against the skyline in the distance Iris noticed a dark figure loosely garbed, and wearing a broad-brimmed hat. It appeared to be reading as it walked along.

"Who is that?" she asked.

"That," answered Newton almost savagely; "why, it's one of the monks from X! 'Rats in shovel hats' (he quoted disdainfully). How the old Guru hated them! It's lucky their eyes are always glued to some devotional work, or they'd soon have found an excuse for spoiling our innocent amusement."

There was a pause.

"I wonder where the old Guru is now?" he said at length.

"Are you speaking of Svaroff?" asked Reginald, who had just strolled up with Gerald.

"Yes," Newton answered; "you'd have liked him, Reggie."

"I expect I should. Why wasn't I born twenty years earlier? Just think of all that I've missed!" And friends echoed the sentiment.

"You've missed the War," said Iris dryly, and she noticed that Gerald winced.

Had she hit upon a sore spot? She felt sorry. She had no wish to hurt him.

"Where's Clarissa?" she asked.

"Preparing the stage," was the answer, and in a few minutes they all walked back and Newton read his masterpiece.

It was the sort of thing that minor poets bring out for private circulation amongst their friends, and was as minus any great idea as such productions usually are.

After adequate congratulations Newton retired to the hut, returning in a few moments with a number of hirsute sun-bathers fresh from their diurnal worship.

The dance followed. In lieu of tom-toms Iris was asked to bang a tea-tray. Reginald crowned himself with leaves and wore a leopard skin, Newton merely wore leaves and Claude played on a penny whistle. What did Gerald think and how would he describe them? He was leaning on one elbow, the picture of indolent grace, and was faintly smiling to himself.

Clarissa was most enthusiastic, "What a colour scheme, what a design for my autumn wallpaper. It would have been better if you had not broken up the line with those strips of white; but of course I shall leave that out," she added placidly.

Iris thought of the invocation of Isis in the days before the war—the genuine enthusiasm that had marked those times, the gay mirth, the irresistible humour.

What a difference! He had retained a certain careless good nature, it was true, but in other respects Newton had now become a mere poseur, a person who read *risqué* poems to a coterie of foolish admirers, a sad-faced jester who capered about with too little on.

A sudden tiredness seized her. "I'll really have to be going," she said, "or I'll miss the Southdown bus. My train goes soon after eight. Thanks most awfully." And she bade the group farewell.

As she crossed the road that skirted the Haven she saw again the figure in black. It was coming towards her, and soon it would be passing her. There was something about the walk and the set of the shoulders that seemed vaguely familiar. Where had she seen it before? She noticed the hand that held the breviary, and suddenly she remembered. Last time she had seen that hand, or one like it, it had been carrying a strangely carved ivory cane, and the little finger had been covered with a serpent ring.

The figure looked up, and their eyes met. The monk smiled.

"Is it Father or Brother Svaroff?" she said.

"We are all of us brothers," was the answer, with just a touch of amusement in the eyes.

He'll always be Svaroff wherever he is, she thought. Aloud she said, "I've a train to catch at eight o'clock. It is possible I may never see you again; may I ask you a few questions?"

"Certainly."

"Then we'll turn aside here," she said, "if you don't mind."

On their left was an unused orchard containing a number of dwarf apple trees, with here and there a cherry tree.

"I don't want to meet any of the Haven crew just now," she explained, as she led the way into the field. "Thank you, but the suit-case is quite light. May I be very crude and inquisitive?"

"If you like," was the smiling answer.

"What made you do it?" She had asked the question almost before she was aware, and at once realised how coarse and unfeeling it must sound.

But, if anything, the smile only deepened. Svaroff paused, as though debating within himself, then, "Do you remember Celia S.?" he asked.

"Wasn't she a pretty little thing with a mass of tawny hair?"

"Yes. And did you ever meet the boy, Vladimir?"

"Once, I think," she answered. "He was a very shy, sensitive child—much darker than his mother, wasn't he?"

"Yes."

Svaroff spoke slowly. "Three years ago I met that boy again and under the most extraordinary circumstances. I had not seen him for nearly twenty-five years, and had entirely ignored his existence. His mother was dead. I found he had taken holy orders some years before, and knowing what he did about his father, had never once ceased to pray for him since the day he had entered religion. I felt there must be something very powerful about a faith that could produce such forgiveness in one so cruelly wronged."

Iris was silent, and Svaroff continued almost as though to himself, "I had a long talk with the boy and it set me thinking. I realised that with no travel, with little or no education (as compared with that that I had received), he had yet got *something* which I had not—the very *something* for which I had been looking all my life, which I might yet find if I took the God-sent opportunity. I decided to put it to the test—and here I am! But there was another thing which helped me to decide. It was that that really first made me realise, I think."

"What was that?" said Iris.

"I realised that the boy had got the same *something* that you had got, that both you had 'arrived,' and I was still wandering, still searching.

"My pride had received a severe blow; at first I think, it was chiefly pride which set me upon the right road; but many roads lead to Rome and what matter the road if the pilgrim arrive?'

"My Yoga practices and other youthful austerities were now of help to me in the matter of discipline, and I took the plunge. After my varied career, it would have been useless for me to enter the secular priesthood. So that, in brief, is the whole story."

"Are you happy, Father Vladimir?" Iris asked.

"Do I look it?"

Iris studied him gravely. "I think you do," she said.

"In these days I am what I look," he answered.

They talked for a few minutes longer, and Iris then said good-bye.

"Pray for me, Father Vladimir," she said simply, as she took her departure; "perhaps I may need it more than you think."

"I will," he said, "and I remember *him* each day at the altar; indeed, I remember them all—though some of them wouldn't thank me for doing so," he added, with the old familiar chuckle. Yet there was a deep glow in his eyes as he unobtrusively made the holy sign.

"Good-bye, soror," he said, "and may God be with you."

"Good-bye, Father Vladimir."

Iris walked away quickly, feeling a strange lightness and warmth at her heart. Could this thing really be true or had she dreamed it? Half-way down the field on her way to the road she turned for a last look.

The sun was setting, a rosy glow was upon leaf and shrub, and the orchard seemed on fire with a strange, unearthly radiance.

Against a dwarf apple tree, whose branches grew in the form of a hierophantic cross, was Svaroff, and he was once more reading his office. The light touched the edges of his broad-brimmed hat, turning the large circle to a larger halo; his garments were surrounded by a roseate gleam, the tree was flashing, the whole sky seemed one immense flame. She thought of those exquisite lines of Fiona Macleod. How strangely apropos they were!

> "Lay me to sleep in sheltering flame
> O Master of the Hidden Fire;
> Wash pure my heart, and cleanse for me:
> My soul's desire.
> In flame of sunrise bathe my mind
> O Master of the Hidden Fire
> That when I wake, clear-eyed may be
> My soul's desire."

And from across the spaces of the years she seemed to hear the answer:

> "The silent voices of the Dawn
> Are waking round—Life is still—
> And Death in transport seems as Life,
> The Higher Servant of the Will.
> I know not if I die or live
> Or if I move or cease to be
> Save only that within my heart
> Lies love's untrammelled ecstasy?"

"He has found his haven," she said to herself softly, "Shall I ever find mine?"

AN AMAZING SECT

EDITOR'S NOTE

THE following are the three articles originally published in *The Looking Glass* and referred to in the twelfth chapter of the novel. They are unsigned but presumed to come from the pen of the paper's editor, West Fenton de Wend-Fenton. In later years Crowley was to claim that de Wend-Fenton had approached him for the purposes of blackmail prior to publication. They appeared on the 29th of October, 12th and 19th of November 1910, respectively.

Much of the details recounted in the third article—the "Rosicrucian Order" in question being of course the Hermetic Order of the Golden Dawn—were allegedly supplied by Samuel MacGregor Mathers, the *de facto* head of the Order, who had finally broken with Crowley after his many transgressions and nursed a grudge against him and Allan Bennett for publishing a set of kabbalistic correspondence tables hitherto reserved for acolytes of that society. That material eventually appeared as *Liber 777*.

AN AMAZING SECT I

WE propose under the above heading to place on record an astounding experience which we have had lately in connection with a sect styled the Equinox which has been formed under the auspices of one Aleister Crowley. The headquarters of the sect is at 124, Victoria Street, but the meeting or séance which we are about to describe, and to which after great trouble and considerable expense we gained admittance under an assumed name, was held in a private room in Caxton Hall.

We had previously heard a great many rumours about the practices of this sect, but we were determined not to rely on any hearsay evidence, and after a great deal of manoeuvring we managed to secure a card of admission, signed by the great Crowley himself. We arrived at Caxton Hall at a few minutes before eight in the evening—as the doors were to be closed at eight precisely—and after depositing our hat and coat with an attendant were conducted by our guide to a door, at which stood a rather dirty-looking person attired in a sort of imitation Eastern robe, with a drawn sword in his hand, who, after inspecting our cards, admitted us to a dimly lighted room heavy with incense. Across this room low stools were placed in rows, and when we arrived a good many of these were already occupied by various men and women, for the most part in evening dress. We noticed that the majority of these appeared to be couples—male and female. At the extreme end of the room was a heavy curtain, and in front of this sat a huddled-up figure in draperies, beating a kind of monotonous tom-tom.

When all the elect had been admitted the doors were shut, and the light, which had always been exceedingly dim, was completely extinguished except for a slight flicker on the "altar." Then after a while more ghostly figures appeared on the stage, and a person in a red hood, supported on each side by a blue-chinned gentleman in a sort of Turkish bath costume, commenced to read some gibberish, to which the attendants made responses at intervals. Our guide informed us that this was known as the "banishing rite of the pentogram."

More Turkish bath attendants then appeared, and executed a kind of Morris dance round the stage. Then the gentleman in the red cloak, supported by brothers Aquarius and Capricornus—the aforesaid blue-chinned gentlemen—made fervent appeals to the Mother of Heaven to hear them, and after a little while a not unprepossessing lady appeared, informed them that she was the Mother of Heaven, and asked if she could do anything for them. (She may be seen in the photograph on page 140 sitting on the chest of "the Master"—Mr. Crowley—and apparently endeavouring to perform some acrobatic feat.) They beg her to summon the Master, as they wish to learn from him if there is any God, or if they are free to behave as they please. The Mother of Heaven thereupon takes up a violin and plays not unskilfully for about ten minutes, during which time the room is again plunged in complete darkness. The playing is succeeded by a loud hammering, in which all the robed figures on the stage join, and after a din sufficient to wake the Seven Sleepers the lights are turned up a little and a figure appears from a recess and asks what they want. They beseech him to let them know if there is really a God, as, if not, they will amuse themselves without any fear of the consequences. "The Master" promises to give the matter his best attention, and, after producing a flame from the floor by the simple expedient of lifting a trap-door, he retires with the Mother of Heaven for "meditation," during which time darkness again supervenes. After a considerable interval he returns, flings aside a curtain on the stage, and declares that the space behind it is empty, and that there is no God. He then exhorts his followers to do as they like and make the most of this life. 'There is no God, no hereafter, no punishment, and no reward. Dust we are, and to dust we shall return." This is his doctrine, paraphrased. Following this there is another period of darkness, during which the "Master" re-cites—very effectively, be it admitted—Swinburne's "Garden of Proserpine." After this there is more meditation, followed by an imitation, a Dervish dance by one of the company, who finally falls to the ground, whether in exhaustion or frenzy we are unable to say.

There is also at intervals a species of Bacchic revel by the entire company on the stage, in which an apparently very young girl, who is known as the "Daughter of the Gods," takes part.

On the particular occasion we refer to the lights were turned up at about 10.15, after a prolonged period of com-plete darkness, and the company dispersed. We leave it to our readers, after looking at the photographs—which were taken for private circulation only, and sold to us without Crowley's knowledge or consent, and of which we have acquired the exclusive copyright—and after reading our plain, unvarnished account of the happenings of which we were an actual eye-witness, to say whether this is not a blasphemous sect whose proceedings conceivably lend themselves to immorality of the most revolting character. Remember the doctrine which we have endeavoured faintly to outline—remember the long periods of complete darkness—remember the dances and the heavy scented atmosphere, the avowed object of which is to produce what Crowley terms an "ecstasy"—and then say if it is fitting and right that young girls and married women should be allowed to attend such performances under the guise of the cult of a new religion.

New religion, indeed! It is as old as the hills. The doctrines of unbridled lust and licence, based on the assumption that there is no God and no hereafter, have been preached from time immemorial, sometimes by hedonists and fanatics pure and simple, sometimes by charlatans whose one thought is to fill their money-bags by encouraging others to gratify their depraved tastes.

In the near future we shall have more to say about this man Crowley—his history and antecedents—and those of several members of the sect—and we also hope to be in a position to give a description of the happenings at the flat in Victoria Street on the occasions of what we may call "private matinee performances."

AN AMAZING SECT II

THE ORIGIN OF THEIR RITES AND THE LIFE-HISTORY OF MR. ALEISTER CROWLEY.

A FORTNIGHT ago we published an article under the heading of "An Amazing Sect" in which we gave an account of a meeting or séance which we had attended of the Equinox Sect, of which Mr. Aleister Crowley is the presiding genius, and which we illustrated by exclusive photographs. After describing in detail the performance of which we were an eye-witness, we promised, in conclusion, that in the near future we should have something more to say about Crowley's history and antecedents. We now proceed to redeem that promise.

The Ancient Rites of Eleusis.

We propose in the first place to give a brief sketch of the ancient rites of Eleusis, from which presumably Mr. Crowley has derived the performances of which we gave an account in our previous article.

The Rites of Eleusis take their name from Eleusis, a city of ancient Greece, and though little is known of their form by reason of the fact that the mysteries perished with the destruction of Eleusis in A.D. 396, yet tradition has handed down some data from which it is possible to reconstruct their general outline. Demeter, so the legend runs, incensed at the rape of her daughter Persephone, betook herself to Eleusis and there dwelt for the space of a year, plunged in solitary mourning for her child, in a temple built for her by the pious natives. Her advent, however, was in the nature of a calamity for these pious folk, as during her year of residence the Earth brought forth no increase, and the human race would have perished had not Zeus, on whom she had some sort of claim—possibly on the score of arrears of alimony, he being the father of the said Persephone—relented and ordained that Persephone should return from Hades. On the return of Persephone mother and daughter are reunited, the corn grows again, and once more all's well with the world. With a parting benison to the good folk of Eleusis, Demeter prepares to exchange her austere temple for the more congenial atmosphere of Olympus. But before quitting Eleusis Demeter laid down the lines of the services which were to be held in her honour after she had gone. These were what came to be known as "the Eleusinia"—the rites of Eleusis.

The Original Ceremonies.

So much for their origin. With regard to the ceremonies themselves the details are most nebulous, and there is marked divergence of opinion among the authorities. Lobeck in his "Aglaophamus," published in 1839, gives most minutia. We are told that during the nine days before the festival the pious fasted, taking sustenance only between sunset and sunrise. At the commencement of the ceremonies, which started at Athens, a proclamation was issued ordering the immediate departure of all strangers, murderers, and undesirables. From this apparently comes Mr. Crowley's "banishing rites of the pentagram," to which we referred in our previous article. On the following day the initiates were bathed for outward purification, and were then decked in a fawn skin as their only garb. This was followed by public sacrifices to Demeter and Persephone, and by a private sacrifice of a sacred pig to Demeter by the initiates; and various ceremonies were also gone through *in camera* by the Order. From the time of the purification of the initiates by immersion the ceremonies were of a dual character, the public ceremonial and festival open to all—barring such aliens, murderers, and undesirables as had come under the ban of the opening injunction—and the private ceremonies open only to the initiates of the Temple. These last were under the leadership of a priest known as the Hierophant, a man vowed to a life of strict and saintly chastity, whose duties were to show and explain the sacred symbols. Besides the virtue of chastity the Hierophant had to possess a good, clear voice for intoning. His right-hand man was known as the Daduchus—the torchbearer—whose office it was to bear the sacred torch and relieve the Hierophant in the chanting. He, too, had to combine the virtue of chastity with a good voice and presence. For the female portion of the retinue the qualifications were not quite so searching, for the Hierophantis—priestesses dedicated to Demeter—were required to live a life of chastity "during their term of office."

Initiates and their Myths.

Initiates to the Order were required to pay a large "fee", and the aim of initiation into the mysteries was that they should be gradually weaned from things of earth—in which category presumably was included the aforesaid premium—and have their higher impulses stirred. From this point the portrayal

271

of the Mysteries of Eleusis is given by the Hierophant and his retinue, and from these rites all but the initiated were rigorously excluded. The mystics commemorated first the myth of Demeter and Persephone, starting with the rape of Persephone; and M. Stephani says that there can be no doubt that the scene of Baubo was given in all its indecent coarseness. Next was shown the union of Jupiter with Demeter; the resistance of the goddess; the god's ruses and final attainment of his desire, from which consummation sprang Persephone. In the next myth is shown how Zeus in guise of a serpent rapes Persephone, who gives birth to the god Bacchus. Then followed the complete myth of Bacchus—Zagreus. Finally the initiates drank a libation and consumed their nocturnal meal. The nine days' abstinence are said by some writers to correspond, to the nine nights' continence of Roman ladies in honour of Ceres. . . . As a French writer pithily puts it: "Nulle part il n'est question de l'emploi des journées qui s'intercalaient entres les nuits mystiques. Il est en effet probable que l'on n'y faisait rien de particulier et que les mystes les donnaient au répos, puis qu'il veillaient toute la nuit."

A Tolerant Critic's Opinion.

It is generally held that the rites contained scenes of the greatest licence, and that there were many symbols of a coarse nature; for example those represented by the Hierophant and the Priestess portraying the union of Zeus and Demeter, and later of Zeus and Persephone, which entered into the higher worship. Clement of Alexandria, most temperate of writers and tolerant of critics, says "in any case it is true that the priest is chambered with the priestess alone, to give to the spectators the verisimilitude of conjugal union between the god and the goddess," and concludes, "La hardiesse d'un tel rite suffirait à légitimer les protestations et les révoltes des Peres de Eglise chrétienne." Such were the Elusina as handed down by the ancient authorities, and from which the Rites of Eleusis, portrayed by Mr. Aleister Crowley, have presumably been derived.

East and West Intermingle.

The number of rites in Mr. Crowley's series is seven, and he has been apparently influenced in his choice of that number by the fact that it corresponds with the number of the planets, and he has ordered the sequence by the rate of their progress across the heavens.

Into the ancient Greek ceremonies Mr. Crowley has interpolated many Eastern observances, with which his long wanderings and research in the East have rendered him familiar.

The result is the ceremony which we endeavoured to describe a fortnight ago. Our readers will recollect that in summing up we made the following remarks: "We leave it to our readers, after looking at the photographs—which were taken for private circulation only, and sold to us without Crowley's knowledge or consent, and of which we have acquired the exclusive copyright and after reading our plain, unvarnished account of the happenings of which we were an actual eyewitness, to say whether this is not a blasphemous sect whose proceedings conceivably lend themselves to immorality of the most revolting character. Remember the doctrine which we have endeavoured faintly to outline—remember the long periods of complete darkness—remember the dances and the heavy scented atmosphere; the avowed object of which is to produce what Crowley terms an 'ecstasy'—and then say if it is fitting and right that young girls and married women should be allowed to attend such performances under the guise of the cult of a new religion."

The Personnel of Crowley.

We now propose to give a few details of Mr. Aleister Crowley's career up to the present time, and we shall then once more leave it to our readers to determine whether or not our remarks as to his precious "sect" are or are not well-grounded. Alexander Edward Crowley—he assumed the Christian name of Aleister later in life—was born about 35 years ago. His father was an eminent member of the "Plymouth Brethren," and young Crowley was brought up in the odour of sanctity. He was educated privately, and afterwards went to Trinity College, Cambridge. There he made the acquaintance of Mr. Gerald Festus Kelly, and after leaving Cambridge these two spent some years in Paris studying art. From Paris Crowley went to the East, where he disappeared for some time, but subsequently returned to Paris about the year 1902, and became a disciple of Rodin. About this time he wrote an effusion entitled "Rodin in Rime," which he dedicated to his master. During this sojourn in Paris he made the acquaintance of the sister of his friend Mr. Festus Kelly, who was a widow, her husband, Capt. Frederic Skerrelt, having died three years previously. He became very friendly with this lady, and in the following year, July, 1903, they met again at Strathpeffer in Scotland. Crowley proposed marriage to her, was accepted, and the marriage took place on the following day.

A Man of Many Names.

In the marriage certificate he gave his name as Macgregor, but his father's name was given as Edward Crowley. After the marriage the happy pair went to live at Boleskine, Foyers, Inverness-shire, a large house with about 50 acres of land which Crowley had bought some years previously. This house he had fitted up in an ultra-esthetic manner. He had one room covered entirely with mirrors, which he called a temple.

Shortly after his marriage Crowley raised himself, to the peerage, under the title of Lord Boleskine, he having previously, in Paris, gone under the style of Count Skerrett. In 1904 a child was born of the marriage, which died 21 months later. Shortly after the birth of the child, Crowley and his wife started for the East, where they travelled for about a year, and in 1906 they were at Hong-Kong. There his wife was in a delicate condition, but in spite of this he left her alone there, himself going to America, and the unhappy woman had to travel all the way home to her father's house in England, where her confinement took place. Crowley afterwards joined her at Chislehurst, and they then went to live at a house in Warwick Road, Earl's Court, which was taken in her name. In the summer of 1909 she found herself unable to stand Crowley's brutal treatment any longer, and on July 21st, 1909, she left him.

On August 5th she learnt from the charwoman that her husband had had a woman staying with him in the house the previous night. Sometime before that Crowley had asked his wife to take care of a child for one of his intimate friends, and she, of course, presumed that it was his friend's child. However, she accidentally opened a letter addressed to Crowley which gave the address of the mother of the child, a Miss Zwee, and Mrs. Crowley, on going to see this person, learnt that Crowley was the father of the child. This Miss Zwee was a milliner in the Burlington Arcade.

How the Sect Originated.

A decree of divorce, with custody of the child of the marriage, was granted to Mrs. Crowley in the Edinburgh Courts on November 24th, 1909. Shortly before this, Crowley had started a half-yearly magazine called "The Equinox," which purported to deal with mystical and occult matters, and out of which was evolved the sect which we have under discussion, and which is technically known as the A∴A∴. Other stories there are about Aleister Crowley, dark and forbidding stories, but we prefer to confine ourselves to indisputable facts—and we ask our readers, after reading this bare and unvarnished statement of facts, to say whether Mr. Aleister Crowley, with the record which we have outlined above, is likely to be the High Priest of wholesome or helpful doctrines, and whether this is the sort of man to whom young girls and married women should be allowed to go for "comfort" and "meditation."

AN AMAZING SECT III

FURTHER DETAILS OF MR. ALEISTER CROWLEY.

SINCE our article of November 12, further information has reached us from an unimpeachable source as to the past record of this man, who dares to put himself forward as a High Priest, who has the effrontery to defend his doctrines in the columns of a high-class journal such as the "Bystander," and who has the impudence to attempt to draw a parallel between his own case and that of Jesus Christ.

By their Friends Ye Shall Know Them.

In addition to those details of Crowley's career which we published in our issue of November 12, the following facts have come to our knowledge. In 1898 Crowley became a member of the Rosicrucian Order, a very ancient association, whose principal object is the study of the mystic philosophy of ancient religions, and which possesses a vast amount of traditional lore on this and kindred subjects, while requiring from its members due respect and honour for religious ideas, as well as good moral character. Two of Crowley's friends and introducers are still associated with him; one, the rascally sham, Buddhist monk, Allan Bennett, whose imposture was shown up in "Truth" some years ago; the other a person of the name of George Cecil Jones, who was for some time employed at Basingstoke, but of late has had some sort of small merchant's business in the City. Crowley and Bennett lived together, and there were rumours of unmentionable immoralities which were carried on under their roof.

An Exposure in "Truth."

Soon after this, Crowley began to shield himself under different aliases, and Allan Bennett swindled a lady, whose name we have, out of several hundred pounds, under the pretext of manufacturing rubies, and was expelled from the Rosicrucian Order. Bennett then went to Ceylon, and thence to Burmah, where he endeavoured to pass himself off as a Buddhist monk sent by the Ceylonese Himayana Buddhists to those of Burmah. Here, however, they soon found him out, and he was rejected by one Buddhist monastery after another as a sham and a fraud. Later he came to England with two Burmese ladies. He formed an association called the Buddhist Society, and made desperate attempts at advertisement, using the name of Macgregor, to which he had no shadow of title, and stating that he was an M.A. of Trinity College, Cambridge, which was a bare-faced falsehood, his education having been really of a very minor description. However, he was well shown up in "Truth," both by its editor and by a very strong letter about him from the president of the Buddhist Society from Rangoon.

To his other vices was added that of drug-taking to excess, and it is more than likely that the incense used in Crowley's rites is heavily steeped in drugs.

Many Aliases.

To return to Crowley. His aliases would grace an Old Bailey criminal. He called himself Macgregor, with an ignorance so astounding of the history of that name as to tempt one to believe that he had never even read the works of Walter Scott. Like his worthy associate Bennett, he endeavoured to use it for the purposes of advertisement. Count Svareff, Count Skellatt, Count Skerrett, Edward Aleister, Lord Boleskine, Baron Rosenkreutz, are a few of the aliases under which he has figured from time to time.

Expulsion from the Rosicrucian Order.

In 1900 he began to show up in his true colours. Being sent from Paris to London on certain matters connected with the Order, he enormously exceeded his instructions, and stole certain property of the Order, which he took up with him to Boleskine. His next exploit was to steal the jewels of a lady, the wife of an English officer, as well as to extort money by threats. She obtained a warrant for his arrest, but he fled the country, having in the meantime obtained a considerable amount from a well-known singer. He then remained abroad for some years, when he came to Paris. In our article of November 12 we related the circumstances which led to his marriage, his treatment of his wife, and her subsequent successful action for divorce. It only remains for us to add that he was formally expelled from the Rosicrucian Order as a man of evil character and acts, and that he was forced to retract a libel which he circulated about the head of this Order, and make a humble legal apology through his solicitors.

A Challenge.

Last year he went down to Cambridge and started some sort of rites there, in which he endeavoured to induce the undergraduates to join. The authorities, however, received a timely warning, and Crowley made no headway. Many of his poems are of the most obscene and revolting character. Other statements about him we refrain from printing, as they are of too horrible a nature, but we think we have said enough to show that our previous attacks on him and his orgies were more than justified, and we challenge Crowley to disprove any one of the statements we have made.

His article in this week's "Bystander" is too unspeakably feeble to merit even passing comment. Moreover, we do not anticipate that this or any other journal with any title to respectability, will open its columns to Mr. Aleister Crowley in the future.

A PARTIAL LIST OF SNUGGLY BOOKS

G. ALBERT AURIER *Elsewhere and Other Stories*
CHARLES BARBARA *My Lunatic Asylum*
CHARLES BARBARA *Stirring Stories*
S. HEZOLNRY BERTHOUD *Misanthropic Tales*
LÉON BLOY *The Tarantulas' Parlor and Other Unkind Tales*
ÉLÉMIR BOURGES *The Twilight of the Gods*
ADA BUISSON *The Baron's Coffin and Other Disquieting Tales*
CYRIEL BUYSSE *The Aunts*
JAMES CHAMPAGNE *Harlem Smoke*
FÉLICIEN CHAMPSAUR *The Latin Orgy*
ARMAND CHARPENTIER
    Claustrophobic Madness and Other Stories of Death and Love
BRENDAN CONNELL *Metrophilias*
BRENDAN CONNELL *Spells*
RENDAN CONNELL (editor) *The Zaffre Book of Occult Fiction*
BRENDAN CONNELL (editor) *The Zinzolin Book of Occult Fiction*
RAFAELA CONTRERAS *The Turquoise Ring and Other Stories*
DANIEL CORRICK (editor)
    Ghosts and Robbers: An Anthology of German Gothic Fiction
ADOLFO COUVE *When I Think of My Missing Head*
RENÉ CREVEL *Are You All Crazy?*
QUENTIN S. CRISP *Aiaigasa*
QUENTIN S. CRISP *Rule Dementia!*
LUCIE DELARUE-MARDRUS *The Last Siren and Other Stories*
LADY DILKE *The Outcast Spirit and Other Stories*
CATHERINE DOUSTEYSSIER-KHOZE *The Beauty of the Death Cap*
ÉDOUARD DUJARDIN *Hauntings*
BERIT ELLINGSEN *Now We Can See the Moon*
ERCKMANN-CHATRIAN *A Malediction*
ALPHONSE ESQUIROS *The Enchanted Castle*
ENRIQUE GÓMEZ CARRILLO *Sentimental Stories*
DELPHI FABRICE *Flowers of Ether*
DELPHI FABRICE *The Red Sorcerer*
DELPHI FABRICE *The Red Spider*
BENJAMIN GASTINEAU *The Reign of Satan*
EDMOND AND JULES DE GONCOURT *Manette Salomon*
REMY DE GOURMONT *From a Faraway Land*
REMY DE GOURMONT *Morose Vignettes*
GUIDO GOZZANO *Alcina and Other Stories*
GUSTAVE GUICHES *The Modesty of Sodom*
EDWARD HERON-ALLEN *The Complete Shorter Fiction*
EDWARD HERON-ALLEN *Three Ghost-Written Novels*